The Hill

By
Davis
MacDonald

Print Edition

Table of Contents

Chapter 1 - Friday

Sometimes your destiny is pre-ordained; sometimes well planned and thought out ahead. Sometimes it gradually sneaks up on you: you look back, surprised at the distance covered. Sometimes it just falls out one day at your feet like the body of a young girl, rolling lifelessly in the surf.

It was early October in Southern California. The day had been very warm early on, Indian Summery, even a little sticky. But as the afternoon dwindled away, the heat gave way to a slight chill as the thin golden rays of the sun vanished below the sea. Soft light spilled like dust over fallen leaves, manicured green gray lawns, and asphalt alike.

Along the coast, a stiff breeze had come up off the water, whipped up by a storm to the south in Baja, churning the Santa Monica Bay into frosty whitecaps. The wind brought the smell and the taste of the sea to the cliffs of Palos Verdes Estates, a small hidden suburb to the southwest of Los Angeles. The waves crashed with a heavy rhythm against the beach as they sluiced up amongst the rocks. The tide was on the way out, but it was still a rugged surf.

The Judge strode along Paseo Del Mar, the ocean bluff street that tracked the city's rocky coastline. He was a tall man - broad shouldered and big boned with just the beginnings of a paunch around the middle, hinting at an appetite for fine wines and good food. He cut an imposing figure in his dark blue corduroy sport coat, outfitted with casual patch pockets. Under it he wore a light blue dress shirt its over-sized collar open at the neck, and disreputable looking jeans of unknown vintage, faded and threadbare here and there. He had the ruddy and chiseled features of Welsh ancestors, a rather too big nose, large ears, and bushy eyebrows on the way to premature grey.

He had a given name of course, but after he ascended to the bench, people began calling him just "Judge". Even old friends he'd known for years affectionately adopted the nick-name. It had stuck.

As the sun faded, the temperature dropped, and the wind brought color to his cheeks and an added urgency to his gait. With his big hands and feet and his jeans and short-cut dark hair, he might have passed for a dock-worker in another locale.

Except that he had large piercing blue eyes, intelligent and restless. Except that his eyes swept the space around him continually and missed nothing. Except that he thought like a judge. Except that this was Palos Verdes, one of the most affluent communities in the United States.

He walked a golden retriever, perhaps a year old. The dog was big, clearly untrained, and still a puppy in spirit and energy despite her bulk. The puppy, as he thought of her despite her size, (Annie by name) seemed determined to go in all directions except the one The Judge wanted.

The Hill

The puppy was recently acquired. An experiment. Annie was to be his new companion, a fellow spirit to balance out what had become a too solitary life.

So far she had mostly been a pain in the ass. She strained at the leash every 30 seconds or so, testing his resolve to stay on the road. At 60 pounds she could give a good tug, although hardly a match for his 200 pounds. She wanted to romp the bushes alongside. He supposed the bushes held better smells. Allied with the asphalt, he couldn't compete.

This was his routine at sunset. He walked with the puppy from his house higher up the Hill, down to Paseo Del Mar. He went a half-mile in one direction along the cliff, then he reversed. He went half a mile past his entry point and back. It was all so...organized.

The Judge was organized. His life was ordered in tiers of personal interest and professional responsibility. He had been technically proficient as a judge, straight as an arrow on the rules, and enjoyed his part in the drama that worked itself out each day in the courtroom.

It was called the American system of Justice. But it wasn't always just. It wasn't always right. And there wasn't always a legal remedy for those who deserved one. American Justice came down to a system of rules. It operated within its own framework. To the Judge, it was still the closest thing to real justice in this world. There was a certain symmetry to it he enjoyed. It had defined his professional life for more than 10 years. But it was by no means perfect.

In any event, that life was gone now. Whisked away in an instant. He'd been dumped on the street. He was no longer a judge. People continued to call him Judge of course, out of respect, or maybe pity…who knew.

He'd lost his re-election 6 months ago. It was still somewhat of a shock. After 10 years on the bench he thought he'd continue indefinitely, and then retire a judge.

Now he had lots of time to squander on things like puppies and walks. It was very different from being a judge.

50 years old, and no law to practice; he didn't feel up to starting a new law practice again. He'd done it once years ago, before the judgeship. It had been hard. Once should have been enough. But then, what the hell else was he to do?

He told himself he wasn't bitter, at least not exactly. Just a mild sour taste. Dumped by his constituents. Ten years, and out the door one morning, almost by whim.

The light in the sky was fading quickly now. Just like his career, he mused. It had been a peaceful afternoon. He hadn't seen a soul. No joggers, no bikers; none of the neighbors walking their dogs. They always seemed to know the puppy's name. They never remembered his. There was an orange afterglow puddled against the rim of the sea. It had turned from Indian summer to cool fall in the space of an hour, the way it does on The Hill.

Palos Verdes, or "The Hill" as its denizens referred to it, was a discrete series of hills with cliffs jutting up off the Los Angeles plain, surrounded on three sides by the sea.

Midway between LAX and the Port of Los Angeles, it was the only rocky coast along a line of otherwise flat surfing beaches stretching from Santa Monica to the Newport Coast in Orange County, punctuated by the twin ports of Los Angeles and Long Beach, and several piers and boat harbors.

Twenty-five minutes distance by car to any freeway, by LA standards it was an isolated and travel-locked outpost far off the beaten track. It was geographically close, but a time-lengthy to travel to LA's so-called "downtown", to the glitzy Westside, or to Hollywood or the Valley.

The Hill quietly punctuated the Southern California coast line, mostly unknown and unvisited by Angelenos, even though at least one of its communities routinely ranked as one of the ten wealthiest in the United States.

And it was very quiet. People only traveled to The Hill if they lived there.

The Judge approached his midway point again on his last stretch before turning uphill on Via Alma. He noticed a battered penny lying in the road. He looked around to be sure no one was watching and then bent over and scooped it up. When he was young he believed in making a wish on such a find. Perhaps he should try - a wish for guidance.

As he bent over, the leash slipped from his grasp. Annie scooted off in a flash, plowing into the brush alongside the bluff.

Muttering under his breath, the Judge gamely waded into dry foxtails after her. She thought it was 'catch Annie, if you can': a wonderful game to her pea-sized brain. She dodged away from his reach, waving her tail like a flagman, dashing further into the rough, toward the bluff edge, daring him to catch her.

The Judge waded after. He could feel the burrs in his socks and smell the dry dust they'd kicked up, mixed with the salty aroma from the crashing surf 40 feet below. He was almost to Annie now. He was concerned she might scamper over the edge in her excitement.

But she had stopped at cliff edge and was seriously nosing something in the scrub. His eyes caught the flash of baby blue as the dry grass parted around her legs. He slowed his pace and gingerly picked his way closer to the cliff and the puppy.

He could make it out now. It was a powder blue dress, neatly folded on the ground, as if laid out for someone to wake up and put on. For some reason it reminded him of the young girl who house sat his puppy the night before - a pretty high school senior, just turned 18, the daughter of an old friend.

He had gone to San Francisco on Wednesday. By pre-arrangement the girl, Christi, had stayed over and puppy sat Annie Wednesday and Thursday night. Having a puppy was like a small child. He had to hire a live-in babysitter if he left town. It was expected: by the neighbors, by the local vet, by everyone. You couldn't just send the baby to the puppy kennel like in the old days. Lock it up for 24 hours in a secure cage and forget it. Oh, no. The damn animal almost had legal rights.

He'd returned from LAX hours before and paid off his puppy sitter. Annie seemed none the worse for wear. Apparently the Judge was never missed. And why would he be? The puppy had been ensconced for two nights with Christi, a young thing in a pretty dress, a robin's egg blue dress. This looked very much like the dress.

Two hours ago, he'd given Christi cash that she was quite happy to get. She'd left in a bundle of smiles and good cheer, wrapped in blue.

The Judge was suddenly cold. He didn't want to look over the cliff edge, but he did.

It was a long way down. A sheer drop, a crashing sea below. All foam and green in the fading light.

Rocks jutting up here and there served as the splash base for spouts of sea and froth as rollers hit the shore. There was a continual roar, punctuated periodically by the crash of a particularly big wave throwing itself against the rocks. The wind whipped a fine spray of salt and moisture up the face of the cliff. The judge's hair and face were quickly coated with a light mist. He could taste the salt on his lips. It was an awesome sight…All power and wild sea. The Judge panned the scene, taking it all in.

Then he saw what he feared.

A bobbing white and pink form, the shape of a young girl, spinning, rolling, half submerged in the sea.

Crashing up against the sharp rocks.

Lifelike, but lifeless - in endless motion: a bouncing, rolling dancer: captive to sea surge, tide, wind, and the merciless rocks.

Chapter 2 – Friday

The last rays of the vanished sun had pasted colors to bottoms of countless distant clouds: pinks, yellows, oranges; a soft blue like the folded dress. But a deeper purple was spreading across the sky now, swallowing the color. The wind had not dropped much but the temperature had. Is that why he felt so bloody cold?

The Judge and the puppy stood together at the side of the road. Annie huddled close, her ears back in dismay, tail flat to the ground. They were alternately painted in the red of the fire truck lights. The paramedic and patrol car lights had been turned off, perhaps a symbol of their futility here.

The Judge always felt a little unreal standing in the arc of sweeping emergency lights. A little disoriented. Not like the men who ran the machines. The layman had only bad experiences with the arcing red lights…Family emergencies, accidents, death, loss of loved ones, face to face recognition of one's own mortality. He pulled his corduroy coat closer around him and brought the puppy against his leg. For warmth he thought, and maybe reassurance. At least one living thing still cared he was alive.

The Judge had dialed 911 at the cliff's edge. He'd considered bolting down the narrow path to the left, down to the beach. But even from his cliff-top perch it was clear the girl lying face down in the water had been there awhile. She was not moving. At least, not of her own accord. The surf was the puppeteer here. It danced the body randomly about the rocks in grotesque fashion, rolling it around and around and slamming it over and under.

And in the deepening dusk, the trail was slippery and treacherous. For someone out of shape like the Judge it would have been a tricky effort. He might have ended up a second victim. The fire rescue team had been there in three minutes flat, and down on the beach in five. But reaching the body across the rocks and surf was proving tricky even for professionals.

The paramedics had gone down the trail at a flat out run, three bronzed young men in their early thirties. They leaped agilely from rock to rock at the surf's edge. After a quick survey, two of them, both wrapped in a fancy harness anchored to the beach, went into the rocky surf and waded the body ashore.

Two policemen, a detective, and a forensic tech hovered in a tight circle over the body on the sand. There were flashlights spraying in all directions, low voices exchanging notes, and the occasional rogue wave threatening to wash them away. The firemen were busy too, rigging a stretcher for hauling the body up the path to the comparative safety of the top - safety for the living; too late for the dead.

Top side, a small band of neighbors had formed, augmented by a couple of bikers, a lone jogger, and a Latino gardener dressed in de rigor khaki, the uniform of faceless people who tended the gardens and lawns of The Hill. The gardener faded quickly when the patrol car arrived, replaced by a young couple slowing in their car, stopping and getting out to have a look.

"It was another suicide jump, and right in front of my house too," announced a tall, angular woman with clever blue eyes and the feel of Stanford. She wore a violet raincoat, hastily thrown over dark blue pants, ivory blouse and blue sport jacket. Early 50s like the judge, she wore the traditional 'I am a professional so take me seriously' uniform so in fashion these days with the softer sex. Beside her stood a small Asian woman, likely Japanese, quietly staring with sad dark eyes. She was dressed in a pinstriped charcoal suit coat. Perhaps a lawyer or a banker.

The female half of the young couple kept muttering, "Oh my god…oh my god" under her breath…a sort of mantra that seemed aimed at making the whole scene disappear. She was a brunette, dressed to show. She wore scruffy tight jeans and a tight T-shirt low cut in front to display budding breasts, rigged with an undergarment to push up from below, in defiance of nature and the law of gravity. Her male counterpart was quiet and pale, watching with sad eyes as the stretcher jostled its way up the cliff, borne by the firemen. He was dressed in tan pants and white polo shirt under a blue striped office shirt, the tail hanging out at the back. He had his arms around her to keep her warm, just a bit too high to be discrete. The Judge supposed he'd do the same if he had a pretty girl like that.

The young detective, short in stature and squeaky in voice, strutted over to the Judge, pulling out his flip-top notebook. "You found the body, sir," he said, more statement than question.

The Judge hated being addressed as "Sir". It felt like a sly slur, an ugly reminder that the younger person had eternity stretching before him while the Judge was on the edge of the abyss. Actually, he supposed it was true. How nice it was to be young and certain you'd live forever. The Judge could vaguely remember the fantasy. It disappeared with the years, as did many things. Of course, the Judge was quite happy to be addressed as 'Judge', but that wasn't going to happen as much anymore.

"No," he said, "I found the blue dress. Then saw something in the surf below. So I called 911." It sounded like quibbling, even to the Judge, but the hell with it. He didn't much like this detective. He didn't know quite why.

"I'm detective Broadman," he announced, handing the Judge a card. "We think we have an ID: one Christina Benson, just turned 18, a local girl. There was a license in the dress."

The Judge's countenance remained impassive, but his heart sank. Then it was Christi.

"Did you know her?' asked the detective.

"I know Christi Benson. Is that her being carried up the cliff?"

"We believe so," said the detective. "Come have a look".

The Judge handed the end of the puppy leash to the tall angular woman, who quite happily took the dog. An opportunity for distraction from the gruesome scene playing out for the cluster of neighbors.

The judge and the detective walked with measured step over to the top of the trail. His feet felt like lead. The firemen were just carrying the stretcher over the top, a terribly small bundle strapped to it, with a grey blanket thrown over. The detective instinctively positioned them so their broad backs more or less blocked the view of the small knot of community looking on. He raised the blanket, shining a flashlight under.

It was Christi. She wore a skimpy, white two-piece swimsuit. She was still beautiful, even in death… but different. Her blue eyes stared up blankly at the judge. Brown, matted, sand-caked hair above pale white skin, marked with cuts, scrapes and bruises, and a huge welt at the side of her head where she must have hit the rocks. Her expression was one of surprise, frozen in time. The image would haunt the Judge.

The lively flashing blue eyes, quick smile, infectious laugh she had used to punctuate statements sometimes, the warmth and the glow of a just-flowering young woman. Poof…poof…gone.

"Yes," croaked the Judge. "Yes…Christi Benson". Mercifully, the detective dropped the blanket back in place. The Judge started to move back toward the relative comfort of the small cluster of neighbors, his eyes cast down, unseeing. But the little detective briskly cut him off, flip book in hand again.

"When was the last time you saw Christina Benson?" he asked. His squeaky voice had all the warmth of a dental drill.

"About three hours ago," the Judge replied. "She house sat, or dog sat, for me last night and the night before. I was out of town."

The detective's eyes narrowed thoughtfully. " So…. you may have been the last person to see her alive?"

The Judge shook his head, "I don't know".

"How did she seem? Depressed, pensive, sad, moody, down, anything like that?"

"No. She seemed happy and full of life. My impression was that she had a date."

"Why did you think that, sir?" That 'Sir' again. "Did she say she had a date? That she was meeting somebody?"

The Judge paused a moment to reflect. "I don't know; she left running fingers through her hair, and doing her lipstick. She seemed happy and…I don't know…animated. No, she didn't say she had a date."

"What was she wearing?" asked the detective.

"The blue dress."

"Sure it's the same blue dress?"

"Looks the same color," snapped the Judge. "I don't know whether it's the 'same' dress.".

"Of course," said the detective, making another note.

An older white Mercedes screeched to a halt at the curve across the street, causing them both to turn and look.

A distraught woman in her mid-forties leaped from the car, making for the stretcher, panic in her face.

Oh God, thought the Judge, it's Maddie - Christi's mother.

Maddie made a determined bolt between two officers, but they impeded her forward motion with their bulk.

With the help of a fireman, they encircled her and blocked her access. Maddie was one of the Judge's few friends on The Hill, a rapidly dwindling group. But this wasn't time to feel sorry for himself.
He ignored the detective and his flip-top book, and stepping around him, went over to take Maddie into his arms.

She started to sob uncontrollably into his shoulder with the grief of a mother who's lost a child. Finally she came up for air, pulling herself together and hoarsely muttering, "I want to see her".

"Are you sure, Maddie?" he said softly. "It's not the way you want to remember her."

"Yes," she said in a voice suddenly cold and far away. "I have to."

The Judge turned to the two officers who had positioned themselves between Maddie and the body.

"She needs to see her daughter now," he said.

One of the officers started to object, but the Judge held up his hand imperially, displaying the prestige and force of personality he'd so often used from his bench. Both officers instinctually moved aside.

Maddie walked slowly over to the stretcher, her head held unnaturally high and straight. The Judge moved with her, step for step.

One of the firemen lifted the stretcher blanket and tried unsuccessfully to soften with his hand the light from the flashlight he shined under.

Maddie gasped, steadied herself, and with trembling fingers, reached down and caressed the face of her child. She bent down to give the cold sandy forehead a small kiss, and then slumped away, seeking the judge's shoulder again for support.

He walked her unsteadily back to her Mercedes and offered to drive her home. She handed him the keys without comment. She trusted him. They'd even been lovers once, so very long ago. Before she met and married Jake, her ex. Before Christi.

Once lovers, always a special connection. Human beings were built to share intimacy. Once shared, it wasn't something that could be put back in a bottle as if not opened. Even when things don't work out and you move on, you carry some part of that person with you into your future.

They'd been good friends on The Hill since her divorce. Strictly platonic, of course. But he'd watched Christi grow up. For some reason, fate had brought him to that cliff edge, and now to Maddie's side when she again needed support..

He helped her into the car. She sat there staring blankly out the passenger side window. He retrieved Annie and loaded the puppy in the backseat. Then he drove the three of them slowly away, wondering what words would make any difference.

Chapter 3 - Friday

The Judge slowly drove Maddie's old white Mercedes down Yarmouth Road and into her driveway, a modest house in lower Lunada Bay. Actually, there was no such thing as a modest house. The land value alone assured astronomical values. In 2010, Palos Verdes Estates was the 81st most expensive community in the United States. And it was only a poor cousin to the adjacent Rolling Hills.

Lunada Bay was one of the communities spread across the shelf above the Palos Verdes cliffs, but facing more out to sea rather than looking across the Santa Monica Bay.

Maddie's place was a Cape Cod style house, grey shingles and white trim. The cherry red front door was the only mark of independence in a bland structure. Very much in conformity with the community's local Art Jury view, which dictated such matters on The Hill.

Night had descended over them suddenly like a cloud. No moon yet. The dark seemed darker and bleaker now.

Maddie leaned on his arm and his shoulder up the pathway to the red front door. He left the puppy in Maddie's car.

They stepped through the door into her living room, all stark white walls with old-fashioned windows. Floor length beige linen curtains hung beside each window in silent attention. The wood floor was heavily stained a deep walnut, but covered by two large rectangle beige rugs sonly the edges showed.

To the left of the fireplace was a built-in bookcase filled with pictures of Christi.

Christi as a baby. Christi toddling. Christi playing soccer on The Hill. Christi taking horseback riding lessons. Christi in the school band, playing the oboe. Christi in a formal white gown with a smiling, heavyset young man, perhaps a tackle, likely taken last spring.

The two remaining walls each had large modern oils. Shapes in burgundies, reds and dark blues popped out from the stark white walls.

Under the oil on the left was a double shelf glass and wrought iron trolley with four brands of vodka. Bottles were down by a third or a half. There was also a small tumbler filled with round green limes, and a crystal ice bucket filled with melting ice.

There were small bottles of tonic, soda, and cranberry stacked up like soldiers on the second shelf along with heavy cut crystal tumblers, a couple of wine glasses, and a jar of pale green olives stuffed with bright pimiento.

A half-finished drink sat on the coffee table. Abandoned when Maddie had bolted for the door. Next to it was an open paperback lying face down. On the cover a swarthy pirate wrapped his arms around a distressed blond heroine in a skimpy nightgown.

Maddie composed herself as best she could into hostess mode, asking if the Judge would have tea, and bustled toward the small Pullman kitchen to make it.

This would be the start of the grief process. Shock and denial to begin with. Recognizing this only depressed the Judge more.

He supposed he had come through a similar process, albeit on a much smaller scale, with his judgeship loss. Shock and denial, then pain at the loss, then anger, depression, and ultimately acceptance at some level. He scolded himself for such thoughts at a time like this. His election loss was a comparative piss in the ocean.

She came around the corner from the kitchen carrying a bright colorful tray with yellow teapot and cups, chipped here and there, but obviously loved. There was a too bright smile pasted on her face. But her eyes had a faraway look. Some part of her was hiding now in memories of better days

He smiled sadly and said, "I think perhaps a more serious drink for us both, Maddie".

She nodded obediently, put the tray down on the oak coffee table, also chipped and well loved, and turned to the Vodka trolley. She poured 4 fingers of Grey Goose each into two short tumblers, dumped in some ice, and handed one over.

The Judge thought Maddie must be about 42 now. Brown hair cropped short with bangs just above her eyebrows set off soft brown eyes, and lots of squint lines around a narrow face that had seen too much sun. This gave her a horsey look, but it was all good, particularly with the sprinkling of freckles and the ready, open smile she usually wore. But this evening, her face looked grey.

She was wearing a polo looking shirt, fine horizontal light blue and white lines, trimmed with darker blue at the sleeves and around the collar. A single pearl hung around her neck on a small gold chain. She had on charcoal jeans, clipped above the knee, displaying well-muscled legs from playing tennis, and sandals with twisted leather straps. She looked like she belonged on The Hill.

It was said you could go down to Manhattan Beach, Hermosa, Redondo, or the West side, and local natives knew you were from "The Hill". It was your outfit, the way you wore it, your attitude, your mannerisms…and perhaps the smaller tips for service at restaurants. People from The Hill mostly had lots of money, but weren't flashy. And they prided themselves on being thrifty…or maybe it was called cheap, depending on your point of view.

More than twenty years ago, Maddie had been the Judge's legal secretary, first at the big fancy law firm, and then at the smaller law partnership he started, and then briefly his lover. They'd spent five professional years, and then six intimate months together. Then she left to date and later marry Jake Benson, an up and coming labor lawyer, and for a brief time, the Judge's law partner. This was before the Judge left private practice for the bench.

What followed was a new baby: Christi. Later, there'd been another woman on the side for Jake. A painful discovery and an unhappy divorce. An expensive property settlement. And a more solitary life raising a child on The Hill. Jake had moved to the Valley to set up a new law practice and hadn't looked back.

Maddie had taken the house in Lunada Bay and very little else, except for support payments, which would soon run out. "Correction," thought the Judge sourly. "Had just run out."

Life was a financial struggle, particularly since as a single parent she needed work near The Hill. She took part time jobs with local lawyers, sold cosmetic products over the Internet, and counted her pennies at the end of the week. It was a common tale in LA, and even on The Hill. She'd survived.

The Judge had kept in touch through it all, sometimes taking her to lunch or dinner, sometimes providing advice on investments or relationships, mostly just listening. They had never been romantically involved again but were old friends, more because of their shared past then because of any common interests.

More recently, as Christi had gotten older and more independent, the judge's impression had been one of conflict between mother and daughter, a natural result of an only child growing up and away, he supposed.

But there were a couple of late calls to the Judge when Maddie was clearly three sheets to the wind, and reminiscing with some bitterness about her past and shrinking future. He had wondered how it would all settle out after Christie left the nest.

The Judge set his drink down, sat on the sofa next to her, and just held her for a while. Then he stood, saying he really had to go, and asking if there was someone he could call to stay with her.

She turned to him then, ignoring the question, anger in her face.

"Christi didn't jump, you know. There's no way it happened like that. We're Catholic. She'd never do that. She was happy, her life was good; we were making plans for college in the fall. We had really good communication. Nothing was troubling her. She would have told me."

The Judge didn't say anything.

"Find out for me, Judge. Find out what the hell happened to my little girl. Someone did this, or it was an accident. We go back a long way. I am asking you....Hiring you...Calling in a favor... I don't know. Pleading with you. There's got to be more. I need to know."

Then she lapsed into silence again, staring down into her empty glass.

"I'll see what I can find out," the judge said softly. "Who were her friends, Maddie? Did she have girl friends at school?"

"Yes, Katherine is her best friend, and then there's Hannah and Paige. They have been together since kindergarten. She had a boyfriend for about six months. He's a year ahead, in college now. Anyway, they had a big fight at the start of school and she broke it off. She said it was pretty ugly. I don't know what happened. She was really angry. She's been going out a lot lately though. I've suspected a new boyfriend, or perhaps just dating the field. But when I asked her, she said it was just new girls at school she's getting to know - she never said who. We have house rules, you know. Back in the house by eleven during the week; keep me advised if you're going to be out late on the weekends."

"Was she sexually active?"

"Judge! Of course not - she only just turned eighteen last week. I mean, but…"

Tears came. "Oh no, Judge, she isn't any more."

"Any drugs?"

"Never."

"Any adults she was close to?"

"Just me."

"How about her dad?"

"Jake? She hasn't got on well with Jake since the divorce." Maddie sighed. "There was a counselor at school she saw - Katy Thorne. I know her through our tennis club. Will you talk to her? I'll call her and suggest it. And there was someone at her summer internship she got on well with, Gloria something or other. But then they let Christi go two weeks early. Not enough work I guess. I don't think she's kept up the friendship.

"Any teachers she might have confided in?"

"There was a English teacher she was in awe of. She was talking about her class at the beginning of summer school. She'd actually decided to study English and be a teacher and historic writer because of her class, and…Oh…Oh…Oh, Judge….She isn't anymore."

Her face collapsed with the weight of it all.

He bent down and gave her one more hug, and then left, making sure the door locked behind him. He took one last look through the door as it closed. She hadn't moved. As though tied to the sofa, staring into the past at the bottom of her glass.

He retrieved the puppy from Maddie's car, called a cab to meet him on Palos Verdes Drive, and started off at a brisk pace toward the Drive. He needed to walk and to clear his emotions.

Chapter 4 - Saturday

Saturday morning turned clear and cold. The Indian summer seemed to have evaporated as quickly as it had come. The wind had dropped, and the vast Santa Monica Bay spread out below the Judge's breakfast nook window. Point Dume, Malibu, Santa Monica, Redondo Beach Pier, and directly below, RAT Beach, short for Redondo And Torrance State Beach, a legendary surfing locale.

The bay was a bright blue, the surf crispy white, and the rising sun reflected off the skyscrapers in Santa Monica, Century City and downtown to the far right.

He padded into the kitchen and shook out some kibble for Annie, his roommate and nuisance.

The puppy was rapidly becoming a dog, and a show dog at that. She went through periods of chubbiness followed by growth spurts, which left her long and lean. Her soft brown eyes viewed the god with whom she resided with affection and puzzlement. There was no telling what he was going to impose on her next. Life was generally uncertain and complex, since her tools of communication were limited and her memory wasn't the best.

At some level she seemed to understand she had been cheated of alpha status by a lack of opposable thumbs, but she did the best she could, using her paws to pounce, to grip treats, to steal away toys and to leave muddy prints of affection up and down the legs of her alpha master.

Her coat was a mixture of long soft caramel and white fur, including an endless surplus to fall out and drift along the floors of the house to its corners. Her muzzle had that boxy profile, with a large wet black nose at the end serving as a sort of combined flash light and vacuum cleaner, sniffing along the ground and lower surfaces for food and scents. Her tail was more like a brush, extending out in a thick trunk with a heavy fringe of feather-like fur, and in constant motion, telegraphing her moods: mostly happy, sometimes bored, occasionally anxious that the Judge was leaving or that she had somehow displeased.

Lately she had developed a sock fetish for no particular reason. She had a comfortable collection of used socks, all singles, hidden under the sofa in the kitchen. She guarded these with fierce exuberance.

She loved to slip her leash and run off through the parklands and rough surrounding the house, but always with an eye on her master. She hoped he would come play 'Catch Me', a game at which she excelled. But at the least hint that he was turning away to leave, she would bound back in panic, certain she was being abandoned.

His quiet reflection on the puppy was disturbed by an authoritative rap at the door, followed by Annie's high-pitched bark. The Judge got up, pulling his bathrobe around him and cinching the belt as he opened the door. Young Detective John Broadman was standing there, brown suit and brown checked tie, looking suitably official and empowered, his flip-book at the ready.

"Just a few more questions, Judge." He smirked. "Course, I guess I don't call you judge anymore."

The Judge stood a little taller in his purple bathrobe, as though it was his old judicial robe, and said, "You can still call me the Judge, Detective; it's what I go by."

The detective faltered a little, suddenly staring down the twin barrels of the Judge's cold blue eyes, but recovered quickly.

"How well did you know the deceased?"

"You mean Christi," said the Judge.

" Eh, yes."

"Her mother, Maddie Benson, and I are old friends. I watched her grow up, but from a distance. Can't say I really knew her in any close sense."

"Did she have a boyfriend?"

"I don't know."

"Did she have any reason to be depressed?"

"I don't know."

The detective zinged in a fast slider. "Did you give her the blue dress?"

"No," said the Judge, unfazed.

"But you're sure the dress she was wearing was the one she put on at your house?"

" I didn't say that. I said it looked the same as the one she wore at my house. I didn't see her put on any dress at my house, Detective. But she left in a blue dress. There was a blue dress neatly folded at top of the cliff. And Christi was without a dress bobbing at the bottom."

"What was she doing at your house yesterday afternoon?"

"She came over two days before, to house-sit and watch my puppy. I had a stay over trip to San Francisco."

"And you saw her the night before?"

"No, I was in San Francisco for two nights. I saw her on Wednesday afternoon. I was gone Wednesday night and Thursday night."

"She ever house-sit for you before?"

"Yes."

"How often?"

"Perhaps four times over the last six months."

"Did she have anyone over to your house when she stayed? Like a girlfriend or a boyfriend?"

"I wouldn't know."

"Was anything disturbed, any sign of a guest or a party?"

"No."

"What time did you return from the airport yesterday morning?"

"As I said, it was yesterday afternoon. About 3 pm."

"What time did the girl leave?"

"About 3 pm."

"Where did she go after she left?"

"I don't know."

"Did she have a car?"

"I don't know. With the hedge there, I might not have seen it."

"You didn't see one?"

"No."

"Did someone pick her up?"

"I don't know."

"Did you see anyone who might have picked her up?"

"No."

"So you don't know where she went or what she did between 3:15 and about 5:30, when you saw the blue dress?"

"No."

"Or who she was with?"

"No."

"And you were here?"

"Yes, I was working."

"Did anyone come by, or was there a call that would verify you were here?"

"No."

"Did she say anything when she left yesterday afternoon?"

"She said, 'Goodbye.' "

"Was she in good spirits?"

"Yes, she seemed happy to have earned the money."

"So you can't think of any reason she might've wanted to jump off the cliff?"

"No."

"OK, I guess that does it for now. I may have more questions later." He flipped closed his notebook.

"Detective, there is another matter we need to discuss."

"Oh?" said the Detective, starting to open his notebook again.

The Judge chose his words carefully.

"The family has retained me to look into the circumstances of Christi's death and give an independent report of what happened. I'd like to follow along on the investigation, see the autopsy report, examine the physical evidence, and compare notes with you here and there. My charge is to understand clearly what happened last evening with Christi, and as best as I can determine …why."

The detective flashed a patronizing smile.

"I am sorry, Judge." He didn't look at all sorry. "This is an official investigation into a death. I can't allow you access to the investigation or the evidence."

The judge smiled tightly back.

"That's fine Detective. I am sure the Chief will okay it."

The detective looked startled, his patronizing attitude replaced by sudden caution.

The Judge didn't actually know the Chief, but he knew the mayor well, and so did Maddie. They should be able to work it out. It was a small town.

The Judge waved at the detective as he set off down the driveway. *Lots of energy and little experience*, thought the Judge. *Guess I was there once too.*

The Judge decided he would start first thing in the morning and take a very close look the circumstances surrounding Christi's death.

Chapter 5 - Sunday

The Judge had over slept. He padded out to his driveway to retrieve his morning papers and returned to his living room, preparing to enjoy the first one over a cup of coffee.

The living room was a massive California colonial affair. High ceilings with roof beams showing. Dark polished hard wood floors, overlain here and there with antique Ziegler Mahal carpets from Central Persia. Large rectangular windows looking out toward the sea on one side and inner courtyard gardens on the other. Someone had picked one of the best lots to build in 1924, with a view down to the surf and the great Santa Monica Bay.

To the left of the massive oak carved front door was a baby grand piano. To the right, deep plush white leather sofas paralleled one another. A massive old fireplace set in the far wall to the left sported an antique mantle of Italian marble and was big enough to practically stand in and warm your buns. An antique table, cut to coffee table height, all soft caramel wood and intricate carvings, sat between the sofas, and in the middle a large tall vase contained fresh flowers cut the afternoon before from the gardens to the rear.

He finished the *Los Angeles Times* in his robe on the living room sofa and then considered his schedule for the day. He had more questions for Maddie. He had given her a day to begin to work through the shock of losing a child.

It was a little after 10 a.m., a reasonable time for a phone call, unless you'd just lost a daughter, in which case there was no reasonable time. He dialed Maddie's number.

After a time, she answered. Her voice was croaky. Hung over or just woken up. Or both.

"Maddie," the Judge said, electing to jump right into business, "there's a question I forgot to ask on Friday."

"Yes?" she murmured softly. The Judge could tell she was steeling herself.

"Tell me more about the blue dress. Was there something special about it?"

"I don't think so. She said she bought it on sale over the summer. She wore it once, and then I didn't see it any more. I assumed it was at the cleaners. It was very mature for her. I thought it was a little over the top, but teenagers don't take advice from their mothers very well. So I didn't say anything."

"Did you see Christi that morning?"

"No." There was a catch in Maddie's voice now. "I had an early meeting. Her first class started at ten, and of course she'd spent the night at your house."

"What about the day before?"

"No. I…we are both busy; she was watching your house… and…no, I didn't."

There was a small sob.

"What about her car, Maddie. Where's her car?"

"I don't know. I suppose it's in the garage. I'll have to look. She walks…walked…to school. Saved money…for exercise. It's close, you know."

"Maddie, how did she get to my house in Malaga Cove?"

"I don't know. Must have gotten a ride."

"How was she going to get home?"

"Someone must have picked her up."

"What's the name of her boyfriend, the one she had the fight with?"

"Jeff…Jeff Harwood."

"From the high school?"

"Yes, but now he's in college. USC I think. I thought he was a nice guy…On the football team. Seemed to like Christi a lot."

"When did they break up?"

"I'd guess it started about the middle of the summer. It was just little things. He wasn't around so much. Didn't call. When he did call, she would duck him. There may have been someone else."

"Do you know who?"

"No."

"You said she wasn't sexually active. Are you sure?"

"I'm sure. We didn't talk about it though. She's just turned 18 you know…I mean… she was…" Maddie whispered. "I guess there were a lot of things I didn't really know."

"Have you talked to Jake yet?"

"Yes. I called him after you left Friday night. He was in shock and very angry. He yelled a lot, said it was my fault, and I raised her all wrong. Said he'd never forgive me…I'd destroyed the only thing in his world, crap like that. So I just hung up."

"Did she seem unhappy lately? Anxious? Maybe over stressed?"

"No."

"Was she on any kind of medication?"

"Just multivitamins."

"Was there any reason at all you can think of for her to commit suicide?"

"Absolutely not. She was happy and excited about life. Looking forward to college. …She had everything going for her."

Maddie started to cry softly.

"Ok, Maddie, get some rest…Oh, one more thing. The detective on the case is not inclined to let me look over his shoulder in the investigation…surprise, surprise. You need to call the Mayor. Ask him to make an informal request to the police chief to allow me access."

"Okay," she whispered. Then she hung up.

Chapter 6 - Sunday

The Judge made a few notes on his conversation with Maddie, and then shaved, showered, and dressed. He selected light brown chinos, a deep blue golf shirt, a tan golf jacket, and brown loafers.

He headed down to the Yellow Kettle, a local brunch café, small and intimate, tucked away in the Plaza in Malaga Cove. He had his coffee and the forbidden coffee cake his doctor forbid, along with his second newspaper, the *Wall Street Journal.* He'd watch people sitting on the patio and ones strolling by. He would pretend they were friends. They weren't exactly friends, of course. They were neighbors; familiar faces from living on The Hill a long time. But he didn't really know any of them he supposed. He hadn't been so good at making friends. Naturally shy, he'd focused his life on being a judge.

He hadn't noticed there was no one else…just the work. But now, the work was gone.
Now that he was 'retired'. Was that the right word? For being voted out of office? 'Retired'? Maybe it was more like, 'run off the bench' or 'run out of town….The hell with it.

He was totally alone. Except of course for the new pooch. He'd left Annie at home this morning. He wanted to focus on Christi. Annie would be hurt and moody on his return, but she'd forget in an hour or two.

Unlike a human female, Annie had a very short-term memory for such slights. And for practically everything else for that matter, especially prohibitions on climbing the sofa, snatching food off the kitchen counter, digging up the lawn, and worst of all, disappearing with his socks.

What happened on that cliff that led to Christi's floating among the rocks? What went wrong? Who shared responsibility, perhaps failing to catch warning signs, or to act? What could have been done to save her?

The Judge was nothing if not analytical. Were it not for Maddie's grief, the puzzle of it would have been most enjoyable.

A young woman in a white tennis outfit that showed off her long pale legs came around the old brick office building that anchored a corner of the small plaza for the Yellow Kettle patio.

The judge wasn't above admiring the local flora and fauna. After all he was still a male, although well past his prime, he mused.

But this girl's large blue eyes pinned themselves on the Judge, daring him to look away.

The Judge suddenly felt caught, like a peeping Tom. He supposed his glance had contained a certain amount of sexual energy that she had sensed.

He thought about glancing casually around the rest of the plaza in a show of disinterest. But the girl would have none of it. She winked of all things, and then headed right for his table, prematurely extending her hand as she approached.

He automatically rose and extended his hand as she got closer. He didn't know what else to do. He had no idea who this pretty creature was.

"You're the judge," she said, giving his hand a firm shake.

Her dad had taught her well.

"I've seen you a couple of times walking your puppy, but you don't know me. I'm Katy Thorne. I work at the high school. A counselor there." This all came out in a nervous rush. "I called Maddie to say how sorry I was. She said you were looking into what happened. She asked if I would share my impressions of Christi with you. Oh…and she said you would be at this table at this joint about this time today. I guess you're a predictable guy, Judge."

These sentences came out in quick bursts, giving little chance to cut in. But they came out in a good-natured way, forthright, and with a smile. The judge suspected Ms. Thorne must be a little low on breath now, so he waded into the one sided conversation.

"Would you like to sit down?" he asked, letting go with his best charming smile, one he hadn't used for some time. He felt faintly like the Cheshire Cat.

She pulled out the chair across from him at the table and gracefully slid into the seat.

Ms. Thorne was tall, perhaps 5' 8,", slender, all arms and legs. Her blouse was open at the top, perhaps a button more than the Judge might have approved if she been his daughter. But she was past the age of taking advice from parents. She had long brown hair, twisted together in a ponytail that bobbed around when she talked. She had small delicate features and smile lines.

Her nose was a bit long and narrow, but in that it matched her head, also more oblong than round, but all very delicate.

Her face was pale white, as though never in the sun. It faded into the white of her clothes, lending to a slightly washed out appearance in the bright light.

She had the most extraordinary eyes, vivid blue like the Caribbean, large and intelligent, with long lashes. He bet she'd look like dynamite in a brightly colored cocktail dress, all pale white skin and blue eyes.

Then he caught himself and gave himself a mental kick. She was easily 20 years his junior. Just a kid.

"How well did you know Christi?" asked the Judge.

"As school counselor, I see most everybody, in the halls or in my office," replied Ms. Thorne. "I knew Christi better than most.

"Maddie sent me a signed authorization, as the surviving parent, giving me permission to talk with you, Judge, about my conversations with Christi as a counselor. She requested I tell you whatever I could. As to Christi, I saw her all of twice. She wanted to talk about relationships with men."

"Did she have a boyfriend?"

"Yes. But they weren't getting along. I heard they broke up for good several weeks ago. Said she was feeling trapped in the relationship; the boy was too immature. She didn't know how to gracefully exit. He was very involved emotionally. They had been together for six months - a lifetime when you're in high school, or in his case now, transitioning to college.

"Did you tell her to have the 'let's just be friends' conversation?" asked the Judge.

"Oh, no," said Katy. "I think that's needlessly cruel."

"Oh," said the Judge, thinking privately that the old wisdom was still the best. Straight up honesty: it's over honey, face the death of the relationship head on, shake hands, wish one luck, and out of there lickety-split. Preferably orchestrated in a crowded restaurant to minimize tears and hysterics. These young females liked to complicate everything to accentuate the drama.

"I told her not to call names. Not to criticize. But to be forthright and real about what she was feeling. If she felt trapped, perhaps wanting to date other boys, she needed to communicate that in the context of her, not him. It was her life. She needed to direct herself along the path she thought best."

"Oh," the Judge said again. He was out of his depth, and he knew it.

"Did you talk to the boyfriend at all?" asked the Judge.

"No. I wouldn't have, even if she'd told me his name, which she didn't."

"Did she say anything else about the relationship, or what was going on in her life?"

"Not directly," said Katy, "but there was a feeling I got…"

"Go on," said the Judge, after forcefully reminding himself that this was not a courtroom. The rules of evidence didn't apply. Feelings and impressions could be relevant. Very relevant.

"Christi went on to talk a lot about maturity. How older men were more interesting: more interesting stories, more accomplishments, a more mature perspective on things. Wisdom gained through experience. Christi said she felt safer in some way with an older man, stronger, successful, established. She contended older men were emotionally experienced, understood emotional commitment, were more receptive to a partner's emotional needs, and so on. The usual rubbish men foist off on inexperienced young women."

The Judge was pretty certain his experience did make him more interesting. Evidently that didn't count for much in the eyes of Ms. Twiddle Dee.

"Are you inexperienced?" The question just popped out. The Judge hadn't meant to say it, but he had. Damn.

Ms. Thorn's eyes flashed up at the Judge, a bit of fresh color coming into her cheeks.

Then…she smiled at the Judge. And the Judge was bowled over.

It was like a rainbow of warmth, starting in her lips and then spilling up into the sparkling blue eyes.

The Judge couldn't help himself. He looked deep into her eyes…And he smiled too.

This seemed to satisfy her in some unfathomable way. She modestly looked down for a second, and then continued her story as though nothing had passed between them.

But something had. The Judge wasn't quite sure what. He was confused, but not uncomfortable.

Whatever had happened, something inside him wished it would happen again.

"Anyway," continued Miss Thorne, "I had the feeling that she had someone specific in mind."

"Did you ask her about it?"

"No. In my business you can listen, you can give advice if you're asked, and you can often subtly communicate some suggestions, but you can't act like a parent. You can't interrogate, cram down information, make judgments, or dictate or demand decisions. You step over those boundaries and you lose trust. You become just another prying adult. Whatever perspective or suggestions you've previously made are filed under 'adult advice: ignore'. You have to tread lightly…let a relationship develop, and then let a particular subject or topic ripen."

Miss Thorne punctuated this with a sly look from under her eyelashes, which the Judge supposed was for emphasis.

"Did you see her with anyone else on campus?" the Judge asked. "Or perhaps off?"

"No. Sorry Judge, no solid evidence." The Judge got a smile here. "Just my impression. I don't know, maybe I should have pressed her more. I thought she might come and talk again, but she didn't. Of course, I had no idea she would throw herself off a cliff."

"Did she?" asked the Judge.

Ms. Thorne got very quiet and her eyes went a bit wide. "Didn't she?"

"I don't know," said the Judge, "but I'm going to find out."

They both looked out at a large cluster of bicyclists in brightly colored Lycra rolling into the Cove Plaza, mixing with other cyclists parked at, departing, or generally milling around the central fountain. Much like a flock of colorful pigeons.

The Judge mused that if he just had the right pigeon food, he could throw a handful out. They would all jump on their bikes and cluster around him. Perhaps if he threw out a bucket of greenbacks…

"So, I understand you're not married," said Ms. Thorne, blue eyes pinning his again.

"What?" said the Judge, totally taken aback by this pivot in the conversation. Damn this woman. She was a nosy son of a bitch.

"Ah, no. I was once, but it didn't work out."

"Sorry to hear that Judge. Do you date?"

Jesus, thought the Judge, *this young woman is really out there.*

"Is this a counseling session, Counselor?" asked the Judge, stalling for time and, if he was lucky, perhaps a wave off.

Ms. Thorne wouldn't be deterred.

"I have a friend that needs to be fixed up, and you'd be perfect."

That was too much for the Judge. Both hands shot up out in front of him, palms flat.

"No, no, I'm a very solitary creature. If I wanted to go out there's no limit to the people I know, and besides this whole conversation is way too personal." It was time to call a spade a spade, or in this case, impolite as impolite.

The Judge was restraining himself from using the "Judicial Voice", although something about those blue eyes made it difficult to get angry. The blue eyes were full of amusement now, no embarrassment, no remorse for prying, no apology, just amusement…and perhaps a twinkle.

The Judge felt extraordinarily uncomfortable, like an insect pinned into a collection box, and yet…It had been a long time since a pretty young female had given him personal notice.

"Okay, Judge," Ms. Thorne said, standing up. "But I'm going to inquire anyway. Maybe I'll just have her give you a call." She threw him a smile that matched her eyes.

"You never know what can happen; you turn a corner, and it can all be new. You've got to keep a little bit of the romantic, Judge. But let me think some more about my conversation with Christi. Then we'll talk again. Perhaps I can help you figure out why it happened."

This all came out in a rush again as she prepared to leave.

"Alright," the Judge said, after the barrage of words subsided.

He belatedly realized that his "alright" could be construed as implied consent to both further help and also to a blind date call. He bit his lip, then opened his mouth to elaborate.

But it was too late. She had turned and was steaming away across the patio toward the Plaza, a young woman on a mission.

Why did every Tom, Dick and Harry female assume he needed to be fixed up? the Judge groused. *Why did he bring out this 'fix you up' instinct in females? Why couldn't they see he was a solitary old reprobate, sort of a Henry Higgins type, who was perfectly happy? How'd that song go?* - "Just an Ordinary Man"…*Why couldn't they just leave him alone?*

But what a smile. He sighed. He wished he were thirty again. But that number had come and gone like the wind, and was only a dusty memory back a long, crooked road.

The Judge returned to his paper and coffee, shaking off the melancholy, determined to enjoy his solitude.

Chapter 7 - Sunday

The Judge backed his 40-year-old Jaguar convertible down his twisty driveway and then out across the street, turning to creep downhill at a leisurely pace. The odometer had stopped at 65,000 miles some 20 years before. The Judge saw no particular need to fix it then, or since. The car was dearly loved. To the Judge it was like a second skin.

Some contended it was a phallic symbol. The Judge chose to ignore folks with this view. The car…his car…the "E", reminded him more of a sensuous woman. She was a 1969 XKE roadster convertible, tricked out in British Racing Green, and her top was always down. She had slender hips at the rear, a large curvaceous body, and sleek sidelines that bespoke breeding and speed. She had a generous mound on her hood that caught the eye and excited, and her chrome, spoked wheels gave her dancing feet. Her engines purred through twin tail pipes, and her slanted headlights added an exotic touch.

The Lucas electrical system gave her the temperament of a female. You could not be sure the engine would start or the lights would work; it was always a little dicey. That was her intrigue.

There was one small flaw. At 6 foot 3, the Judge didn't really fit in the E. In fact, the top was always down because it was hard for him to drive it otherwise.

Once behind the wheel, the Judge stuck up above the windshield like a carrot top. He suspected he looked silly driving the car. An overage man with overage weight squeezed into a young man's racing machine, albeit a 40-year-old one.

But the Judge didn't care. He liked the car. He was loyal to the people and the things he liked. He'd bought the E new. He'd seen it well loved and well driven, initially as a fancy new car that turned heads, then as a prestigious part of the Jaguar line…that still turned heads, and more recently as a vintage sports car…that *still* turned heads.

The Judge swung down to Palos Verdes Drive West, the ocean rim road, and then south toward Bluff Cove, catching expansive views of surf and rocks. It was three in the afternoon. The sun was warm, but the air had a hint of colder days to come.

He pulled into Lunada Bay past the Ranch Market and then turned right down Yarmo Road, Maddie's street.

He pulled into Maddie's driveway, again marveling at the sale prices commanded by these modest bungalows. No one answered the bell. When he'd called she hadn't answered, so he'd assumed she was out.

What do you do two days after your daughter dies, he wondered. Go to the market?
Pay the utility bills? Go to church, to a shrink? Go to an undertaker, to Forest Lawn?
…Perhaps to the drug store for pills. Knowing Maddie, more likely the liquor store.

He walked up to the double garage door, a weathered light blue, tugged up on the handle, and the door slid up. Christi's car was there, a compact Mini Cooper convertible, perhaps three years old.

It was steel grey, with black and white checker details under the windows, and a black convertible top. He tried the door and it opened. He slid in behind the wheel, adjusting the seat back for his bulk.

The car smelled of Christi. The slight scent of the inexpensive perfume was familiar. It had wafted around his house when she arrived to sit the dog, and as she'd left two short days before.

There were school books in the back seat, a set of grade notices tucked in the driver's side visor, sunglasses in one side pocket, Kleenex in the other. A comb, a brush, a pocket mirror, some Chapstick, and Juicy Fruit gum.

He fumbled around a bit and found a lever to release the trunk and went back to have a look. A well-used, mostly tread bare spare tire, jack kit, small tool kit, and a flashlight.

He turned on the flashlight, illuminating the darkest recess of the interior. There was a small zipper bag tucked way back in a corner. He reached way in, pulled it out and opened it. It contained shampoo, soap, a toothbrush, toothpaste, and something royal purple neatly folded.

It was a pair of woman's silk panties, unusual in that an area in the lower crotch had an opening, doubled hemmed on each side.

Something had dropped out as he had unfolded the panties: a little black plastic case. He unsnapped it, and the contents slid out: two unopened condoms, Trojan Magnums.

Chapter 8 - Sunday

The Judge turned into his driveway, put the E away in her garage, rubbed the puppy's ears a little as a hello, and headed for his office in the library.

The Judge's library was a big room, 20 by 30 feet, built as a south wing of the house. A huge cavernous wooden space, defined by the windows and sea view on the one side, and a large fireplace framed by its granite mantle on the other.

The ceiling was divided into 4 by 4 molded wood frames, each containing a hand painted country scene in the 18th century Italian style. The walls were paneled in pine and stained a soft grey. The floor was darkly stained inlaid wood, with three large antique Persian rugs running across it.

Tall windows on the right looked out over the lawn and the vast blue Santa Monica Bay. Heavy curtains in soft blue tones, embroidered with a geometric pattern, hung on each side of the windows, tied in swags by blue silk cord. Glass doors opened outward at the end of the room to a small half-circle brick patio surrounded by garden and high shrubs on three sides, and the sloping front lawn and sea view on the fourth.

The fireplace centered a wall of books, which ran the length of the room, broken here and there by windows opening onto the sheltered rear gardens. There were law books, a collection of first editions from the 20s and 30s, a leather bound set of Shakespeare Classics, various reference books, a couple of large atlases, and stacks of law journals.

An informal sitting group of leather sofa and two leather upholstered arm chairs in darker browns were arranged to the left of the entrance, the sofa positioned to take advantage of the view. The room had a slight smoky leather scent.

The Judge's desk, a carved library table from the 17th century, sat diagonally in the far right corner of the room, with an antique buffet placed behind for laptop and supplies. It was stacked with files and an old rotary telephone the Judge retained with affection. Two soft brown leather upholstered arm chairs, also old and Italian, were arranged in front of the desk

On the floor around the desk's far side and against the wall were a half dozen stacks of legal binders and files, some green, some manila, some brown, cluttered, but with a sense purpose. A bright red copy of the California Corporations Code sat upright on the floor in easy reach of the chair, along with a blue bound volume of the Civil Code. The leather chair behind the desk was well worn.

Even though it was in the most southern corner, the library was, in all respects that mattered, the very center of the house.

There were framed photos of past exploits and travels: fishing in Alaska, sloop racing in the Bahamas, Serengeti ballooning, whale watching in Iceland, Carnival in Rio, and a couple of black and whites of a young Judge, standing tall and straight before the volcano on

Bora Bora, and in front of Mont Saint-Michel. There were no pictures of a wife, children, or other family.

A recent snap of a 9-week-old puppy had been hastily pinned into a temporary cardboard frame and perched on one shelf. It sat beside a tall cut crystal flower vase. Dry and dusty, it hadn't seen a flower in a very long time.

The Judge brought his laptop from the bureau and settled in at his desk. He opened up Google and typed in "Palos Verdes High School. He found a listing of the senior grad students in an online copy of the yearbook, and skimmed through the names until he found Jeff Harwood.

Jeff had big features, small eyes, a square jaw and a rough and ready smile. He had broad shoulders judging from the headshot, and a blond crew cut. He looked the sort that belonged on the school football team, and so he was. A tackle.

The Judge dialed information and asked for the Harwood residences in Palos Verdes. There was only one household listed and the Judge took down the number, and then dialed.

"This is Jeff," said a deep, confident male voice. The Judge explained who he was, what he was about, and asked if he could meet up to ask a few questions.

"You mean now?" asked Jeff. "It's kind of a bad time."

"It'll take just a few minutes," said the Judge. "It often helps to talk some. What you might remember now, Jeff, while it's recent, could make all the difference..."

The Judge droned on until resistance faded. He could be very persistent, much like a car salesmen. Eventually people gave up and gave in.

The Judge headed for the garage and backed the E out of the driveway again.

Jeff Harwood lived with his family in an area of The Hill called Rolling Ranchos. The family would be very well off. It was the most expensive part of The Hill, hidden behind guarded gates and laid out in large, at least one acre lots with open spaces, riding trails and vast views of the ocean and the city from the top of the peninsula.

Once through the gates, the Judge drove along winding roads framed by white picket fencing until he found Conestoga Drive, and turned down it. It was a heavily wooded area. Tall eucalyptus trees lined the road, providing a canopy above the E's open top, while patterns of light splayed through the leaves onto the E's dash. The Judge could smell the eucalyptus, mixed with the earthy scent of the manicured riding trail adjacent to the road.

Jeff 's parent had a large rambling ranch style house, white clapboard and broad windows, with a large circular driveway in front providing the boundary for a huge expanse of deep green lawn. Stables were off to the left and slightly back from the house. On the right a large grazing pasture was framed by the mandatory white rail fencing.

The Judge had been buzzed in at the guard gate, and he supposed that Jeff was the young man leaning against his mailbox, waiting for him.

The Judge pulled up and extended a hand out the E's open window to shake. Jeff obliged.

"Nice to meet you," said the Judge. "Very sorry about the circumstances, and thank you for talking to me.

"Christi's mom, Ms. Benson, has asked me to ask around a little; see if we can find out why she did it. It would help her a lot to understand. This is all off the record. I'm not a policeman or anything. So I hope you'll help us. And I hope you'll be as candid as you can. Christi's gone now, but maybe someone else can be helped."

Jeff listened with a blank stare. The Judge suspected he didn't really give a shit.

The silence hung between them for a beat. Then Jeff blurted out: "Nice car. What year?"

"1969", said the Judge.

"My favorite number," said Jeff with a sly smile.

The Judge had a feeling he wasn't going like this Harwood youngster much.

He got out of the car, sliding on his red USC baseball cap, a token reminder of his days at the University of Southern California, or the University of Spoilt Children, depending on your view. He walked slowly over to Jeff, putting on his 'at the funeral' face, and shook hands again with the young man.

Jeff Harwood was big. Tall, broad shouldered, a bit over six feet, with light brown hair, smallish brown eyes set a tad too close for the Judge's taste, and a strong stubborn-looking jaw. He was dressed in a light brown polo shirt that complemented his eyes and blond hair. It also highlighted his muscular arms and chest. There was a smell of rich boy. Maybe it was the expensive brown loafers or the tan designer jeans. Perhaps it was the manicured nails and designer haircut. Or maybe it was the arrogant way he leaned on his mailbox, or the occasional smirk when he talked.

"You're a Trojan," stated Jeff.

"Yes," said the Judge. "Undergrad and law."

Jeff thrust his hand high, making a "Victory" sign with his fingers. "Go S.C.! My Uncle Richard is on the Board of Trustees; I'm on the Junior Varsity football squad…well, an alternate. I was a tackle on the varsity PV High team."

Jeff was muscular, solid built, even a little chubby. Perhaps 230 lbs. worth of blocking power there. He looked the sort that would like to bang into people.

"How old are you?" asked the Judge.

"Just turned 19."

"Cool", said the Judge, wishing he were 19 too, or anywhere close. "I am very sorry about your girlfriend."

"My ex-girlfriend." A touch of bitterness now crept in behind Jeff's smile. "We dated. But she was pretty lame."

"So you broke up?"

"She broke up."

"When was that?"

"End of August. Just before college started."

"Can you tell me about her, Jeff? How did you two spend time together? "?"

Jeff smiled tight.

“She pretty much wasted my summer."

"How was that?"

"I gave her a lot of time. Lot of my money too. She was always broke. Took her out lots: shopping, movies, Disneyland, Magic Mountain. Then there were lunches; dinners. We spent time in La Jolla and Santa Barbara; did lots of stuff. Treated her like a queen. Introduced her around to my surfing buddies. Got her in the inner circle…dudes like me from behind the Gates.

"She had no friends at the beginning of the summer, ‘cept her three lame girlfriends. By the end of the summer she knew all the best surfers here on The Hill. It’s a special fraternity you know. We had good times together I guess, but it apparently meant more to me than it did to her."

"She broke it off?" asked the Judge.

"She dumped me as soon as school started. Couldn't get rid of me quick enough. Threw me away, just like that. One day she says she loves me, next day she snaps her fingers and I'm toast. Like I turned into a frog or something.”

“Did you two always get along when you were together?”

“Not always. She was a female, right? They have the times of the month where they kind of go nuts. And sometimes she'd get really bitchy, for no reason. We had some awful fights.

"She knew how to get to me. Could say some really mean things. Wouldn't take any of my advice. She was Miss High and Mighty a lot. Could use all my time, spend all my money, and then just abandon me to flirt with some other guy right in front of me. She was kind of mean that way.

"If you go together, certain responsibilities go with that. Returning calls, sharing schedules, being available...the usual stuff. She had a lot to learn about relationships. I tried to teach her some. But she was selfish, stubborn; I don't know, a lot of the time just mean. And boy what a sharp tongue."

"So you weren't a big fan of Christi's in the end?"

"She didn't love me, despite what she said. Didn't appreciate me. Didn't value our relationship. By the end of the summer it felt like she was just trashing me every chance she got. Flirting with other guys in front of me. Always demanding I spend more money on her. Calling me cheap, immature, shallow. Breaking dates for no reason. Wouldn't answer my calls or texts at certain times. Always very critical of what I thought; condescending almost.

"Well, you can see where it got her. She should have stuck with me, made a bigger effort, built something with me. If she'd done that, she'd be alive."

The Judge's blue eyes snapped to Jeff's. "Why do you say that?"

"I...I mean...well...she...she'd had no reason to jump off a cliff with me. Treated like a frigging queen. The new guy probably screwed her over. Broke her heart or something. Good for him. How the hell do I know? I don't want to think about it anymore."

"What new guy?"

"The guy she left me for. Turns out she wasn't exactly exclusive while we were together. She was seeing some other guy. Cheating on me. Porking him. All summer I think."

"Did you have a sexual relationship?"

"I won't answer that." Jeff's voice rose an octave and his eyes flashed. "You're not even a cop. I don't have to answer."

"You just did. You think she was having sex with this other guy too?"

"She was screwing him big time. My surfer bro saw them…on the beach…Bluff Cove." Hah, Bluff Cove. Guess it was buff cove for her."

"That made you angry?"

"Hell yes, it made me angry.

"She's supposed to be my girl. She's spending all of my money for me. She's sucking up all my time and attention, or she was. She weasels herself into my exclusive surfer gang, then starts flirting with every damn one of them. Suddenly she's belittling everything I say. Ignoring all my advice. Suddenly I can't do or say anything right.

"Then I find out she has this other guy and she's sleeping with him behind my back. It made me sick.

"I almost think she deserved what she got." Jeff folded his arms, suggesting the issue was closed.

"What did she get?" asked the Judge, again pinning Jeff with his eyes.

"I mean…I don't know…I mean, whatever happened with her lover boy."

"Who was her lover boy?"

"Don't know. Some old fart I suspect."

"Why do you say that?"

“Cause she called me immature. Too young for her. Not man enough, crap like that.”

“Who’s your surfer friend? The one who saw them.”

“Mark Daniels. He’s a twilight surfer like me.”

“So you’re not sorry Christi’s dead?”

“I didn’t say that."

"I guess I'm sorry. But my surfer buds all knew she played me. I looked stupid.”

The Judge could sense raw emotion. Perhaps the young man was not as nonchalant as he pretended…. about the breakup…about her death…about any of it. The second stage of grief after shock was anger.

“Was there a confrontation when she broke if off?”

"Yes." Jeff's voice had gotten hoarse now.

“What happened?”

“It was in the high school parking lot. Beginning of the semester. We had a shouting match.”

"What happened?"

“She called me a dickless wonder.” There was residual shock in the young man’s voice.

“Me…Can you believe it? Said I couldn’t hold a real woman, not mature enough. Called me a real jerk. All this crap came out of her mouth. Said I had a pencil dick. Fuuuck…” Color was coming into Jeff’s face as he re-lived the clash.

“What started it?” asked the Judge.

“Wouldn’t talk to me. Wouldn’t return my calls. All communication just suddenly stopped. So I waited in the PV High School lot cause I knew she had to register. USC starts later, so I had time. I caught up with her by her car after registration. Asked her what the hell was going on.

"That was before I'd heard about her doing this other guy. She wouldn't talk, tried to ignore me. Tried to walk around me. So I grabbed her, held her hands so she had to talk to me. She really got mad then, really lost it. Called me these names. Dumb jock. A bully. An asshole. Told me to stop stalking her. Me…stalking her, little Miss goody two shoes. I couldn't believe it."

"So then what happened?"

"I got mad too. Grabbed her car keys. Threw them as far as I could onto the baseball field. So she couldn't leave. Figured she have to stay and talk. Called her a tramp. Didn't know how right I was. Told her she was dead as far as I was concerned. Told her she'd be sorry for stringing me along. Called her a ho. She didn't like that." Jeff smirked, recalling her fury.

"That's when she slapped my face."

"So I hit her back. The bitch. I don't give a fuck, I'm glad I did it. Nobody hits me in the face and gets away with it. Nobody.

"Then she pulled this female shit in front of everybody coming onto the campus. Pretended I hit her too hard. Kind of slid down the side of her car to the ground, like she was stunned or something. Like she couldn't stand. I didn't hit her that hard. Wish I had.

"Anyways, she starts to cry. Someone said the security asshole was heading over. One of her friends said they'd called the police. So, I left. Assholes, all of them."

"Did you threaten her?" asked the Judge.

Jeff took a long breath in and then let it out slowly, reflectively…making a sound like a surfacing whale.

"I was angry. I don't know what I said. I've discussed all this with the detective. I didn't mean any of it. Just got angry. Said a lot of stupid stuff."

"But you meant to hit her."

"She hit me first….what the fuck? If a woman wants to hit a guy, she should expect to get it back. That's equality, like they're always talking about."

"So was it a punch, or just a slap?"

"Oh come on, it was just a tap. Probably a good lesson. I don't know why she fell."

"Did you lose your head again on the Malaga Cove Bluff, on Friday ?"

Jeff looked stunned. "No. I don't know anything about that. When she took her big nose dive I was here studying for a test."

"With your parents?"

"My parents were out of town over the weekend."

"So can anyone vouch for you being here all afternoon?"

"No, but this is where I was."

"How often did you see each other when you were together?"

"Twice, three times a week. Then in the middle of the summer she suddenly didn't have as much time for me anymore. By August maybe I'd see her once a week. And she was always moody and unresponsive."

"What else did you two do when you were together? "

"She was always pushing for me to take her shopping, so we went shopping for her a lot. God, I hate shopping. She'd come to the beach and watched me surf. We'd hang with my surfing buddies. Just stuff."

"Was there any hint of depression?"

"No."

"What about when you had your breakup fight? Did she seem depressed? "

"No, just mean."

"Who were her other friends at school?"

"Katherine, Hannah, and Paige. Her three stooges. Might have been others in their little clique, I don't know."

"Were there other guy friends?"

"You mean besides the guy screwing her? Don't know."

"Were there any older adults she was close to? Adults besides her mom and dad; perhaps a cousin or a neighbor or teacher?"

"Don't know."

"She told me she visited the school counselor once or twice. She liked her English teacher, Mrs. Roth. And spring semester she had the new history teacher. She liked his class. I got real tired of hearing about history. But she wouldn't have talked to either of them outside class. Teachers at PV High are unapproachable."

"Was she close to her Dad?"

"Didn't ever talk about him. I've never met him."

"Did she ever wear a light blue dress, or talk about a blue dress?"

"Hell, Judge, she's a girl. They wear all the colors. She talked to me about dresses only when she wanted me to buy, and that was all the time. A lot of my god damn allowance went to cover her back."

"But you don't recall any blue dress she might have worn?"

"Nope."

"Ok, Jeff, You've been very helpful. Thanks for the time."

As the Judge walked back to the E he pondered this new Christi, so different from Maddie's image. He wondered if there was a relationship or a connection between Jeff, with his smoldering anger even now after several weeks, and Christi's plunge off that cliff. Maybe she was pushed, despite the folded up dress.

He considered his own limited relationship with Christi. Did he miss some telltale sign of potential self-destruction? This triggered a new memory. Two afternoons before, when she had come to house sit and he was packing, they had talked a little. She'd asked a funny question. What was it?

Something about records. Could you get in trouble for record destruction? Something like that.

He had replied offhandedly, as he had thousands of times to those who asked questions out of the blue, seeking free legal advice.

"No, not generally if they are your records. Unless the records are subject to a subpoena for record production, or you are destroying evidence of a crime, or stuff like that."

He hadn't seen her face; he was packing his case. But he'd sensed her stiffen. Damn, he'd forgotten about that.

Anyway, Christi didn't strike him as a candidate for a jump off a cliff. That was one of the reasons he'd agreed to look into it - it just didn't feel right. Of course, frankly, he didn't have much else to do.

Chapter 9 - Monday

Dawn was crisp and clear on The Hill. Stockbrokers roared out in their fancy show cars around 5 a.m. to work, followed around 8 by bankers in prestigious, but less flashy autos, and by engineers in smaller economical cars, all newer models with the latest gadgets.

Moms were out between 7 and 8 a.m. on bus runs, dropping school kids, and around 9 a.m. lawyers sped away, heading for offices downtown, Century City, or Beverly Hills, driving as competitively as they practiced.

At 10 a.m. the real estate brokers departed for their local offices, geared up with pocket listings and smoldering negotiations they needed to fan.

The departing denizens of The Hill were met by an onslaught of incoming traffic. A few doctors returning from all night surgeries, some driving vintage sports cars only they could afford, mingled with a plethora of gardeners, housekeepers, window washers, pool cleaners, home repair contractors, food purveyors for The Hill's handful of boutique restaurants, and so on, the invisible people who kept life on The Hill 'civilized'.

Since the Judge wasn't a judge anymore, he had the luxury of getting up anytime he wanted. But old habits aren't easily dropped. He popped up like toast a little after 6 a.m., padded into his kitchen in royal purple robe and slippers and made himself coffee. The machine made one cup at a time from a small canister. He'd learnt that if you ran it twice and switched cups half way through each time, dumping the second half of the brew, you got a reasonable cup of coffee.

He hadn't slept well. Images of Christi dancing on the edge of the cliff, and then throwing files into a bonfire, competed with the lonely image of the cold body on the stretcher. He shook this all off around 3 a.m., after making himself some hot chocolate, and had settled into a deep sleep which lasted until his internal alarm went off. Or maybe it was just a need to take a whiz. He wasn't sure, but he seemed to wake up around 6 a.m. most mornings.

He supposed he was a sight, his hair at odd angles and his face still filled with sleep, his robe pulled tight around his continually expanding paunch, marching across his wet lawn to retrieve his newspapers. But there was no one to dress for except the puppy. She was very forgiving about how he looked. Her affection for him was unconditional.

The Judge settled in behind his desk with the LA Times and his cup of coffee, saving the New York Times and Wall Street Journal for later. The third page of the local section had a small picture of Christi and a story of her suicide. It was reported the body was discovered by local residents.

The Judge got no mention for sounding the alarm. A bit shallow in reporting he thought, slightly miffed.

He had called Maddie yesterday evening, to see how she was doing with the funeral arrangements, and to ask a few more questions. Christi had been an intern most of the summer with the firm of Harley & Johns, long time real estate developers, building and operating apartments and shopping centers on The Hill and throughout the Greater South Bay area of Los Angeles.

She worked for a small wage and for the experience. They didn't pay interns much these days. Any sort of internship was in demand for the experience, the resume boost, and the chance of a real hire later.

Christi had worked for Gloria as an office assistant. Maddie wasn't sure of Gloria's last name.

Finishing the LA Times, he padded off to his bedroom at the other end of the house to shave and shower. He dressed, bundled the other two papers under his arm, and decided to walk down to Malaga Cove for a full breakfast again at the Yellow Kettle. He liked it there, particularly early on Monday mornings, when everyone was busy coffeeing up or eating and then dashing off to work. It was his kind of place. He felt less alone with all the people sitting and bustling in and then off in a swirl of activity around him.

As he walked around the corner to the Yellow Kettle cafe and its patio, there was Ms. Thorn. And she was sitting at the Judge's usual table.

The Judge made a break left for another table at the other end of the patio, discretely avoiding eye contact. But Ms. Thorn spotted him immediately and began waving both hands up in the air, arms extended, as though she were a soccer coach and her team had just scored. She even called across the short distance, "Oh Judge …Over here, Judge…Over here!"

The Judge was trapped. There was no polite way to avoid her. Heads were already turning at other tables to see who had made the goal.

The Judge let go of the prospect of enjoying his coffee and paper in quiet solitude and reluctantly turned back toward Ms. Thorn, who was now all smiles, having clearly gotten past his defense.

She was dressed all in canary yellow. A short skirt displayed her spindly legs discreetly folded at the ankles under the table, and a blouse with puffy shoulders and descending V-neck line completed her ensemble. The Judge couldn't help but admire what he considered to be a lot of "V" in the V. His generation was far more conservative in their displays, but he grudgingly admitted to himself that she filled the outfit out nicely.

Small high breasts, or at least the dress suggested so. You never really knew these days with the clever advances in structural support. The cleavage displayed was provocative, but within, he supposed, acceptable good taste under current mores. The dress fitted closely around her narrow waist, and then flared around the hips. He visualized the tennis shorts of the day before to fill out her hips and thighs within. The yellow fabric gathered at her middle left more to the imagination than her tennis shorts, but the Judge had a good imagination. It was automatic. He was male.

She wore a wide dark brown belt, and matching 3-inch heels. If she stood, he was sure he would be looking up at her.

There was very little that intimidated the Judge, but for some reason the Judge felt awkward and uncomfortable.

This young lady looked like a large soft butterfly, perched on her chair, but ready to take flight. But was she was going to fly away from the Judge…or at him?

"Come on, Judge, sit down. I'll buy you a coffee." Her sea blue eyes scanned his, almost a twinkle in them. "I heard you're usually here around this hour. Often even at this table."

The Judge had a brief vision of being stalked, like a beetle suddenly aware of the shadow of a descending butterfly, but it passed. A ridiculous notion. Butterflies don't stalk beetles. Besides, he was The Judge.

It was his turn to extend his hand for that firm handshake, but only because she had gotten to his table first.

Ms. Thorn immediately turned business-like, reassuring the Judge he was reasonably safe.

"So Judge, I went through my notes on my conversations with Christi, and I have a bit more to report. Since it's Monday, I thought well, I'll just report to you now before school, and maybe buy you a cup of coffee. Last time I saw you, you looked like you needed someone to buy you coffee."

The Judge was about to take exception, but there was suddenly the smile again…all perfect teeth, likely a set of expensive golf clubs for a dentist when she was younger. It wasn't the smile per se --it was a wonderful smile of course-- but the way the smile spread up her face and into her sparkling blue eyes, which opened wide and gazed directly into his. It was both a smile and a shared intimacy, somehow just for him.

The Judge couldn't resist it. He smiled back. That made her smile widen even further, and somewhere inside her he thought he caught the brief glimpse of a victory dance. *Don't be crazy*, he scolded himself.

She pulled a couple of yellow legal-size pages out of a folder, and then looked around cautiously to be sure no one would overhear.

"I'm not bound by the Hippocratic oath, but the school would not be happy if they knew I was discussing notes with someone other than a parent, although I have Maddie's signed paper work. Still, Christi's gone now, Maddie wants you to have all information available, and it was an opportunity to see you again…" This last with another flash of the smile and teeth. "Let's just not tell anyone we had this conversation."

"It's totally off the record, Ms. Thorn," said the Judge.

"It's just Katy, Judge. Anyway, I saw her twice, once near the end of the spring term, and once at the beginning of the term this fall. In the spring, my notes pretty much reflect what I told you before: personal conflict about what to do with her boyfriend, unsatisfied needs in a relationship, and so on. Pretty much girl talk I don't think you'd understand." Another soft smile to soften her rebuke.

The Judge let it pass. For some reason, the Judge let a lot pass with this young woman. It just felt good to listen to her and watch the smile flag on and off.

"The meeting this fall was different. She wanted to know about birth control, how effective condoms were in staving off pregnancy. I gave her the statistics, 14% to 15 % failure rate over 12 months of use without a spermicidal agent, 95% effectiveness with. We also discussed proper technique."

"Do you learn that first hand getting a college degree?" asked the Judge. He couldn't resist, it was the devil in him coming out. He felt…almost jealous.

She blushed, a sunrise sort of affair, rising from her chest up her throat and into her cheeks. It was quite satisfying to watch. And reassuring too: some part of this very modern young woman was still modest. He suddenly felt like a bully picking on a small kid, ashamed at his petty victory.

She looked at him closely, and concluded, as was true, that the comment had just slipped out. He wasn't trying to be sarcastic. And maybe there was something more…A test had been passed. She was somehow now on a different footing with her Judge.

So instead of taking offense, she flashed the teeth and smile again, all the way up to the blue eyes, which focused on his.

"Christi seemed disturbed by the statistics. But she immediately switched topics, giving me no chance to probe."

"Switched topics to what?"

"It was a legal question, Judge. Your world not mine. She wanted to know if destroying records in the middle of an investigation of a company could get her personally in trouble."

"What'd you say?"

"I said she ought to talk to you, I wouldn't have a clue."

"You knew I hired her from time to time to house-sit?"

"I did. Through the grapevine I guess. But I've been watching you walk that puppy on your lonely walks since the beginning of school."

"What's lonely about my walks? I like my solitude. And I have the puppy for companionship. It's the time I do my reflecting. The scenery is magnificent, the walk is healthy, and I can step out of my door to start. What could be better? Some men don't need a gaggle of people around them to feel alive and relevant…"

The Judge ran out of breath, realized he'd said more than he intended, and slammed his mouth shut. It sounded defensive, even to him.

The teeth flashed in a smile again. Another victory sign, the Judge suspected.

Katy immediately took the opportunity opened by the Judge's retort. She was quick, the Judge had to give her that.

"Well, I talked to my friend, and she would like to meet you. You know, for sort of a traditional, non-internet blind date. She's a little younger than you, but very nice, sort of an old fashioned girl." Again, the teeth.

The Judge was stunned; he heard himself asking how much younger, before he could clamp his mouth closed again.

"About 20 years I guess."

Damn, damn, damn, why couldn't females just leave solitary old men alone? The Judge could feel himself starting to blush, but controlled it.

"Ms. Thorn, I really don't need to be…fixed up," said the Judge, trying with all his might to get his old judicial burr into his voice, but with little success.

"Call me Katy, Judge. This girl's very nice. Works hard at a professional job she takes quite seriously. But she's lonely. She's not a fancy lawyer like you, but she'd be very…sociable. A homebody type; she'd be fun to date once and see. She'd make someone real happy in a relationship. Besides, she's a neighbor in your community, Judge. She's seen you walk your puppy, thinks you're quite handsome, in a rugged sort of way. And she's not unattractive by any means. She'd enjoy having dinner with you at a restaurant she probably couldn't afford. She works at the high school teaching the next generation of this country for peanuts. You can't just clump around and ignore her. You owe her at least one dinner. A chance to see if there might be chemistry. Cause you're the Judge, a single male, and her neighbor. You have to be fair about this."

This came out in a rush, climaxed with the teeth, but this time was there a hint of desperation behind the smile.

The Judge was startled by this onslaught. He almost felt in court again. But he was determined to put a quick end to it.

"Look, Ms. Thorne…".

"Katy."

"Look Ms…er, Katy. I'm an old guy. Someone 20 years my junior, a generation younger, has no interest in the likes of me. We'd have nothing to talk about. There'd be no sexual attraction on her part. In fact, someone like that would only be interested in an old reprobate like me for money, lifestyle, security, all the wrong reasons. I know about these 'move-up' females in LA, the ones who marry serially, moving up to richer husbands each time, leaving a trail of vanquished dreams, shredded assets and large legal bills."

The Judge was almost on a rant now. He looked across the table to see if he'd made his point, if he'd put an end to the absurd proposal.

What he saw made him very uncomfortable. The teeth vanished and Katy's face started to crumple. There was no other way to describe it.

She looked like a little girl whose ice cream has just toppled off to the ground. She dropped her eyes to her coffee. Her shoulders slumped and she suddenly seemed smaller and frail. It was like watching a balloon with a large leak.

The Judge felt guilty and mean, for no rational reason he could fathom. Like a scrooge pricking people's balloons. Or maybe just a prick.

He'd always been a sucker for little girl charm. For some reason, he hated to disappoint this young lady.

"Look Ms.. Thorne… ah, Katy," he said softly in his kindest voice. "I don't want to disappoint your friend, but I've been alone a long time now. One gets set in their ways, and quite happy with their solitude, and…"

His voice trailed off as her blue eyes came up again to hold his, her chin now pointed out like the prow of a ship.

"Look, Judge," she said, "…I'm the date…"

"Oh!" That was all the Judge could manage.

She immediately took that as an affirmative and before the Judge could gather his wits and protest, she jumped up, leaned over to pat to top of his hand with one of hers while displaying a most distracting view of her V-necked blouse, and steamed off, leaving the Judge with an over-the-shoulder, "Great, Judge. Got to go. Late for work..."

Chapter 10 - Tuesday

The morning broke with a cloud bank thick as cotton laid out over the Bay and the L.A. Basin. The Judge looked out his study window across the thick white layer to the distant tops of downtown LA's skyscrapers rising above the mist. He felt a little like Jack at the top of the beanstalk, surveying the distant tangle of towers from across a plain of white.

After papers and coffee, this time at the comparative safety of his desk where he wouldn't run into Ms. Thorn, he shaved and dressed, slipping into his daily uniform, grey slacks, blue striped dress shirt open at the collar, blue blazer and soft brown loafers. He piled into the E and headed off for Palos Verdes High School. The previous afternoon he'd talked to the principle and cleared his presence on campus to interview a few people who knew Christi. He wanted to be there before classes started.

The Judge drove the E around the large block which contained Palos Verdes High looking for suitable parking, which was tight, and drifted down a long alley-like road at the back of the school itself, snaring a good parallel spot when another car pulled out.

The E turned heads as it always did. But this wasn't an old crowd who could really appreciate a '69 E convertible. Heads were probably turning as much in amazement at the old fart driving, his head towering above the windscreen, squeezed in like some over-ripe melon, as to admire a legendary car that few had likely seen up close in their young lives. The attention still gave the Judge some measure of satisfaction.

Well just so it doesn't get scratched, thought the Judge frostily. He didn't 'not' like kids, he supposed. A clear double negative in his thinking, and untidy. It was just he'd never gotten around to having one. And now…beginning his 50s, time had pretty much run out. It seemed unlikely to happen.

He walked past the small shrine of flowers that had piled up at the school entrance, a tribute to a loss the entire school felt for one of their own, and struck off into the maze of covered corridors, and doors and windows that was the high school.

Wondering if he'd be lucky enough to catch a glimpse of Katy, he threaded his way toward the principal's office to check in. For some reason had the feeling of a temporary office, as though it belonged in one of those Quonset Huts erected during the Great War and not in the modest brick building that housed it.

He pushed his way in through one of the double doors and looked around. A long counter ran along one side with a woman in her mid-40's manning the station and looking reasonably harried. A grief counselor was talking softly to a distressed young girl in one room, and a poster on the opposite wall proclaimed a candlelight vigil for Christi Benson that evening.

He identified himself to the counter lady, explained that he'd been asked by Christi's mother to look into the death, and that he wanted to speak to a couple of Christi's teachers. He also produced a hand-written note from Maddie.

The secretary got out a small map of the school and carefully penciled a route through the labyrinth of classrooms he wanted to visit, marking a step by step trail all the way to each from the principal's office, and a complete return from each with a wide red marker.

Either he looked lost and confused, which he doubted, or she had lots of experience with lost and confused teens and parents, and had adopted this scorched earth approach to giving directions in the hope that search and rescue parties would not later be needed.

He dutifully scooped up the map and headed for the door, thanking her politely for her help.

He started with Mary Roth, Christi's English teacher. He found her in her room preparing for the day's classes, as he knew he would. She had the reputation of being conscientious. Her room was at the end of a long block of classrooms that stretched off like several spokes from the school's central axis hall.

Mary was about 45, tall, thin, and horsey looking, with short-cropped blond hair, squinty blue eyes, and something of a puckered smile. She was a regular sort that would always be the first to volunteer, the one to do more than her share on any project, and the first to critique your performance if you fell a little short.

The Judge introduced himself and explained the reason for his visit. She readily agreed to talk about Christi, and the words came out in gushes of breath, like bellows that operated on the intake and the out take both.

"I loved Christi," she said. "I am distraught and anguished at our loss. Christi would have been a wonderful novelist. That's what she was going to do, you know. She was going to start by writing historical fiction."

"What was she really like?" asked the Judge.

"Oh, Judge, she had a wonderful gift. She was very creative in her writing and not afraid to take a chance. Always diving into novel themes and controversial issues. Her essay on the sham of our marijuana laws was amazing. Showed a depth of understanding and experience far beyond her years. And her fictional story on gay rights made you believe she'd actually lived in a gay household. She did a piece on the sexual rights of woman too. She contended that women of the current generation, only partially liberated, are by definition, thereby still partially exploited. She explored the thesis that the institution of marriage is just another technique for female exploitation. She was very determined, Judge, and a good student - bright. Occasionally I saw flashes of a temper, but she usually got herself under control pretty quickly. I teach my class that if you want to be a writer, you have to go out unafraid, and unabashedly experience life, and the world first hand. I believed that's what Christi would have done."

"Christi doesn't sound like a suicide candidate," said the Judge.

"In my opinion she wasn't, Judge. I don't know what happened over in Malaga Cove, but I find it impossible to believe she voluntarily jumped of that cliff and ended her life."

The school buzzer announced that the first period was about to commence, with a finality that shut off further conversation.

He ambled back to his car and drove uphill through the winding streets of Lunada Bay, and around Bluff Cove to Malaga Cove and home.

He arrived back on campus minutes before noon, checked in at the principal's office again, and followed the red magic marker footsteps on his map toward the history classroom just as the lunch buzzer rang.

As he turned a corner of the first adjacent classroom building he almost ran into a striding teacher. The Judge recognized the teacher from his picture in the yearbook. It was Christi's history teacher, Hamilton something Smith.

"I'm looking for the history professor," said the Judge, though he knew he'd found him.

"That'd be me," Smith said. "I'm Hamilton Anderson Smith." He extended his hand to shake the Judge's in the best ingratiatingly Ivy League manner. "Originally from Boston," he added, as if it was somehow a further credential after his name. "Do you have a student in my class?"

Smith had a deep resonant voice that carried well, reminding the Judge of a stage actor. His handshake was firm, he looked the Judge in the eye as they shook, and he seemed to loosen up a little now that his pedigree had been firmly established.

He was handsome and youthful looking, in his early-thirties. Square jaw, large brown eyes set wide apart, well-proportioned nose and features, a buff body, and an outgoing friendliness that felt just a tad too…friendly. Much like the car salesman who is always so interested in you and the names of your children.

Smith wore a tweedy sport coat in soft browns over a dark green cashmere sweater over a soft beige dress shirt, buttoned up, with the top covered by a natty green bow tie. His bottom half matched - soft brown Chinos and dark brown loafers, sans socks.

Smith could have been a TA or a young professor at an Ivy League school on the East Coast, the Judge considered, except for the missing socks and the fact he was a tad too old. The Judge considered the lack of socks. He'd heard it was a style in fashion right now. Personally he considered sacrificing warmth for style quite silly, but then he wasn't an East Coast guy who needed to keep up his image on this Western frontier.

Smith seemed overdressed for his part as a history teacher at a southern California high school, even though it was on The Hill. And the clothes looked expensive. Maybe he had a working engineer wife or something.

The Judge surmised that young impressionable high school girls would think Smith the cat's meow.

But they don't use that expression anymore, thought the Judge. No, Mr. Smith would be cool, or 'rad', or brilliant, or whatever the popular flavor of the day. Each generation seemed to take special glee in changing the language just enough so as to make the prior generation feel a little old and out of touch. In his case, way out of touch. He smiled at the thought.

Smith was attentive as the Judge spelled out his mission. “Good for you, Judge,” he said. “How can I help?”

“It's nice to meet you, Hamilton,” said the Judge, a little unsure of etiquette here. Should he use ‘Hamilton’, his given name, or perhaps ‘Professor Smith’ as sort of rank and serial number? The Judge, considerably older, decided by rights he could call Hamilton what he liked.

“I was wondering if you’d given any thought as to why Christi might have committed suicide, Hamilton? And I guess the alternate question is…” added the Judge “…Does anyone come to mind who might have wanted to do her harm?”

The Judge waited while Smith furrowed his brow.

“I didn’t know her that well, Judge, so I don’t know why she'd commit suicide. I didn’t see any warning signs. But I had very little personal contact with her."

"She was a good student; smart as a whip. Often an unusual slant on topics. Had a temper though, didn’t take criticism well, and a tendency to stubbornly argue a position after it was untenable."

"I teach in the Socratic method in my class. I ask lots of questions and the students have to find the answers.” He paused to reflect.

"I have to admit this fall she wasn't the old Christi I grew to appreciate in the spring semester. She did seem a little down, depressed, moody. More sensitive than usual. She'd pout if I criticized. She’d close up. Become uncommunicative.

"I figured it was teenage hormones. But now, with her leap off that cliff - I guess there were much deeper issues we didn't appreciate.

"Perhaps the pressures of high school and relationships overwhelmed her, left her in a state where suicide seemed an alternative. Who knows with these young people?

"But I had no inkling she would do anything like this.

"As for doing her harm, her boyfriend was very angry about their breakup I'm told. In fact I heard, indirectly, that he hit her when she told him they were through. Said she'd been leading him on just to hurt him. Called her an evil bitch. Wished she were dead. Stuff like that."

"That was Jeff Harwood?" asked the Judge.

"Yes, I think that's his name."

"Well, I've got to get to my classroom and prepare for my next class over lunch. Nice talking to you, Judge. Sorry I'm not much help. I have very little contact with my students outside of class."

He pranced around the Judge and started full gait in the direction of his classroom.

An engaging character, mused the Judge, although a little too Ivy League for his taste.

Chapter 11 - Tuesday

The Judge turned and wandered back to the main hallway, and then left, toward the cafeteria and the outside patio where benches and tables were occupied by students at lunch. He was told the small clique of girls he wanted normally met at the southeast corner of the patio near a drooping olive tree.

They weren't hard to spot: three girls in scruffy jeans and bright tops, decked out in almost a matching dress code, enjoying their lunch and talking incessantly. He recognized the girls from the yearbook - Hannah, Katherine, and Paige.

He approached; introduced himself. They were startled and hesitant. When he finished his explanation, there was an awkward silence while they looked at each other with large round eyes.

Finally, Katherine spoke. "I'll tell you what I can Mr. Judge if it might help. We're all in shock. It's just so terribly sad and upsetting, to lose a friend, and like that."

The others dumbly nodded their heads in agreement.

"What was she like?" asked the Judge.

"She was our friend," Katherine said simply.

"She was really bright," said Paige. "She used to help me with my homework all the time. She knew how to break it down and make it simple to understand. And she was a good friend. If you needed to borrow a dollar or something to make a movie ticket, or needed to be picked up 'cause you couldn't get your mom's car, she was the first to offer the dollar and the ride."

"She was a nice girl," said Hannah. "She wasn't mean, or jealous, or catty like some girls. Easy to get along with. Not picky. Course, she did have a quick temper. If she thought you were treating her unfairly, she'd be quick to set you straight. She stood up for herself. Didn't take any crap from anybody. I especially liked her for that."

Then their words started to come quickly, tumbling out over one another in a blur of memories, fondness, and disbelief that she was no more.

"She knew how to dress. She bought her own clothes and had great style."

"She had a great sense of humor. We'd laugh together a lot."

"But she could carry a grudge sometimes."

"Yes, if you crossed her, she never forgot. There are a couple of girls even today she would ignore if she passed them in the hall."

"She didn't have as much time for us after she got her boyfriend last spring. But then it didn't work out and I thought we'd see more of her, but we didn't."

"That Jeff was a controlling jerk."

"Mean to her. Remember he called her fat in front of us?"

"Jealous too. The way she told it, she couldn't even look at another guy or he'd fly into a rage."

"Always dictating where they were going to go, what they were going to do. Wouldn't allow her time with us. I wouldn't want a boyfriend like that."

"You've never had a boyfriend ever. I'll bet you'll take what comes along."

"He was always hinting he was getting some. Remember how he used to smirk? I don't think he got squat. But it made Christi look bad."

"She told me once he slapped her around toward the end of the summer. They were parked in his car down by the bluff. He got jealous the way she'd looked at one of his surfer friends earlier. He just started yelling and slapping her in the face. On the head. On her shoulder. She said she had a slight black eye she had to cover with makeup the next day."

"Remember when she came to school and she had those two humongous bruises on her one arm? It looked like someone had clamped down on her arm as hard as they could with both hands and squeeze real hard to make it hurt."

The girls nodded at each other, their eyes big and round.

"And what about that humongous fight when they broke up? In the school parking lot. Jeff slugged her, I saw it".

"I heard he threatened to kill her."

"I heard that too."

"My psych teacher says some women like to be controlled and abused, or at least they think they do.

They just keep attracting the same sort of guy, over and over."

"That's crap," said Katherine. "No girl wants to be treated like that."

"Anyway, Christi dumped him, and then she got the new boyfriend. It was her big secret. We all tried to guess who he was."

The girls nodded again in unison.

"We finally just gave up. We guessed everyone we could think of, then we pleaded, we begged. I even tried to bribe her to tell us who he was. She wouldn't."

"Was she a good student?" asked the Judge.

"Mostly got B's and A's. But she worked hard for her grades. She was always looking to see how things worked. Always able to spot what was going on behind the scenes. Very good at details. Nothing escaped her."

"And competitive. You'd never play 'dare' with Christi. She'd do anything to win."

"Remember when she boasted she could take her bra off in public without taking off her blouse? So Hannah dared her to do it right then. And she just did, right here at this table, in front of the whole school."

"She was a little out there," said Katherine.

"What do you mean?" asked the Judge.

"She means Christi had sex with her boyfriend," answered Hannah, matter of factly.

"Or so she said," chimed in Paige. "Maybe it was just talk. I think this secret boyfriend was a wild affair." "Remember how she told stories about the where and the what?" In the backseat of a car, under a tree, on the beach. She said they had a secret place where they'd leave notes, and occasionally meet up for fun."

"Oh…and that special dress…" They all giggled with satisfaction recalling tales .

"She told us he bought her a special dress, but on the condition that she could never wear a bra or panties under it. So she didn't."

"She wore it to school once. When we asked, she said nope, no underwear."

"It must have been chilly. Remember how careful she was sitting and walking outside. I don't think she dared bend over." This elicited further giggles.

"What color was the dress?" asked the Judge.

"Blue. A kind of light blue, real low cut in front."

"I think she had pads snuck down in the front to hide her nipples that day she wore it to school."

"Wouldn't you?"

"Yes. Yes…You'd have to in public."

"Do you have any idea who her secret boyfriend was?" asked the Judge.

"No," they said in unison.

"She told us a lot about the 'What', and the 'Where', but never the 'Who'."

"He must be as distraught at her death as we are, or more."

The three girls turned silent, reflecting on their lost friend.

"Was there any sign she was thinking of suicide?" asked the Judge.

"No," said Katherine. "She was kind of a Catholic. Used to go to church occasionally. Confession and stuff. Maybe she slipped on the cliff or something. I just don't see her killing herself."

The others nodded in agreement.

"How'd she get along with her parents?" asked the Judge.

The girls looked at each other, silently balancing how much information to share.

"Christi lived with her mom, who was devoted to her, but worked nights a lot," said Katherine. "Christi had a lot of time to spend on her own. She told me once she used to lock her bedroom door when she went to bed, then crawl out her side window and have her boyfriend pick her up. She was a little wild, but her heart was good. She never got in trouble, never caught drinking, or caught with drugs; never caught speeding."

" 'Caught' is the operative word there," said Hannah. "I think she was damn lucky."

"That's not right," said Katherine, "she hated drugs. She told me once her dad had done drugs and that's what broke up the marriage. She had zero tolerance for anyone even occasionally doing pot. She was very opinionated about that, I know first-hand."

The other two turned to look at Katherine, as did the Judge.

"I mean…well…'course I don't know first-hand you understand…but we had conversations."

"That's right," said Paige. "Christi said she bailed on her fancy summer internship job 'cause of drugs."

"What internship was that?" asked the Judge.

"With Harley & Johns, the big developer, at the top of The Hill."

"What'd she say about drugs?" the Judge asked.

"Not much. Just it was a corrupt firm 'cause of drugs. She'd never go back to work there."

"But wait, wait, remember she said her secret boyfriend had her try marijuana?"

"Oh that's right. Guess she changed her mind for him. Whoever he was, he had a lot of influence on her.

"Anyway, she and her dad didn't see each other much. She didn't like his lifestyle, didn't like his friends, didn't like the drinking and drugs, didn't like that he'd bailed on his family. I guess you couldn't blame her for that."

"Was she close to any of the faculty?" asked the Judge.

"She was friends with Katy Thorne, the student counselor," said Katherine, "and she spent some time in out-of-class projects with her English teacher, Mrs. Roth, who she really liked. Oh, and she loved the new history teacher. What's his name…Mr. Smith. Guess he's not so new now."

"So," said the Judge, "Christi was a good friend, bright, hard-working, generous, but competitive, with a quick temper, could hold a grudge, sexually active, hated drugs but tried pot, a part-time Catholic, liked to share stories about her escapades, but secretive about her new boyfriend. Did I get it right?"

The girls looked at each other and then nodded at the Judge, their eyes suddenly moist.

"Did she seem down, or depressed or moody recently?"

All three shook their heads.

"Thank you for the help, girls," said the Judge.

The Judge walked back to where he'd parked the E, slid in and crept down the street that ran along the ocean side of the high school, carefully dodging young people who had no fear of stepping out in front of his car. The Judge sighed. When you're young, you're certain you're going to live forever.

Chapter 12 - Wednesday

The Judge walked down toward the cliff road with Annie. But instead of his usual jaunt along Paseo Del Mar, he and the puppy crossed over and carefully picked their way down the rugged path in the cliff to the rocks below.

The tide was out and pebbles were making a rattling sound on parts of the beach as each wave slid in. The sun was settling into the water like a ruddy orange.

He sat down on a large rock with the puppy and watched the parade of surfers paddling in as the last of the sun vaporized into the sea. Pink and orange entrails stretched across the sky, lighting the cloud bottoms. A faint pink corridor of sea cut across the blue, stretching from where the sun had almost disappeared to the slurry of foam and water sluicing up the sand at the Judge's feet.

It was cold, with a crisp salty breeze blowing off the water. But it was invigorating and magnificent too. Far better than inside a courtroom. That's where he would still have been at this hour a short six months ago. The first pair of surfers walked up the beach after unhooking tethers. This was the great divide of surfers. The bulk of them climbed the path back up the cliff in the fading light, tired, cold and happy. But a select few would proceed further around the point to the Palos Verdes Swim Club.

If your family was part of the affluent membership, a warm Jacuzzi, hot shower, fresh towels, and hot food at the snack bar awaited you. Then a long climb of what seemed like a thousand steps up to the road. But unencumbered by your board, which would be stowed safely in the Club storage. The elite did have a nice life, mused the Judge, funded of course by Mom and Dad.

As the surfers approached, he turned the puppy loose to greet them, a sure conversation starter. As they reached down to rub her ears and fur, he inserted his question.

"Hi guys…you know Mark Daniels?"

"Sure, he's coming in now, the guy with the yellow board."

The Judge waited patiently as several other surfers passed, and then turned the puppy loose on the yellow board surfer. The puppy never failed. She was awesome.

"I guess you're Mark Daniels," said the Judge.

The young man looked up, suddenly alert, not expecting to be known.

"I'm a friend of Christi Benson, and I spoke with Jeff Harwood."

"Know who you are," said Mark. The Hill was really a small village.

Mark looked like a nice young man, perhaps 18, decked out in a purple and black wet suit that clashed badly with his yellow board. The Judge bet he didn't care. He had a crew cut, soft brown eyes and a friendly smile.

"A terrible thing about Christi," Mark said, shaking his head. "Jeff must be devastated."

"Christi's mother asked me to figure out what happened.... and why. Jeff helped with some insight. Hoping you could too."

"I really don't know anything, but if I can help, I'm in."

"You a member of the Beach Club?"

Mark smiled. "I am."

"Can we grab some fries and a shake or something, and just chat for a couple of minutes at the Club? I'll buy." The Judge had been a founding member, back when they couldn't give memberships away. Now there was an eight-year waiting list.

"Sure," said Mark, "let's go to it." He strode off down the beach leading the way, puppy and Judge in tow.

They settled in on the upper terrace, next to the Snack Shack. Their vista overlooked the adult Jacuzzi, the Olympic pool, and the now dark expanse of the Santa Monica Bay. The Queen's Necklace of lights, named after Bombay, stretched out to the west, marking the boundaries of RAT Beach, Redondo, Manhattan Beach, and El Porto, while occasional planes took off over the water from LAX, darting up like fireflies in the distance. "So, Mark, did you know Christi very well?"

"I knew her from school, classes and such. She was a hot chick. When she started dating my buddy, Jeff, I saw a lot more of her. But I didn't really know her, if you know what I mean. We weren't close or anything. She seemed nice though.".

"Know any reason why she might kill herself?"

"No. She seemed level-headed, not hyper or anything."

"Did she seem down, depressed, nervous or anxious over the last several weeks?"

"Can't really say. I just didn't see her around much since she and Jeff broke up."

"But you saw her with some other guy? "

"Well, I don't know whether I should talk about that. I mean she's dead and all. Does it matter now?"

"It could matter a lot. It could be a key to explaining her death," said the Judge.

Mark sighed.

"What did you see?"

"My tether had broken that day, so every time I lost the board, I had to go chase it. One time a quirky undertow shoved it kind of around the end of the beach at the South. I had to catch it in a hurry or it would have washed into the rocks. That's a dangerous area."

"And?"

"Well, that's what's embarrassing. I didn't realize there's a kind of skinny sliver of beach there when the tide's out, pretty hidden from view. Christi was there with another guy."

"Did they see you?"

"No. They were way too busy. I was only in view a couple of seconds getting my board."

"What were they doing?"

"Well, neither one had their clothes on. He was lying on his back on a towel, and she was sitting on top of him, and they were doing it, and I mean hot and heavy."

"Are you sure?"

"No. But that's what it looked like. She was having a real good time. Her boobs were bouncing around. She was grinding and howling, and he was too. Or that's the way it looked."

"You're sure it was Christi?"

"Yes. She was facing me. No doubt."

"Who was the guy?"

"Couldn't tell. He was on the bottom. Feet pointed up the beach. Could only see the top of his head. He had brown hair, and a bald spot in the middle. Looked sun burnt." Having a real good time, looked like.

"So it wasn't Jeff."

"Oh, no. I think the guy must have been older. Bald spot, hairy legs arched up behind her."

"Did you see them again?"

"No. But I saw her earlier that day. My board made the same trip. It was a little weird."

"Earlier she'd taken off her dress and left it on the sand at the south end of the beach, and I thought she was going to swim out. But instead she crawled across the face of the cliff there in her swimsuit. Later when my board got away and I retrieved it, I saw her poking around the cliff crevices at the back of that same sliver of beach. Couldn't figure what she was doing up there. Maybe looking for fossils."

"When was this?"

"Maybe six weeks ago."

"What was she wearing?"

"She wasn't wearing anything, Judge." Mark smiled.

"I mean earlier."

"Oh, she was in a light blue dress."

"You didn't see them leave?"

"No."

"Ever see them again along the beach?"

"No. I saw her lots with Jeff over the summer. She'd come down and sit on the beach while we surfed. But she didn't surf. Never saw her with another guy, except that once."

"Was this before or after they broke up?"

"It was before. I didn't plan on telling Jeff. Figured it was none of my business. I stay clear of relationships: they're always more complicated then they look. But after they broke up and Jeff was so angry and unhappy and all, I broke my rule. I told him what I saw."

"How'd he take it?"

"Not good. Should have kept my mouth shut."

"What did he say?"

"He got even more angry. Said she was a ho. Said she wasn't even a good fuck. Going through the world screwing guys up and down, both sides. That's what he said. Said she'd pay. It was a real rant. Hasn't talked much to me since. Guess he lost face. Maybe blames me 'cause I saw her like that. Maybe 'cause I didn't tell him right away. I don't know."

"So there's no way of telling who the guy was?"

"Well, I did see his board. It was leaning on the rocks off to the right. It was cherry red. A Billabong. Had the big logo across the bottom. Kind of unusual too. Don't see them in cherry very often. Beautiful boards; expensive."

"Ever see anyone else with a board like that around?"

"There was a guy had one. I haven't seen him around lately. A twilight surfer like us. Came down near the end of the day. Caught the last rays and waves with us. His nickname was Lam, or Ham, or something like that. Funny name. Had a cherry colored surf board, don't know whether it was a Billabong though, don't think I ever saw the underside of his board."

"How old?"

"Older guy. Maybe mid to late 30's. Good surfer though. Knew what he was doing."

The Judge felt ancient. His thirties were a faint memory.

"Do you think this other guy with the cherry board could be the same guy that was Christi's new lover?"

"Have trouble believing that. Guy I've seen is old…Maybe 35...38. Why'd Christi be attracted to an old fart like that? She could have had any of us on her arm once her breakup was old news."

"*Ouch*", thought the Judge. What would this young man say if he saw the Judge kissing someone, say, 20 years younger? Probably be disgusted. After all, it was a ridiculous notion.

Stop that, the Judge commanded, shutting down his inner voice. *Just stop it. Focus on business.*

"What does this other guy, the one with the cherry colored board, look like?"

"God, I don't know. Average height I guess. Looks like he works out, short brown hair. Heard he's a little arrogant. Doesn't share waves very well, but he's a real fine surfer."

"Bald spot on top?"

"Never noticed."

"Hairy?"

"Aren't they all when they get old?"

"Know where he lives, what he does, maybe what car he drives? Know any friends he has?"

"Nope. All I know is this guy had this cherry Board, wears a cherry RipCurl wet suit to match. Must have some money, a real job. No surf bum like me. That's all I know."

"Thanks," said the Judge.

They stood up. Mark took the Judge's hand, pumped it vigorously, turned and started over the upper path toward the Beach Club's 1000 steps. The Judge took the puppy's leash and began a more leisurely traverse of the same steep slope. There weren't really a thousand steps, of course. It just seemed like it when you were going up.

Chapter 13 - Wednesday

Returning from his breakfast next morning, the Judge found a voice mail from Jack Martin, the Palos Verdes Mayor, on his answering machine. He fired up the E and headed down The hill to visit Jack at his real estate office in Malaga Cove Plaza.

Jack was old, no one knew quite how old, but definitely old. Old, skinny, and a little bit bent over. But he still scuttled around Malaga Cove with enormous energy, tending to real estate clients, and his tenants.

Jack was the stereotypical City Father. He'd been on The Hill forever. This was his third or fourth stint as Mayor, most people couldn't remember. He knew everybody and was universally liked - an older gentlemen of grace and manners stranded amongst a new age of people too rushed to be polite.

Jack's real estate office was in a prime location, all glass in front, facing the plaza fountain.

"How are you, Judge?" Jack asked, extending his hand and a warm smile. He may have been old, but he had a firm handshake, a keen eye, and was sharp as a tack.

"What a shame about this little girl. She was a bright young thing, full of sunshine and promise. Don't understand why she'd do it." Jack shook his head mournfully. "These kids grow up on The Hill with everything, silver spoons, spoilt. When real life comes along they can't handle it. Not like in my day. There were just a few houses here in the thirties, a bunch of truck farmers mostly, and some summer homes. We had to work hard during the war and after. No one had money, but we all got on real good. Shared what we had. Respected each other. We all had our dreams; knew we had to work for them. No one jumped off cliffs. Now it seems like every year we get a jumper. It's these young people today, Judge. They've got too much. Value the wrong things. All the stuff they think they have to have…chase after. And they think the golden life goes on forever. Life throws a curve, and they just crumble. Do silly things. Jump off cliffs."

Jack had wound down his soliloquy now. The Judge had enjoyed it. Guess that meant that he was getting old too. Starting to think like his dad.

"Maddie asked me to look into it, Jack. She is desperate to know what happened, how it happened, and most of all, why".

"Yes, I know. She called me too. That's why I called. Figured it's better if we don't generate an email record," said Jack.

The Judge nodded.

"I don't think you've met our new Chief of Police. Nice enough young man, about your age, plenty of experience. Takes a practical approach," said Jack. "Thought I'd make a warm introduction, kind of smooth things along." Jack gave the Judge his big smile again.

They walked out of Jack's office together, across the Plaza, and around the corner, heading for City Hall across Via Corta. The Police Station was a part of the same building. They walked shoulder to shoulder, Jack leaning into the Judge's space a little as they walked, conveying intimacy and warmth in an Old World sort of way.

"Christi interned this summer at Harley & Johns, Jack. You ever done business with them?"

Jack turned to the Judge, his soft brown eyes pinning the Judge's blue. "Once or twice," Jack said carefully. He was suddenly alert.

"Know much about them?"

"They got together about 20 years ago; smart guys. Figured the South Bay would grow as people moved closer to the water. Get out of the smog and the heat. Figured there'd be a need for commercial and residential space. They were right. Done real well I hear."

"What're they like?"

"Well Pat Harley, he's a clever builder and marketer. Great at picking the right site. That's 3/4ths of it you know. Negotiates well, detail oriented, squeezes the last nickel out of his subs down to a rat's ass I hear. Pardon my French, Judge. That just slipped out."

"Now Mel Johns, he's very quiet and shy. Doesn't like the limelight. But he's the money guy. Seems to have sources with unlimited capital."

"There's been good times and bad times in the last 20 years in real estate around here. Comes and goes in cycles. Tough to predict. A lot of builders get over extended. Have to be an eternal optimist to develop real estate. Builders often wash out, lose their projects, lose their house, lose everything, sometimes their wife. Have to start over. Hell if I'd gotten out from under my wife, might have been worth it," Jack cackled.

"Harley and Johns got over extended several times on the down cycles, like everyone. But the way I hear it, Mel Johns, he'd just come up with more capital. Must have a very rich uncle somewhere. I've seen them eat maybe a couple hundred thousand a month in negative cash flow. And hold on at that rate for three or four years with no outside help."

'Till it turned around. Always does, sooner or later. Always cycles."

"Any idea where all that capital comes from?"

Jack looked around discretely as they walked. No one was within earshot.

"I heard rumors. Heard they had unlimited funds available from a deep, deep pocket investor. Anonymous, if you know what I mean. No bank accounts, no loan documents, just a handshake. Might be a tax dodge, or someone's secret money they're trying to move back on shore, I don't know. I also heard they had a big time Latin American partner once."

"All just idle gossip, likely. Mostly from busted developers who were jealous. That's all. These guys are so active, rumors fly around like rain in the wind. Never saw anything to support any of it. All I know is when everybody else is tapped out for cash and the banks aren't lending, Mel Johns always has unlimited cash to make deals and carry his projects through. Always."

"Did they ever raise capital locally, maybe a syndication or something?" The Judge knew the answer, but asked the question anyway. That was the case he hadn't gotten because of his election loss. He wanted to see what Jack had heard.

"Oh that," said Jack, with a scowl. "Yeah, the one time they raise money locally, they end up in a law suit. Wouldn't you know it. Damned miserable attorneys…'course I don't mean you, Judge."

"How's the lawsuit going, have you heard?"

"You probably know more about that end than I do. I hear the Plaintiff's attorneys are unhappy with the judge. Say the judge continually stomps their discovery motions made on Harley & Johns."

"You mean 'quashes'? The judge is quashing discovery motions?"

"What, Oh, yeah I guess…stomped on, quashed, I don't know. At every turn the judge shuts them down. I guess the lawyers are trying to peek at things they aren't supposed to. It's been real uphill work in that courtroom, so I hear. Serves them right," Joe snorted. "I don't much care for class action lawyers. Anyway, like before, it's just gossip and all."

They'd reached the door of the Police Station. Jack led the way in.

"The Chief in?" asked the Mayor at the front desk..

It was a modest police station in keeping with the low profile of a rich and private community where nothing much happened.

It was said there only three roads off The Hill, and that if a serious crime happened, a fleeing suspect never got off The Hill once those three roads were locked down. It acted as a deterrent to the roving violence that plagued South-East LA and other parts of the coastal plain circling The Hill.

It was a nice fantasy, but not entirely true. There were many small tributaries off The Hill if you knew where to look. But then if you were to break into an occupied home on The Hill, you'd likely hear the unmistakable sound of a shotgun being cocked. That was the real deterrent. Much of The Hill was armed to the teeth. .

The Chief came out to shake hands with the Mayor. Jack turned on his big smile again.

"This is Bill Wright, our new Police Chief."

The chief was six feet tall, broad shouldered, and had the look of a former athlete now starting to go to soft. The beginnings of a robust tummy were pushing through his white starched shirt above the belt, making it look a tad too tight. He had a bald head, preferring to shave it all rather than suffer the indignity of puffy side hair surrounding a shiny dome. He had brown eyes with crinkle lines around the edges, likely from squinting into the sun. His square jaw with tight lines around the mouth hinted at past stress and sun damage in a career started years before. Likely in South East LA.

He gave the Judge strong handshake with a massive hand and looked the Judge straight in the eye while doing it. The Judge could see he'd had lots of experience reading people. This was a man the Judge wouldn't play poker with, unless of course he had to.

The Judge stared back. He could see that the Chief knew why he was here. The Chief didn't look happy. His request had quickly blown up the chain of command.

The Chief wouldn't like to bend rules. On the other hand, the Mayor was technically his boss, although he reported to the City Council. His job was political as much as law enforcement. He would protect his job first, his men second, and the law third.

Jack spoke softly so the conversation remained between the three of them.

"The mother of that little girl who jumped off the cliff has asked the Judge to undertake an investigation of the facts. I and the mother and the Judge go back a ways. And we all knew the young lady well. I would take it as a personal favor if you would keep the Judge informed on the progress of your investigation, assist by answering any questions you can, and allow him access to physical evidence and reports. Treat him as an unofficial assistant on the investigation with full access."

The Chief's jaw squared and moved a notch or two toward the ceiling, sending a signal contrary to his words, which were conciliatory.

"We really don't need any help, but we'll be glad to share our findings with the Judge."

This left an uncomfortable silence, which the Judge allowed to linger.

The Judge read that as a grudging, foot-dragging sort of commitment, but shrugged it off. He had lots of sources in the DA's office, the Coroner's and elsewhere. Besides, this cop's job was to see if a crime had been committed. The Judge's job was to find out not only what happened, but why. It was the "why" that was important to Maddie. The Chief had no interest in the why, unless it established a motive for a crime.

The Chief finally broke the silence. "Why don't you come back to my office, Judge? I'll tell you what we know." The two men went into an anteroom and down a small corridor, while the Mayor left the station.

The Chief ushered the Judge into a small Spartan office with a large window looking out over Malaga Cove and the Santa Monica Bay. A wooden desk faced toward the door, nicked with cuts and bruises from long use. A new overstuffed leather chair behind it fit Bill Wright perfectly as he settled in. The Judge was left with a choice between two uncomfortable looking grey metal chairs in front of the desk. He chose the one with the best view over the Chief's shoulder and out to sea.

The wall on the left had grey metal bookshelves with various codes, statute books and manuals neatly marked and organized. The opposite wall had a locked gun cabinet containing an assortment of shotguns and rifles. On the Chief's desk was a picture of a middle-aged blond woman and two older looking boys who had the look of expensive college tuition.

The Chief sat behind his desk, quiet and unmoving, waiting for the Judge to break the ice. The Judge sensed the desk was almost a protective barrier for a chief: a clear delineation between him and everyone else, including whatever person was sitting on the other side, making trouble or giving him headaches. It represented authority, prestige, and security, much as his raised bench had been for the Judge.

"So, what do we have?" asked the Judge.

The Chief pulled a file folder out of his side drawer and flipped through the documents inside.

"We have the body of a female Caucasian, just turned 18, blue eyes, brown hair, appeared in good physical health. Pronounced dead at the scene, likely from the leap off the cliff. Wearing a white mini two-piece swimsuit, no jewelry, no tattoos, no shoes. Bruises, abrasions and scrapes all over her body, likely from rolling in the surf among the rocks.

"Mother identified the body at the scene. You called in the report from a cell phone on the cliff above. Firefighters responded in three minutes, pulled her out of the water eight minutes later after making their way down the cliff and rigging equipment to reach her among the rocks.

"A blue dress, identified as hers by her mother, found on the cliff above, from the point where she jumped. Couldn't get any prints off the fabric. No marks, tears, or rips in the dress. It appeared to have been carefully folded and placed on the ground. No suicide note. No purse or wallet found, only her driver's license in the pocket of the dress. No cell phone. We've interviewed the neighbors up and down the street from the cliff location. No one saw anything.

"We'll have the Coroner's report in about a week.

"Open and shut, Judge. She jumped to her death. We don't know why."

The Chief closed the file and folded his hands over it, clearly done, not offering to share further details if he had any.

"Can I see the file?"

The Chief hesitated, considered his options, and then reluctantly slid the file across the desk.

The Judge took his time studying its contents, ignoring the fidgeting Chief.

On top were photos: the body at the scene, the folded blue dress, the body at the hospital, the body laid out at the morgue, full length photos, close-ups of her battered face. There was a deep wound on the left side of her head at the temple, perhaps when she landed.

Last was a blowup of a picture of Christi in school clothes, likely taken for her high school yearbook.

Beneath the pictures were the reports of the arriving officers, the firemen, the detective, and the hospital staff. Then there were interview notes: interviews with Maddie, the Judge, the neighbors at the scene, the firemen again, and the high school principal. There were also notes of a telephone interview with Jake, Christie's dad. It was all depressing.

The Judge looked at each photo carefully and then studied each report and interview. Nothing stood out.

"What time did she hit the water?" asked the Judge.

"We'll know more about that when we get the autopsy report," said the Chief. "And we'll confirm the cause of death."

As the Judge closed the file, he asked, "How'd she get there without her car?"

"We don't know", said the Chief. "We didn't find a car at the scene."

"Where are her purse and wallet?" asked the Judge.

"We don't know."

"Why did she take her dress off?" asked the Judge.

"We don't know."

"Where was she between the time she left my house and the time she died?" asked the Judge.

"We don't know."

"Have you interviewed her friends?"

"No."

"Her boyfriend?"

"Yes, someone talked briefly to him."

"Her school counselor?"

"No."

"Have you searched her room?"

"No."

"Her car?"

"No. I said we didn't find a car." The Chief's voice betrayed aggravation now.

"Judge - we are a small city with a limited budget. This case is pretty clear. We don't have the manpower to chase geese."

"I understand," said the Judge, sliding the case file back across the desk. "Thank you very much, Bill. I'm going to dig a little and see if I can fill in some of the missing pieces."

The Judge stood up, shook hands with the Chief over his desk, and turned to leave.

The Chief didn't stand up and see him out. He just watched from his chair behind his barrier desk. The Judge could see the Chief didn't like sharing information, didn't like someone looking over his shoulder, and particularly didn't like the Judge.

Chapter 14 - Thursday

The Judge had slept in late, fiddled with some marketing plans for his contemplated new practice as a mediator, and had forgotten about breakfast. It was almost noon. His stomach started to growl.

The Judge had forgotten to feed Annie, too. She gave him a woeful look as he entered the kitchen and mixed up a god awful smelling mixture of dry doggy kibble and creamy plain people yogurt. The vet said it would keep her healthy. She seemed quite happy with it despite the smell. But then again, she'd eat just about anything, including his favorite socks.

He changed into beige chinos and a bright green golf shirt, and headed out to the Palos Verdes Golf Club for brunch. The Club was a small modest building, dating from 1924, and remodeled in 2007 in a way that kept its low-slung feel. Its dining room provided spectacular views over its golf course, wild parklands, and the Santa Monica Bay, often with a speck of a tanker docked at the El Segundo Refinery in the distance.

Besides the view, the food was superb, and the staff provided service in an old-fashioned style that had gone the way of the buggy whip elsewhere in L.A.

He strolled in past twin pots standing as sentries on either side of double carved doors, protected by a bright green awning proclaiming the name of the club. It was all quite festive.

The staff knew him, of course, and a waiter led him across the dining room toward his favorite spot, a small two-person table against the view window. It afforded the Judge the opportunity to sit with his back to a side wall and look out at both the view and the other diners. He could even pretend he wasn't alone.

He glanced around the room at neighbors he didn't know, but with faces he recognized. He supposed they thought it odd he ate alone. But he really had no one to eat with. And he'd grown accustomed to having his coffee and eggs here and reading his newspaper at least once a week.

He'd almost reached his table when he saw Ms. Thorne sitting at the other end of the room, facing his direction, and chatting animatedly to a tall young man whose back was to the Judge. She looked at her companion with a measure of warmth and affection reserved for someone closer her age.

The Judge was a bit envious, but dismissed the feeling and immediately shifted his eyes to the panoramic view, pretending he hadn't seen her. He settled into his usual table, but this time planted his back to the room and his face to the view, hoping he wouldn't be noticed. He ordered eggs over easy with coffee and buried his nose in his Wall Street Journal as added defense.

He supposed that by saying "Oh", and then remaining silent, he'd agreed to take her to dinner on Sunday. He hadn't considered it a date. He was way too old. She was way too young. He was going to buy her an expensive dinner because…because he could. Or so he had rationalized.

But upon reflection, he'd decided to call it off. She had pretty much tricked him into the dinner invitation with all her patter about fixing him up a blind date, then springing her trap, and dashing off. And the tears, well…almost tears. Anyway, it had been all very dramatic. He'd foolishly allowed the record to look like he'd acquiesced into an acceptance of what had really been her dinner offer. Hell, she should buy.

But it was a dumb. It might be only a joint dinner, but it implied a date. And that made no sense. No sense for an old independent duck to go chasing off after a much younger woman. She wasn't even 30. Practically a teenager. The age of his daughter, if he had one.

He surreptitiously peeked back toward her table on the other side of the room. The view of her and the handsome young man confirmed all his doubts. He assumed the young man was handsome. All he could see was the back of his head. But he was certainly young. He was aggravated at himself for the small pangs of jealousy as she lavished warm attention on the man.

He buried his nose back in the Journal and waited patiently for his eggs to arrive.

He was engrossed in an article on world shipping activity as a leading indicator of where the economy might head when he felt a presence. Then, a small hand was placed lightly on his shoulder and lingered a tad too long before moving away. As he started to turn, her low pitched voice drifted down over his shoulder.

"Fancy meeting you here, Judge."

He could smell her scent and feel her breath as she spoke. She was leaning close over his table. Too close, he thought; too, too…intimate … into his personal space…but damn. He could feel himself stir.

It was an unfair power women had over men. Simply injecting their physical presence into the man's personal space produced volcanic hormonal change.

Was this true for all women, wondered the Judge, or particularly this woman?

Pulling himself together, the Judge turned in his seat and said, "Why Ms. Thorne, you snuck up on me." He looked up into her smile with all the teeth, and the dancing blue eyes. She was clearly pleased to see him. He wondered what her boyfriend thought.

"I'm so glad we ran into you," she said. "Can I steal you away from your Journal for just a minute or two? There's someone I want you to meet."

The Judge was dumbfounded. He wasn't accustomed to have his peace and solitude disturbed during his brunch ritual. But damn, she was charming.

He put on his best smile, smoothed out his voice, and rose, saying, "I'd be delighted, Ms. Thorne," in as best a low, warm voice as he could muster. Jesus, it was hard to be polite.

"Katy, Judge. Katy."

As he stood, she snatched up his hand before he could move it out of way. She towed him across the room, acting as both tug and pilot.

The young man had been joined at the table by an older woman. She was eyeing them both. The Judge sensed skepticism and cynicism in her gaze. She didn't look particularly friendly, or anxious to meet him.

Katy seemed totally immune to this, towing him smartly into the fire zone and docking him at the table between the woman and the young man.

"I'd like you to meet my mother, Judge," she said with a flourish, much like a fisherman showing his 200-pound sail fish freshly hauled up the side of the boat.

"A pleasure to meet you," he mumbled.

"And a pleasure to meet you too, Judge" said the regal woman, who didn't stand but sent a thin pale hand across the table for the Judge to take. "Name's Florence Thorne."

She had a surprisingly firm hand shake: that of a rancher, or a farmer, he thought. And her blue eyes, similar to Katy's but a bit paler with age, pinned his with the same sharp intensity. A line from Don Quixote drifted into his mind, "still strong in tooth and claw". She was all of that.

He guesses she was in her early 60s, but a reasonably slender figure and elegant carriage gave her a more youthful appearance.

"Oh, and this is my kid brother," Katy rattled on, "Tommy."

Tommy also extended his hand, and looked at the Judge with genuine curiosity. He looked to be a couple of years younger than Katy, perhaps 24 or so.

"What's your given name?" asked Mother.

It was a question the Judge was often asked, but rather than ducking it as he usually did, he blurted his name out, instantly regretting the decision.

"Is that Irish?" Mother asked suspiciously. "Irish Catholic?"

"Welsh," he responded.

"Oh," said Mother in a very non-committal way. "Well, we've heard quite a bit from my daughter about you."

"Oh?" said the Judge, giving Katy a quizzical look.

"Perhaps you'd like to join us for brunch, since you look to be sitting alone," continued Mother.

He could see she was savoring the thought of a full interrogation. She watched him now, much as a webbed spider might watch a passing fly.

That was the final straw.

The Judge stood a little straighter, his equally regal presence flipped on as though by switch. He said with almost his bench bark, "Oh, I think not Mrs. Thorne. Thank you for your invitation, though. It's of course a pleasure to meet you, and you too, Tommy, but I think I'll leave you to your family get together and return to my Wall Street Journal."

Katy started to look distressed. This wasn't going the way she'd hoped.

The Judge turned to her, gave her his best smile, partially to stir up the mother, and said, "It's always a special pleasure to see you Ms. Thorne." Then, to the group, "I hope you all enjoy your breakfast".

He unhitched himself from his tug and started to steam back under his own power toward the safety of his table and Journal.

"I'm looking forward to our dinner Sunday," Katy called after him, a bit desperately he thought with some satisfaction.

He pretended not to hear, mostly out of meanness he supposed, reached his table and dived with relief into his Journal without looking back.

Chapter 15 - Friday

On Friday morning, the Judge looked up the telephone number for Harley & Johns and dialed their number. He asked the reception lady for Gloria, the name Maddie had remembered from Christi's internship.

"Gloria doesn't work here anymore," she replied.

"Got a forwarding telephone number?" asked the Judge.

"No," said the frosty receptionist, "I don't."

"Can you give me the spelling of her last name?"

"No, I am not allowed. No information's to be given out."

Very curious, thought the Judge.

"I represent her brother's estate. I need to confirm she's the sister."

"I have very specific instructions on this person, sir. As far as our firm is concerned she never worked here. We have no information about her. I can't give out her last name."

"When was she let go?" asked the Judge.

"Last week… I mean, I can't tell you that. I can't talk to you any further." She hung up.

The Judge called Maddie, explained his lack of success in reaching Gloria, and asked if Maddie had a last name, or phone number. She seemed glad to have something to do.

Two hours later, Maddie called back. She had found Gloria's name and cell phone in some personal notes she took in case of an emergency when Christi started working there.

"Gloria Tomlin," she said, giving a local San Pedro number. "I contacted her just now, and we spoke briefly. Told her you would call. She seemed pretty down. They recently fired her. One month's severance - that was it. She lives in the projects. And Judge, she sounded a little tipsy."

The Judge called Gloria Tomlin and made arrangements to come over to visit. From the brief phone conversation it sounded like the Judge needed a face to face. And yes, she sounded tipsy.

The Judge pulled his other car out of the garage, an old beat up Chevy, four-door, marine green, with some 200,000 miles on it. The E couldn't go to San Pedro because it might never return.

The Judge headed for the subsidized housing on First Street in San Pedro. These were Section 8 projects. Nice enough buildings originally, but now run down from successive generations of poor tenants. They were also gang infested.

Gloria Tomlin was in a second story walkup. He rang the doorbell next to a faded grey door marked and dinged with abuse.

Her place was a mess, and so was she.

She was perhaps the Judge's age, 50 or so, unhealthily thin except for large breasts, no doubt enhanced. Maybe 5'8", dyed red hair, split at the ends, loosely pulled back with a scrunchie holding a ponytail.

Pale blue eyes, and deep scarlet lipstick unsteadily applied.

She wore a faded pale yellow housecoat with red flowers. Perhaps silk, but it had seen better days. It was loosely closed in front, exposing too much cleavage. Her pale thin legs stuck out of the bottom, the pasty white skin set off by a bruise here and there, suggesting she occasionally ran into things, or perhaps just fell. She wore pale yellow slippers with open toes, displaying bright fuchsia toenails.

And she'd been drinking.

Two empty bourbon bottles stood sentry at one end of the railcar galley to the left. Empty takeout packages were dumped in the sink. The counter was strewn with the morning's newspaper and a cup filled with cigarette butts. The bed in the corner was unmade. Worn yellow sheets and an old army blanket left in a contorted position suggested troubled sleep.

The place had a musty smell, blended with the odor of old smoke and old food.

She moved to a small sofa covered in a soiled brown plaid. The Judge sat down in a bendy plastic patio chair across from her.

He asked if she'd heard about Christi. She had.

He explained that he was looking into Christi's death for her mother, who was trying to understand why it all happened.

"I know who you are Judge," she said. "This thing with Christina is tragic. I really liked her. Those bastards canned her first. Terminated her internship three weeks early. Refused to write her a recommendation. Just get out and don't come back.

Bastards. I worked there 10 years. One little mistake, and poof, I'm on the street. Fifty years old. Where the hell am I going now?" Gloria took another sip from her paper cup.

"Why'd they let you go, Ms. Tomlin?" asked the Judge, very curious about why the company's receptionist had been instructed to erase Gloria's presence from the firm's collective consciousness.

"Going to tell you, Judge. I don't give a shit about their confidentiality agreement. All those threats to keep my mouth shut. Screw them...They can go pound sand. What they going to do? Sue me? I've got nothing to take. Bastards."

"What exactly happened?" asked the Judge.

"They asked me to get rid of some files. They were in a hurry to see them gone. Had their fancy lawyer come from the Valley to talk to me first. Jake Benson - turned out he was Christi's dad.

"He was kind of slippery. Didn't give me a card or anything. Jesus, usually you lawyers have a damn card changer on their belt." She cackled at this. "I liked Christi, but her dad, this guy Jake, he was a real cold fish.

"He explained to me real careful like. Said the company had a Record Retention Policy. Said this was the Annual Record Retention Review. Said, based on the review, these records needed to be destroyed at once. What a load of crap. There wasn't never a Retention Policy before. There'd never been an Annual Retention Review. I was there 10 years. Hadn't been anything like that. All made-up bullshit. This guy, Christi's dad, he was just wiping their ass in case it came up later. I told Christi that. Told her how I felt, even though it was her old man. I don't care. I say how it is. And now I've told you."

"What did Christi say?"

"She said that's just how he is, real tricky. Said you always have to watch your back."

Anyway, it was a big job and they wanted it done in a hurry. So I asked Christi to help. Christi's a smart girl. Maybe too smart.

"We started shredding these paper records. Accounting records, ledger sheets, copies of checks, emails and other stuff.

"But she got to worrying about it. You know how young people get. Christi had been working for John's secretary. She'd seen a subpoena for records.

"Looked to her to be the same records we were destroying. So, she asked some questions. Asked Harley's secretary if the documents were covered by the subpoena. Asked if she might get in trouble. Guess she knew her old man pretty well.

"Anyway, then the shit hit the fan.

"Harley's secretary, Emma, told her to shut up and do her job. Then Emma must have reported her to Harley. Harley called Christi into his office for a private chat. They were in there a good half hour. Then Christi came out. She's all red and flustered, looks kind of sick to her stomach, won't say a word to anyone. Goes back to helping me shred more documents.

"Next morning Christi comes to work and Emma hands her a one sentence letter. You're fired. Emma tells her to remove her things from her desk and get out. Don't talk to any of the employees. Just go.

"Christi turns white as a sheet. She goes to her desk, takes a couple of personal things, and leaves. Poor thing. We weren't allowed to say goodbye. Bastards. Pure bastards.

"One week later they let me go. Say my work hasn't been up to snuff for some months; showed me a bunch of doctored records. Notes about poor performance and meetings with me to discuss my failures. Never happened. All bullshit.

"Said I could sign a confidentiality agreement and get one month's severance check, or I could refuse and just get nothing. Either way I was not to come back. After 10 years. Threw me away like a disposable cup." Gloria paused to take another sip from her disposable cup, then sat back and glared at the Judge. As though it might be the Judge's fault."

"Do you know what the records were about?"

"I don't know…It was records involving large cash deliveries from offshore, and cash payments to vendors, unions, inspectors, and other public officials. Monies they'd paid to various people to get deals done, I think. They paid money to brokers and lawyers, syndications, officials, inspectors, trusts…blind trusts - I don't know what that is. Trusts don't have eyes to start with. 'Course stuff on the computer we just erased. Used one of those fancy wipe programs. Christi figured out how to use it. I think the money they were spending all came from their big swinging Dick Mexican partner."

"Was Christi very upset about being let go early?"

"For sure. But she wasn't suicidal. They weren't paying her much for Christ sakes. Mostly there for the experience and a nice recommendation letter, which they refused to give. She was concerned about the subpoena though. Troubled her she might be doing something illegal."

"Can you think of any reason why she might want to jump off a cliff?"

"No."

"Did she seem down, moody, unhappy, angry that last week before she left?

"No. She was real angry when they fired her though."

"Did she discuss her friends with you, her love life, her school work, her home life, anything personal?"

"Not much, Judge. Said her plan was to study history, get her masters, and become a history professor. She seemed certain that's what she wanted to do. Just turned 18, Judge. So young.

"She did confide once she was changing boyfriends. Said she'd met someone older she'd fallen in love with. Was having a hard time breaking with her current fling. The guy had been real possessive and controlling. Often jealous and mean. Told her there was no way they were breaking up. He'd rather see her dead.

"I think she was a little afraid of him. What he might do. Said he had an ugly temper.

"I told her boyfriend's get over it quick. I've had lots. Too many boyfriends in fact. Told her men are short-term animals. You may hold one for a while. But to hold on forever and keep him interested…that's impossible. Once they get what they want, they'll be off chasing some other twist. It's how they're built. Told her not to get too involved with this new guy either. You can't count on them. None of them. Guess she didn't listen."

"Did she ever wear a blue dress to work, or talk about one?"

"Her 'fuck dress'," cackled Gloria. "She told me the story. Her new friend bought her a special blue dress. But she couldn't wear any underwear with it. That was the condition of the gift. Sounds damn cold to me, Judge. This time of fall I'd truly have witches' tits without my undies." Gloria cackled again. "This new crop of kids gets a little carried away with sex. But jumping off a cliff like that. Over a guy. Just plain nuts."

"You said Harley & Johns had a Mexican partner?" asked the Judge.

"I don't know nothing 'bout that," she said quickly. Perhaps a little too quickly, thought the Judge.

"Thank you for the help," he said, standing and heading toward the door.

"You're welcome Judge. You're a good man. Real sorry 'bout what we did to you."

"What?" said the Judge, stopping in mid stride, turning back to face Gloria.

"What did you do to me, Gloria?"

"I mean the firm, not me."

"What did Harley & Johns do to me?"

"Lost you that election. Got you thrown out as a judge. You didn't deserve that."

"How'd they do that?" the Judge asked softly.

"They got a lawyer to set up some other fellow to do a surprise run against you. Paid the lawyer handsomely I heard. Put $300,000 into one of their blind trusts, or something, for the lawyer to spend on their guy's campaign. They called in favors with two local newspaper guys to do some smear articles. I heard the lawyer even sent people out to pull down your signs. Lots of behind the scenes nasty tricks. I helped them print the copy for the mailer that went out. Sorry about that. Never felt good about it. Didn't seem right smearing a judge, least of all you. Everyone respected you. Knew you couldn't be bought. But people believe everything they hear and read. Big secret campaign sprung on you last minute. Guess you didn't have much of a chance."

"Guess not. Any idea why they went to all the trouble?"

"I heard there was some case coming up. A lot at stake. That was the scuttlebutt. But very hush, hush. We weren't supposed to know about it."

The Judge stood still by the door, suddenly not moving, considering the implications of what Gloria just said.

There had been a case he was going to judge. And Harley and his partner had been, and still were defendants in it. A case involving a syndication and alleged fraud. He'd lost the election before the case got to him. The case was automatically assigned to the next senior judge for complex business matters at the Torrance Branch of the Superior Court: Judge Henry Potter.

"Thank you Gloria, you've been very helpful," said the Judge, moving again to the door.

"Nice to meet you in person, Judge. You ever get lonely, come on down here and we'll party. You know us 'Pedro' girls really know how to party."

The Judge turned at the door, smiling.

Encouraged, Gloria gave the Judge her best smile, adding a small shoulder shake that allowed the housecoat to slide open a bit further revealing the better part of a large breast. Then she winked.

"I'll keep that in mind, Gloria. Good luck. Hope things work out."

Chapter 16 - Saturday

At ten o'clock sharp the next morning, the Judge got into the E, and called Maddie as he backed down his driveway.

Maddie was home and he invited himself over.

The E whipped around the corners and bends on the way out of Malaga Cove like the thoroughbred she was. The day had drawn up cloudy and grey with a forecast of rain in the evening. It was also damn cold with the top down, but the Judge didn't have a choice.

He'd always been too tall for the car. Now he was too fat too. He used to look like a tall carrot, his head sticking well above the windshield, his hair flopping in the breeze. Now he figured he looked more like a damn toad, his bulky shoulders protruding out on all sides, his paunch squashed under the steering wheel. It was becoming increasingly uncomfortable to squeeze into the E. He supposed there was an old man's car in his not too distant future.

The Judge bounded up Maddie's driveway and steps, mostly since he was freezing from his ride, and rang the doorbell. She opened the door at once.

"Hi Maddie, how are you doing?"

"Hi Judge." Her voice was distant and dispirited. "I'm doing. Not sleeping well. Sometimes I just start crying. It's hard. Part of me won't accept she's gone. It keeps expecting her to pop in the front door with a 'Hi Mom'. I don't know how long I can take this."

"I'm so sorry," said the Judge. "It'll take time, some considerable time. It won't ever be the same, I'm afraid, but it will get easier. Slowly, but it will get easier."

"Have you made any progress, Judge? Can you tell me why my baby's not here anymore?"

"I don't have the entire picture, Maddie. But I'm trying to piece it all together. I'll get there. I'd like to look at her room."

"Right now?"

"Yes, I think so…if it's okay, Maddie. Just for a minute."

"Sure. I can't bear to go in there right now. You'll have to go by yourself."

Maddie pointed to the door at the other end of the interior hall, off the living room.

The Judge opened the door and walked into a small bedroom.

It was a corner room at the front of the house and the morning sun gave everything a warm glow. The room had the faint scent of perfume, a stronger scent than she would have used later in life, and the fainter smells of deodorant and shampoo.

The posters taped to the wall identified it as a teenage lair. A young male vampire movie star in goth rock concert garb looked out from one, staring across the room at a heartthrob leading man. There was also a stack of movie magazines: *Cosmo* and *Running*, a half empty six-pack of diet coke. Three stuffed animals from bygone days, still loved, perched on the bed. A poster board on the wall was layered with assignments, to-do notes, old concert programs and tickets, and impromptu snapshots of friends and outings stretching back to younger days.

One picture caught the Judge's eye: Christi in jeans and purple blouse, seated in a photo booth on someone's lap. She looked radiantly happy, make up all done up, jeans and a low cut top.

The head of the lap's owner was cut off, but he was obviously buff. Beige tweedy coat over dark brown slacks didn't hide a powerful physique. His arms wrapped around her waist and his hands were resting territorially toward the inside of her upper thighs. The Judge had the sense this was an older man, not a youthful teenager out with his date. The Judge wondered if Maddie had focused on the photo, and what she thought about it.

The Judge moved to the bathroom, taking his pen out to poke around. The white tile counter around the sink had a collection of powders, lipstick, blush, and other potions foreign to the Judge. Also mouthwash, power toothbrush, blow dryer, and what the Judge suspected to be a curling iron. Things were spread all over the counter in some underlying order known only to Christi.

The 21st century teenager traveled anything but light, mused the Judge. High school girls on The Hill were well groomed and dressed all the times. Far different from the Judge's day when girls dressed down in jeans and sweat shirts to look like the boys. Girls on The Hill were fully kitted out.

The medicine cabinet contained Tylenol, toothpaste, floss, a hairbrush, Band-Aids, a bottle of prescription sleeping pills, out of date but almost full, aspirin, and pills for cramps. The cabinet drawers had nail polish, various brushes and combs, and a variety of odd-looking items descended from Middle Aged tools of torture, or so it appeared. One drawer was jammed with Kotex, Kleenex, and cotton balls.

Another drawer contained makeup in a variety of colorful and expensive looking dispensers, along with cleansing pads, makeup remover, various fancy soaps, and other female accoutrements.

The Judge carefully lifted the top of the toilet tank. Taped to the side was a tightly wrapped baggie, and within, a second baggie. Inside were three joints, one partly smoked. He wrapped them up and taped the package back.

He moved back to the bedroom and sifted through the closet. There seemed to be a choice of outfits and colors for every occasion. The Judge owned one blue tweed suit for work, one black wool suit for funerals, and three dark blue sport coats, interchangeable, which rotated back and forth to the cleaners. He would have been totally befuddled, he mused, if he had to contend with so many choices. Christi was apparently a clothes-horse, or perhaps the Judge was just out of touch with teenage life. Sometimes, he regretted never having kids.

In the pockets he found a couple of movie ticket stubs, an expired coupon for pizza, a couple of credit card receipts. The Judge came to a pair of black and grey striped slacks, the lower half of a very business-like outfit.

Stuffed in the left side pocket were two crumpled pages, apparently jammed into the pocket in a hurry. The first page was a photocopy of three separate checks for $25,000 each, issued by a company called GreenShoots, Inc. There was no address on the check, but each was signed by Jake Benson: Christi's dad and the Judge's old law partner.

They were each made out to "Henry Potter", the replacement judge on the "No Limit" Civil Panel who took over after the Judge lost the election. The checks were dated monthly, starting in July, just after the Judge's loss. Each check was drawn on the Bank of America, Rolling Ranchos Branch. The memo line was completed with 'legal services'.

The second page was a photocopy of a page from an accounting ledger. It listed a series of payments, $10,000 each, noted as "paid in cash", and paid the previous March to ten separate individuals. There appeared to have been a project name at the top, but someone had taken a dark pen and blocked the name out.

The Judge wrote the number of the bank account into the small calendar book he carried, used his cell phone to take a picture of each document, then put the papers back in the pocket of Christi's slacks.

The Judge's search of the rest of the room turned up little of interest: no pills, no hard drugs, no diary, no date book, no purse, no wallet, no car keys. But under the mattress was a bill for $489.00, marked 'paid', from a local Doc in the Box Family Clinic. The description read: "for test and consultation".

The Judge took a picture of the bill as well, and then put it back where he found it.

The Judge returned to the living room where Maddie sat, dispirited, on the red sofa.

"Did Christi carry a purse?" asked the Judge.

"Sometimes, or often just a small wallet she'd tuck in her pocket."

"Did she have a diary?"

"Oh yes. She was always writing in it. She wanted to be a writer. She said you have to experience all sorts of things first before you can write, and it's important to write them down as you go."

"I didn't see it in her room."

"She usually carried it with her."

"Have you seen it recently?"

"No."

"What did it look like?"

"It was kind of a blue denim fabric, a bit beat up from being carried everywhere."

"How about her car keys?" asked the Judge.

"They're on a hook in the kitchen. It's my second car, and sometimes I use it. The rest of the time it was hers."

"Were you using it the day that she died?" asked the Judge.

"No," Maddie said.

"Are you sure the car keys are still in the kitchen?" asked the Judge.

"I think so, we can look."

They looked. On a peg next to the refrigerator hung the keys.

"Maddie," said the Judge, "can you leave Christi's room just the way it is and not let anyone in there for a couple days? I'm going to suggest to the Police Chief that they search the room as a part of their investigation."

"Okay," said Maddie, returning to her post on the sofa. "Whatever you want Judge. It doesn't much matter now. Not much of anything matters."

The Judge sat quietly with her for a little and then got up and made his apology for having to leave.

He closed the door softly behind him. Maddie remained on her sofa, just staring into space. The Judge trudged back to the E and squeezed in, relieved to be away.

Chapter 17 - Sunday

The Judge awoke after a night of troubled sleep.

He'd dreamed he was dancing with Ms. Thorne. The dance floor was crowded. The other dancers, all Katy's age, stared at him, whispering amongst themselves. Suddenly, everyone left the dance floor in the middle of a song; it was 'Some Enchanted Evening', from *South Pacific*. Katy and he danced alone.

The other dancers sat down at their tables, each folding their arms across their chests, regarding him with disapproval.

The Judge looked down and saw that he wore no clothes. His middle age paunch, pink and fuzzy, which he detested, projected out so he couldn't see his plumbing below. But everything was hanging out.

Katy started to laugh at him. Then the entire room started to laugh. They laughed so hard they pounded their tables and each other, tears streaming down their faces.

Then he woke up.

It was most unsettling and confirmed all his instincts. This young lady was far too young for him. He had meant to call yesterday and cancel the dinner date. A sudden illness, an emergency trip out of town, whatever. Somehow he'd just never gotten around to it. It was morning; he'd do it in the afternoon. It was afternoon; he'd do it in the evening. It was evening, but then it was past 10 pm and not a polite time to call.

Once again he wrestled with whether he should call it off. By noon, he was just plain tired of thinking about it. He would just show up and to hell with what people thought. It was only for dinner. They would think he was a favorite uncle or something.

The Judge arrived promptly at 7:30 in front of the townhome address Ms. Thorn... Katy...had given him. He was still unsure about the wisdom of this date, but he'd recalled how happy she'd been when he agreed to dinner. For some reason, her happiness had spilled over and had made him feel good too. It was worth the risk just to see if it would happen again.

The Judge had taken unusual care with his attire too, though he'd never have admitted it.

In lieu of one of his Tommy Bahama shirts, traditional fare for an old guy like him with a paunch, he'd chosen a polo golf shirt, emblazoned with an extraordinarily large polo player logo where a pocket should have been. It was a soft blue (perhaps it would bring out the faded blue in his eyes). The shirt had been given to him for his birthday in September by his elderly aunt. She was considered to have the best taste in the family, having once been the editor of a New York fashion magazine. But he detested shirts with no pockets and generally refused to wear them. He'd been forced to stuff his reading glasses in his pants pocket along with his comb, and had actually left his pen at home, unheard of for the Judge. It was all making him a bit irritable.

He wore soft neutral Chinos, and brown loafers without socks. It occurred to him to remove his socks at the last minute, he wasn't sure why. He'd seen an ad somewhere, and the young man modeling wore no socks. He regretted his decision as soon as he was out of the driveway. It was bloody cold, the shoes were new, and he was going to have blisters. Besides, he suspected it looked truly silly.

He'd left his prize E in the garage. He didn't fit with the damn top up, and it was sure in hell too cold for Katy with the top down. Besides, women always fussed over their hair in convertibles. He was driving the old green Chevy, which had visited the car wash that very afternoon. It had been cleaned, polished and detailed, inside and out. He could still smell the sickly scent of vanilla car freshener.

He marched up her driveway, clomped up on to the front door stoop, involuntarily took a big breath, and rang the bell. She immediately opened the door. Christ, she must have been standing behind it, waiting.

It was a breath of fresh air to see the smile with all those teeth again.

"Come in Judge, and sit down. I just need a minute to put on some lipstick." She winked.

The Judge couldn't believe it. She winked. What was he getting himself into?

His misgiving magnified as he perched uncomfortably on the edge of her sofa. He felt like a prisoner waiting for the firing squad to march out.

He had noted that she was already pretty well dolled up. He wondered why she waited to put her lipstick on until he arrived. Women were such tricky creatures. Maybe he was supposed to look around. Why not? He immediately got up and started to explore.

The townhome had dark wood beams stretched over an open ceiling, giving the small space a lofty feel. Kitchen on the left, and a hall off to the right no doubt led to bedroom and bath. That's where she'd disappeared.

A dark brown wood bookcase stretched across the wall opposite the door, climbing toward the ceiling. Some of the books dealt with psychology and counseling, but there were also cook books, travel books, several photo albums, a walking trails guide, a stack of dog-eared Vanity Fair magazines, and a couple of paperback romances, the kind written by women for women, full of fiery passion. Generally short on plot and character.

The bookcase also sported several photographs in silver frames, a brightly painted Chinese tea service on a lacquered pa wooden tray, and a tall vase with fresh cut white edged purple lilacs. Kind of an old fashioned flower, thought the Judge. Their scent filled the room.

A large glass coffee table held a museum quality art tome on Spanish masters, a large book entitled "A Photographic Journey of the Palos Verdes Peninsula", and three thick manila folders and a yellow notepad, a tip-off that Katy took work home.

He examined a framed photo of Katy's mother, looking more relaxed than at the Country Club, and a man he assumed was Katy's dad. The parents looked all of ten years older than the Judge. This gave him pause.

Jesus, what did they think about his dinner date with their daughter? Correction - he knew what Mother thought.

Father looked quite serious: receding hair line, grey speckled hair, perhaps an engineer or a doctor.

There was a picture of Katy and her younger brother. He was hamming it up. He favored Mother. Katy clearly favored Dad with her long nose and pointed chin.

Katy swept around the corner, extending her hand to pull him away from the bookshelf and lead him to the door. No offer of wine, or better yet, Scotch on rocks. They were going straight to dinner.

She was so obviously pleased to see him that he couldn't hold the way he been entrapped into dinner against her. He supposed it would be impossible to hold any sort of grudge against someone so open and so happy.

Katy had on pale green slacks and a soft buff colored silk blouse, collared, and unbuttoned a little in front. Sort of a Katherine Hepburn look, the Judge thought. Slimming, soft, and professional looking, all at once.

He wondered if her green slacks would clash with his telephone green Chevy. That made him smile. She thought the smile was for her, and smiled back. He marveled again at that smile, all sparkling teeth, and the way the smile spread up into her eyes.

He piled her into the Chevy and they roared down The Hill in his noisy bucket of bolts. It was an old car after all and its 200,000 miles hadn't been kind. Katy didn't seem to mind.

He took her to 'River Gauche', a small French restaurant tucked away across from City Hall in Malaga Cove.

The place had white walls with heavy dark beams running horizontally here and there along the walls and across the ceiling, partly for support and partly for effect. It gave the impression of an old country inn. The small tables were covered with linen. Each had a candle and a vase with a flower or two. The green carpet added to the old world effect, as did the pictures: original sketches and oils of the Left Bank, Notre Dame, the Eiffel Tower and the Champs Elyse.

He asked Jacques, the owner, for a private rear table away from the old piano player, and that's what they got. It was dark, it was tucked away, and it was discreet. Nothing like the Judge's nightmare.

They settled in over drinks made by Martin, the other restaurant partner, a gin and tonic for the Judge and a French chardonnay for Katy. Martin knew how the Judge liked his drinks. His glass had enough gin to float a battleship, with a chaser of tonic just in case, and a small plate of cut limes.

"To prevent scurvy," said the Judge, "you can't be too careful." Her eyes danced at him.

"So here we are," said the Judge, for once a little lost for words. "You've got your date with a judge, and an expensive dinner. Although it's not that expensive. I'm sure you could have afforded it on your own."

She laughed softly, almost shyly at that, a small little chuckle that started back in her throat and slowly worked its way out.

"Yes," she said, "I've got the attention of my Judge. At least for a little." Then she smiled at him again, that smile that started with her mouth and worked its way all the way up to her eyes as she looked into his. And all the tension evaporated.

They talked then, over their cocktails, over the menus, over the soup and then the salad, over the main course, over desert, over coffee, and on and on until it got very late and the other patrons had left. They didn't even notice when the music stopped and the old piano player packed up his notes and crept slowly away.

The Judge talked of his ex-wife, how young they had both been when they married, and how she had left him for another man, shattering everything he'd taken for granted.

She talked of her "live together" boyfriend for five years after college, how as they grew and changed and drifted farther and farther apart, until there was really nothing tying them together. So they had called it quits.

The Judge talked of his college days at USC, the Gould School of Law, and his time at the mega international law firm.

Katy talked of her time at Stanford, majoring in Psychology over the objections of her dad, of her sorority days, and the whirlwind social life at Stanford, followed by hard work to get her teaching credential on her own at UCLA.

The Judge talked of being a Judge, how much he thought he'd liked the job, and how depressed he was when he'd lost the election.

She talked of her work as a counselor, how rewarding it was, how many problems, both old and new, modern teenagers had. She spoke of how she was making a difference for some of these kids, sometimes even providing emotional shelter when there was nowhere else to turn.

They shared stories of growing up, and of parents. Of victories and defeats, jobs and travels. Of siblings, hobbies, likes, dislikes and how they chose to spend their personal time. They spoke of dreams and aspirations, relationships and loneliness, middle age and retirement, of death and of life's wonders.

The Judge liked travel, fine wine and fine food, live theater and concerts, sailing, America's cup, and the USC football team.

Katy liked traveling as well, and movies, gym classes, cooking, hosting cocktail parties, dressing up to go out, book clubs, charity work, small children, puppies, and Hollywood gossip magazines.

They laughed together, and leaned ever closer across the dinner table as they shared ever more personal experiences and feelings. They talked of the funny things that had happened, of the places they had been, and the places they would go, of the good and bad of being single. They talked of pets and cars, of close calls and lucky breaks.

Finally, near the end of the evening, they ran out of talk. They just looked at each other. Her blue eyes dancing with sparkles, her face slightly flushed. Katy's face was alight. The Judge could feel it too, a special camaraderie. Like they'd known each other forever, but only just found one another again. The Judge hadn't felt this comfortable with a woman ever.

Finally Jacques could give them no more time. Hating to interrupt what he could see was a transformation in them both, but needing to let the staff go and go home himself, he quietly brought the bill over and laid it discreetly in front of the Judge.

The Judge paid with a credit card, not bothering to check the bill; not wanting to take his eyes off this captivating creature across the small table. The evening had been priceless. He was sad to see it end.

They were both quiet on the way home, processing this extraordinary evening, neither daring to risk spoiling it with some new intellectual topic. The evening just was.

He helped her out of the car in front of her townhome, and she tucked her hand in his as they walked to her door. As he leaned forward awkwardly to give her a little hug, she stood up on her tip toes and kissed his lips, a quick "gotcha" sort of kiss, gave him her best smile, and then turned, dancing into her townhome. She turned back, peeking at him before closing the door, and said, "I want to do it again, Judge, soon."

Then the door closed…and the Judge felt a light had suddenly dimmed in space and time.

Chapter 18 - Monday

The Judge pulled out his laptop, and punched in "Federal Election Commission", and then "Electronically Filed Independent Expenditures". Then he searched for Carl Randolph, the lawyer that had beat him in the election. Nothing came up. Next he pulled up the California Secretary of State Website on Campaign Finance Activity, or Cal-Access.

Here his search was rewarded with a campaign report filed by Carl Randolph. He pulled up Campaign Contributions. There was only one made. Gloria had been right. It was in the staggering amount of $300,000. Jesus, no wonder he'd lost. The maker of the contribution to the committee was GreenShoots, Inc., and its principal executive officer was Jake Benson

The Judge leaned back in his chair and sipped some coffee.

It was about time he paid a visit to his old law partner.

Jake had a fancy office on Ventura Blvd, on the penthouse floor. The Judge had to look into a fish eye camera at the outer door and identify himself. He was buzzed in to a large lobby with a cobblestone floor, expensive French antiques, large original modern art which, to the Judge's eye, clashed with the antiques, and two low upholstered brown leather sofas one easily sank into, but found it difficult to get up from. Especially if you've got lead in your butt, thought the Judge, as he managed a counter weight standup on this third try by sliding to the edge and leaning way out over this feet.

Copies of *Variety* and the *Hollywood Reporter* were stacked on a once beautiful antique table whose legs had been hacked off to make it coffee table height. There was also the *Wall Street Journal* and the *New York Times* for more stuffy visitors like the Judge who preferred semi-fact to total fiction.

A pretty blonde girl with an expensive set of add-on breasts way too big for her small frame sat behind an expensive looking inlaid table desk. The Judge wondered if she were a danger to herself or others in a high wind.

He sat in the lobby for a full half hour past his appointed time, thumbing copies of newspapers, finally forced to look at the Hollywood dailies. There was nothing else to read. Since there was no modesty panel on the reception desk, the Judge supposed he could have spent his time watching long legs and lacy underwear, but the Judge had admired them when he first sat down and didn't feel a need to view further.

Finally a second young blonde with an outsized re-engineered torso appeared. She showed him to a large corner office. The Judge suspected he'd deliberately been allowed to cool his heels.

There were trophy cases here and there, displaying footballs, basketballs, jerseys, and helmets, all autographed with the names of sports figures the Judge was sure were famous but didn't know. A bookshelf along one wall displayed a set of the California Reporter case law, and a set of California Legal Codes, neither of which looked to have ever been opened.

Built into the middle of the bookcase wall was a small but fully stocked bar, with a sink, glasses, bottles, and mirrors on all planes displaying multiple images in a confused pantomime of the original.

In one corner, a round glass table with four small, upholstered swivel chairs provided the 'de rigor' conference nook for more intimate conversations. Cobblestone flooring, another deep leather sofa, and two comfortable looking wing chairs sat in front of a large glass desk.

Jake Benson sat behind the desk. It was empty except for a blank yellow pad, a single pen, and an expensive crystal tumbler glass. This was the minimalist look, meant to convey that the occupant had more important things to think about than old files. Things like the price of sugar in India, or the water table in Tibet.

The Judge decided that this office was designed for show. He wondered where Jake did his real work, and for that matter, exactly what that work was.

Jake didn't get up, but remained seated behind his desk, perhaps for distance, perhaps for protection, the Judge wasn't sure. He wore a soft lavender shirt with an oversized collar, unbuttoned one too many buttons to expose dark curly chest fur. He had grey slacks, a black belt, and black loafers, all visible through the top of the glass desk. His shoes were polished to a T. A heavy gold Rolex hung on his port wrist, leaving the Judge to wonder if he walked with a list.

He was average height, thin, with sharp features, a large pointed nose, a full head of graying hair cut to a buzz, and soft blue eyes which belied the sharpness of his face, and tended to misdirect people into being at ease.

He'd been a good lawyer back when the two had partnered together: energetic, dependable, persuasive in court, and not afraid of the hard and tedious preparation required to be successful. He'd aged some, but rather than adding weight like the Judge, he'd gotten thinner, perhaps unhealthily so, and his angular features had grown thin and hawk like.

When they'd been law partners, Jake persistently pressured the Judge to take time off for R and R in Vegas. When Jake had finally worn the Judge down, he got them comp'd in twin penthouse rooms at the newest and best casino. But it gave the Judge pause that Jake was on a first name basis with every pit boss on the tables along the Strip.

They went their separate ways after only a year of partnership, the Judge off to serve on the bench, Jake staying downtown for several years. After his messy divorce from Maddie, he had moved out to the Valley to try sports and entertainment law. Apparently he'd been successful.

This morning, in spite of his immaculate clothes, Jake looked like shit. There was no polite way to describe it. The Judge felt sorry for him. But there were questions that needed answering. There'd never be a good time.

There were large dark circles under Jake's eyes from lack of sleep. The blue eyes were slow, without sparkle. His lips were tight across his face in a perpetual grimace. A bourbon and rocks sat beside him, freshly iced but already half gone. His movements were lethargic. It wasn't the Jake Benson the Judge expected; there was no snap.

The Judge walked up to the desk and extended his hand over it, biting his lower lip a bit as he said softly, "I am so sorry about Christina, Jake."

Jake took the Judge's hand, but his grip wasn't firm like it usually was.

Thanks, Judge," Jake said. "It's just…a shock. I can't believe she's gone."

The Judge sat down in one of the two wing chairs in front of the desk while Jake stared out the window behind him for a time.

"We weren't close you know," said Jake, breaking a silence that lingered a bit too long.

"After the divorce, well, she sided with her mother. She was only eight. I fought for custody of course, but what with the Vegas trips, the gambling debts, the people I was partying with…Well, you know, it all came out…I just got a weekend a month for visitation. It made it tough to keep up a relationship." Jake's words came slow and without conviction. The Judge wondered if there had been pills in addition to the bourbon. "After a while we just stopped seeing each other. I got too busy I guess. And I'd moved; it's a long way to Palos Verdes from here."

"It's a long way to The Hill from anywhere," corrected the Judge.

"I just never thought she'd do something like this. I thought now she was getting older I'd have another chance. We'd have more in common. She'd understand better."

Jake's focus wandered as he spoke, and he had difficulty meeting the Judge's eye.

"You know, Judge, it takes two people to make a marriage, but it really only takes one to break it all to Hell."

"There's always plenty of fault to go around, seems to me," said the Judge.

"I suppose…And people do change. Develop different interests, different spheres of friends…drift apart. After a while, the early sexual passion becomes slated, becomes ho hum, then kind of a duty. You don't have it to fall back on when tension mounts over finances, how to raise the kid, who has what duties and chores, or even where to go for dinner.

"There comes a point where you start looking forward to your time apart more than your time together. You don't look forward to coming home anymore. Things deteriorate quickly from there. The years start to go faster, you start to feel mortal. You're not going to live forever. You can feel youth slipping away, a little more each day.

"So, you start to take chances, live more aggressively, suck the marrow out of each moment. Pretty soon "not looking forward to going home" becomes "not going home". There's more fun and excitement with your new crowd. Single people, or on the way to being…like you. Some have the same monkey on their back…running out of youth and time, frightened to be old with their youth wasted. Some still searching for their dream, more desperate and less discriminating each birthday. Some just hopeless children who never grow up, moving from liaison to liaison, destined to be perpetually disappointed.

"You try everything, you do everything and everybody. You work less because your new life takes more time and energy. You find easier ways of making money to support your time with your new crowd.

"One day you come home after a week and a half away. You silently walk into your bedroom and pack your clothes. You ignore your wife, who transitions from angry at your absence, to anguished that you won't talk to her, to terrified you're actually leaving.

"Then it's over. You walk out the door. You never look back.

"Trouble is, it's a lot more complicated with a kid. It's not so easy to turn off all those feelings about your baby. It tears you up. I guess it tears the kid up too.

"Christi and me…We still had a chance." Jake stopped here to take a sip of bourbon, and to control his emotions. "Anyway, it's all shit now. Life sucks, Judge. It just sucks."

"Maddie has asked me to look into what happened," said the Judge. She's desperate for answers."

"Yes, she told me, although I don't see the point. It's all crystal clear." Sarcasm and slight slur slipped into Jake's voice. "Unhappy over a boyfriend...Well, just jump off a cliff. What else would you do?"

"Did you know Christi was working for Harley & Johns?" asked the Judge.

"Yes," sighed Jake. "I helped her get the internship."

"Then you know Pat Harley and his partner, Mel?"

"No…Well…ehhh…. I mean…I know of them, I guess. I talked to the school and suggested an internship for Christi."

"Who did you talk to at the school?"

"Oh, Christ, I don't remember the name, just someone in career search or something. I'm sure they wouldn't remember me," said Jake, flushing, his eyes suddenly snapping on like twin blue beacons.

"I understand you represent an outfit called GreenShoots," said the Judge.

This brought Jake bolt upright in his chair.

" How'd the hell did you hear that?"

"Is it true?"

"You know I can't discuss my clients, Judge," a poker face now sliding down over Jake's countenance.

"Well, among its other activities, old buddy, GreenShoots found time to bankroll the opponent in my judgeship election to the tune of some $300,000. Think about money like that, an orchestrated sneak attack out of the blue, and a series of dirty mailers and ads filled with malicious innuendos. Gave me little chance to recover before election day."

"Well that's unfortunate, Judge, but I guess that's politics," said Jake, a bit smugly thought the Judge, despite his now blank face. "Anyway, I can't discuss the identity of my client, were this GreenShoots actually a client, which I'm not admitting."

"Who do you think was in line to take over my cases in the event of a loss of the election?" asked the Judge.

"Why, I don't know," said Jake, rather archly. "I don't keep track of stuff like that."

"Henry Potter," said the Judge.

Jake didn't bat an eye. "Henry Potter," he said, rolling the name over on his tongue. "No…can't say that I know him. He's a judge I presume."

"Gee, Jake, the way I heard it, GreenShoots is affiliated with Harley & Johns. They fund the entity. You run GreenShoots for them and sign all the checks," said the Judge bluffing only a little.

Jake's eyes widened. "I told you I can't discuss clients," he snapped.

"Even if it might involve the death of your daughter?" asked the Judge.

Now Jake got angry. "You come in here and make innuendos about me, and now, now… now you have the gall to suggest a connection with my daughter's death. You're mad, Judge, absolutely crazy."

"So, there wouldn't have been at least three checks, drawn on GreenShoots, totaling $75,000 of Harley & Johns' money, paid to Judge Henry Potter? Henry Potter, a sitting judge now presiding over a very large trial involving Harley & Johns? Three checks with your signature, drawn on the GreenShoots Bank of America account?

Jake looked like a gaping fish, his mouth working, but no sound coming out.

"How'd you…No…No; I know nothing, nothing about that," he snarled.

"Suppose a copy of such checks were taken by Christi from Harley & Johns. Suppose such copies were found among her effects," said the Judge.

Jake gasped, blurting out, "They'd never do anything to hurt Christi." Then pulling himself together, he said in a low threatening voice, "I'm through talking to you Judge, forever. Show yourself out."

The Judge got up and headed for the door, but turned as he opened it. "I suspect you're right about Harley & Johns. I don't see them as violent, just opportunistic and unscrupulous. But what about the Mexican partner who provides the money? It's their money at risk if Harley & Johns goes down. People like that don't play by the same rules we do, Jake."

"You'd better watch your back, Judge. You're getting in way over your head. You've no idea how much hurt may result..."

"I think you've been in over your head for a while, Jake," the Judge said softly. "Good day."

Chapter 19 - Tuesday

At 9:05 a.m., the Judge called the law offices of Jenkins & Clark, a prestigious class action and products liability firm in the South Bay. They represented the Plaintiffs in the case against Harley & Johns.

He made an appointment to see Dick Jenkins, their lead trial counsel, at 10:30.

"It's a personal matter," the Judge told the secretary, "just 20 minutes is all I need."

Time was money when you practiced law. If the Judge took up too much of Dick's time, he'd expect to be paid. Lawyers were like that.

He backed the E out of his driveway and drove downhill toward the Del Amo Financial Center. It was ahead of its time in 1967 when it was built, with its 178-foot diamond shaped office tower and low-rise pavilions and waterscapes. The project was supposed to include three towers in a full circle, but developers could never obtain sufficient tenants to build more than the one tower. A bit out of date now in some ways, it was still a beautiful property, and the place where well-known South Bay law firms liked to set up shop. The Judge always made a point of parking on the far side of the parking lot so he could walk through the waterscape and gardens on his way to the tower.

Jenkins & Clark took up the entire fourth floor. The lobby was a busy place: people bustling in all

"Excuse me, Betty. I'd better check on my dog."

In big strides, the Judge went quickly back up his front steps, through the house, and opened the door off the kitchen to the rear yard, stepping through to the patio beyond.

Annie was huddled in a heap in the corner of the patio, not moving, lying in a puddle of blood.

As the Judge got close she lifted her muzzle to look at him with difficulty, blood dripping from a slash wound at her neck. Her eyes were glazed and confused. She tried to get up to meet him, but collapsed back down.

The Judge cried out in horror and grief, "Annie, Annie, Oh my God, what have they done?" He sank to his knees beside the animal and held the dog's head in his hands a moment, trying to staunch the blood flowing from her neck. It wouldn't stop.

He picked the animal up and rushed into the bathroom, pulling out larger size irregular bandages from a drawer. Grabbing a longer thin one, he pushed the fur back around the wound, and then plastered it as best he could with the bandage.

Then he carried the animal quickly to the E, put her carefully on the passenger side, and roared out of the driveway, heading for the vet's office in Lunada Bay.

The vet was in, and took Annie right into the surgery center in back, leaving the Judge to pace up and down the small lobby.

The Judge was in shock. Annie was friendliest puppy he'd ever seen. She wouldn't have attacked a stranger entering her house or her yard, or even barked enough to present a danger of early discovery for the thief. She might have licked him to death, but that was all. This was a senseless, malicious, brutal act on a defenseless puppy. And something more, it was a personal warning to him. A very personal warning.

The vet came out about 45 minutes later with a look of relief on her face that reassured the Judge.

"Fortunately the wound wasn't as deep as it looked. Annie still lost a lot of blood. There's no doubt she'd be dead by now if you hadn't got her here so quickly. But the stitches I put in are holding. I've given her a blood transfusion and antibiotics, and barring any unforeseen complication, she should be okay. I'd like to keep her here overnight for observation. Someone will be here around the clock to keep an eye on her."

The Judge nodded his assent, too upset and relieved to say anything.

"How did it happen?" asked the vet. "It looks like someone made an effort to slit her throat."

"That's about it," said the Judge, feeling nauseous now that the crisis was over. "Some sick son of a bitch wanted to make a very definite point."

Chapter 37 - Monday

The Judge had returned to his tossed house the prior afternoon feeling old and tired. He'd rummaged around in the pile of debris behind his desk until he'd successful come up with a bottle out of the pile. It was an old bottle of Laphroaig, his favorite unblended Scotch.

He'd poured himself three fingers over ice and sipped it softly, contemplating the mess around him. Then he'd taken the advice he'd given Maddie days earlier and had called his cleaning lady and her two daughter to come over on an emergency basis early the next morning to put things right. Then he'd gone to bed.

Some people might have felt uncomfortable sleeping in a house violated by an intruder just hours before, but not the Judge. He went into a deep sleep as soon as his head hit the pillow. He was awakened the next morning by the racket of his cleaning lady and daughters moving furniture around his living room.

He lingered in bed for a time, tucked in under the warmth of the covers. Some part of him realized that Annie wasn't back and available to roust him from bed at 6 a.m., ever optimistic for food. The cleaning lady was a poor substitute for Annie's soft brown eyes.

He picked Annie up from the vet late in the morning. The Judge was surprised to discover how much he had missed her.

Annie was weak and lethargic on her return. She had a large plastic cone around her neck of the type often used when some breeds had their ears clipped, a barbaric procedure to the Judge's mind. The cone kept Annie from scratching at the bandage and beneath it, the wound at her neck.

The Judge thought she looked like a walking gramophone, the kind you had to crank by hand. When she turned this way and that, the whole cone moved, restricting her movements, throwing her off balance, and causing her to bang into furniture and walls if she tried to go anywhere too quickly.

Annie felt she'd been deliberately abused for no apparent reason.

She looked at her Judge with sad, slightly accusatory eyes, and was very cautious in her movements lest she bang into walls and knock herself over. She accepted her fate the way loyal creatures do, but with some level of sad bewilderment as to why her master would treat her so.

It seemed to have no impact on her appetite; however, nor on her ability to nab his newest socks when he wasn't looking and chew holes in them. He had to feed her the medicine the vet had prescribed by squeezing the small purple capsules into the middle of some foul greasy substance recommended to him, which Annie seemed quite happy to gobble down in one gulp.

The Judge had been surprised at how much emotion and distress he'd experienced when he'd found the animal in her pool of blood. Much like Henry Higgins, he seemed to have grown attached to the animal in spite of himself, and now quite looked forward to her excitement and always generous welcome on his return home from anywhere, no matter how short the errand.

When he thought about the invasion of his home, and the cruel attack on his innocent companion, he got angry all over again. He vowed to himself that he would settle up with the person responsible.

Chapter 38 - Monday

By 1:30, the Judge had gotten his personal papers and books properly sorted and back in the working stacks where they belonged.

His cell phone rang. He hit the button and put the phone to his ear.

"This is Gloria, Judge. You remember - Gloria Tomlin. The Pedro girl you were going to buy a drink." There was a wicked chuckle on the other end of the call. It sounded like Gloria had already started her drink without him.

"Yes, Gloria, you're unforgettable," said the Judge with a smile reflected in his voice.

"I found some interesting pictures of Christi," said Gloria. "Pictures I know you'll want to see. May explain what happened, why she did it, you know, jumped. And I can also tell you a lot more about Harley & Johns, bastards both of them."

"Thought you might want to buy me a drink, maybe even a late lunch today. Could show you everything I got. You know how us Pedro girls are…we show all." There was another cackle.

"I'd be delighted to buy you lunch. What time and where?"

"There's a bar round the corner from me, called Bobby's. Cheap drinks, good burgers and stuff. We can start there. Then if you're a little frisky…well who knows, Judge. Maybe you'll get lucky."

The Judge said, 'Okay," hiding his distaste at the thought of a liaison.

"Oooowee," she said, "I'm going to put on my best lipstick."

"I'll meet you there in 45 minutes," said the Judge.

The Judge took his old Chevy again. Pedro was Pedro, after all. He wasn't about to leave the E on the street there.

He drove across PV Drive North, dodging the variety of service trucks flitting like moths around The Hill this time of day: gardener trucks, electrician trucks, plumber trucks, painter trucks, carpet trucks, and a few cars driven in wild abandon by housewives returning from their gym, racing to pick up younger kids after the final bell.

He shifted to Anaheim Street at Five Points, the dangerous "down the hill" junction of PV Drive North, Western and Anaheim, roared onto the 405 South, and slowed when the end of the freeway dumped him onto the middle of Gaffey Avenue, the heart of Pedro.

He found a place to park across the street and down the block from Bobbie's Bar and Grill. He spotted Gloria on the sidewalk, in tight purple pants and a low cut yellow top, very low cut it looked, even from up the block. She stepped off the curb to cross to the bar side of the street.

As she did, the Judge noted a dusty green Camaro, battered and banged up in the tradition of Pedro, barreling along up the street from the other direction.

Gloria had stepped off the curb, but cautiously stopped at curbside and waved the car past.

It obligingly sped up, and then at the last minute the driver floored it and spun the wheel, sending the car hurtling over toward the curb where Gloria was standing.

The Judge could hear a sickening thud as the driver's side headlight and front bumper struck Gloria full in the stomach.

The car must have been going 45 or 50 miles an hour. It mowed Gloria down like a stalk of grass, the front wheel thudding over her chest, crushing it to pulp.

The driver spun the car back into the center of the street and kept going, increasing his speed, whisking past the Judge like a freight train.

The Judge saw green metal, a broken headlight, a swarthy driver at the wheel in a white T-shirt, a straw fedora pulled down low over his head. The driver's arm and hand nonchalantly hung out the driver's side window as if nothing had happened. On the back of the hand was a tattoo: an ugly skeleton in a cape holding scales and a ball:

The Judge noted the license as the car sped past, reaching for his pen and a pad to take it down. Then he ran down the street toward Gloria, calling 911 as he ran.

She was there in the gutter, lying face up, a crumpled form of broken arms and legs askew, the imprint of a tire across her crushed chest. Her glazed eyes stared up at the Judge unseeing.

There was nothing to be done for Gloria. The Judge hoped she was in a happier place.

He picked up her purse, a brown tote bag of sorts with a long strap.

Her wallet was inside, her cell phone, the usual kitchen sink assortment: hair brush, lipstick, powder compact, eye liner, Kleenex, a condom she'd perhaps been saving for him. She had certainly been both optimist and Girl Scout. Always prepared.

But there was something else the Judge was sure had been meant for him: four color photographs, all of Christi.

Two were taken at what looked to be an office picnic, likely during the summer. The first one was of Christi standing with Harley next to her, his arm around her back. Christi had on a very low cut pink blouse and looked to be braless, her nipples showing through the light material. She wore darker pink short shorts, cut high at the bottom and low at the top, fitted so tight that little was left to the imagination.

The camera had caught Harley in the act of looking down the front of her blouse, a licentious smirk on his face.

The Judge couldn't blame him for looking. Christi was beautiful. But Harley was a little too old, a little too obvious, and his hand around her back was just a little too low below her waist, almost to her buttocks.

Christi didn't seem to be enjoying the attention. She had a smile on, but it looked to be pasted over gritted teeth, and her eyes weren't smiling at all. Harley was definitely leaning into Christi, his upper leg pressed again her hip, his head tilted in close over her shoulder.

The Judge didn't like it. Harley was way too old to be making that sort of play. What was the age difference? Christi had just turned 18, and Harley was what? Maybe 38. A 20-year difference. About the age difference between the Judge and Katy. This thought made the Judge very uncomfortable, and he shoved it aside.

The second picture was likely the same summer party. Everyone had apparently changed into swimsuits. This was a picture of Harley with Christi sitting on his lap. He had a furry chest and wore dark blue surf shorts. Christi wore a micro bikini: two dots and a dash, in bright yellow, with a collection of yellow strings holding the various parts in place.

Harley had a wolfish look on his face. Christi seemed not to notice, staring at the camera with a sweet smile, trying to be oblivious to the lap she was perched upon.

The third picture looked to be a candid shot from someone's cell phone, snapped in the Harley & Johns lobby. A Latino, dressed in plaid shirt and disreputable jeans and looking shifty and tough, was crossing the lobby heading towards Johns' corner office. He carried a large leather satchel at his side. The Judge could just make out the top part of a tattoo across his hand, a robed skull holding a scythe, the same tattoo he'd seen on the hit and run driver's hand.

The fourth picture was also taken by a cell phone: a picture of a different ledger sheet of entries from apparently the same ledger book as the one from which Christi had made copies. The picture was clear and detailed - bank account numbers, check numbers, payees, amounts, and dates all legible. Some were marked as "cash" payments made. The only thing missing was exactly what the payment was made for.

The Judge waited bleakly for fire rescue and the police to show up. He gave the San Pedro Sergeant a full report of what he'd seen and signed a statement. He'd taken his own pictures of the photos in Gloria's purse on his cell phone before handing them over to the Sergeant, who assured him they would be catalogued into evidence.

The Judge trudged back to his Chevy…angry, weary, depressed.

Chapter 39 - Tuesday

The Judge awoke the next morning after an uneven sleep. Uneven? - Hell, he felt like he'd been rolling around in the waves and the rocks all night. It was grey outside, which suited his mood. He grabbed a light overcoat as an afterthought as he headed out the door, hopped into the E, and coasted down to Malaga Cove. The coffee at his usual table at the Yellow Kettle seemed tasteless. He abandoned it, pulled his coat around him against the chill, and strode purposefully toward City Hall and the Police Station.

He entered the Palos Verdes Police Station, and politely told the attendant behind the glass he wanted to see the Chief. He was left to cool his heels in the reception room for five minutes, deliberately he was sure, and then the great man himself made his appearance, stepping out from a side door with his political smile pasted to his face and his sun-burnt hand outstretched to give the obligatory warm handshake.

The Judge dutifully shook the Chief's hand, and was shown back his office and deposited in the same uncomfortable chair.

"I thought it was time to compare notes on the Christi Benson case," said the Judge.

"As I said before, it was a simple suicide. We've closed the case."

Do you have the coroner's report?"

"No, they got jammed with a couple of high profile cases, and then there was a holiday, so it will likely be next week. But it's just going to say she died from the fall, and got banged around in the surf and the rocks after her death.

"I still believe there is more to the story," said the Judge.

"What else could there be?" asked the Chief, spreading his hands to show they were empty and so was the case, empty of any inconsistent facts.

"There are lots of loose ends. For instance, there's no indication anywhere that Christi was a candidate for suicide. There's an ex-boyfriend that threatened her with serious harm. There's a secret older lover she was having an affair with. There's the suspicious coincidence of Gloria Tomlin's hit and run death yesterday. There have been personal threats made against me. There's the search of my house and the physical attack on my dog. There are rumors of money laundering. There is evidence that suggests bribery of public officials. There are rumors of a partnership with a Mexican drug cartel."

The Chief's face got redder and redder with the listing of each loose end.

He finally exploded in anger, pounding his fist down on the table for emphasis.

"That's ridiculous. There is no evidence of laundering, or bribes or Mexican gangs. You are spreading malicious rumors, sir."

"I asked you to search Christi's room, but I guess you couldn't be bothered. Stuffed in her coat pocket were copies of Harley & Johns' ledger sheets listing cash payoffs to various officials and vendors, and copies of checks issued to the sitting Judge who has the Harley & Johns civil case before him even as we speak."

"If you have such evidence, let's see it," growled the Chief, controlling his anger and now looking just a tad smug, thought the Judge.

"Someone broke in and searched Christi's bedroom. The documents in Christi's bedroom have gone missing."

"Too bad," said the Chief in a crocodile voice.

"Luckily for us both," the Judge smiled, "I found a similar set of documents in Christi's locker, and these I took and have lodged in a safe place. I have the names and dates of the payoffs, and the bank account number on which the Judge Potter checks were drawn."

"You can't use evidence like that," sputtered the chief, "It's an illegal search."

"It might have been if it had been Harley & Johns' office. But this was Christi's school locker. I was given permission to search by Christi's mother, and the cooperation of the school. All admissible, and so are the fruits of any investigation which is initiated by those documents."

The Chief's face was still bright red, and the Judge could make out small beads of sweat along his hairline. Here was a man the Judge could play poker with and win. WYSIWYG…

"Listen, Judge, Harley and Johns are well respected upstanding members of this community. You can't go around accusing them of laundering drug money."

"Why not?" asked the Judge.

"Look, I've got two councilmen chewing up my ass to get you to stop making wild accusations about Pat Harley and Mel Johns. It's got to stop, Judge."

"Which councilmen?"

"Will McCory, and Drew Saffer. You destroy Pat and Mel's reputations based on malicious rumors, and it affects us all. Your rumors could destroy their business, deter them from playing City Father and donating monies to our community. You impact their business, they lose contracts, and the community loses taxes and jobs. Their projects don't get built. Businesses don't come to our city to fill up their finished projects. More lost tax revenues, more lost jobs. The community loses the businesses which would have occupied their now failed projects, and we are all poorer, likely a lot poorer."

"They'll sue you for slander and libel. You'll be on the receiving end of powerful lawsuits seeking to strip your assets away, Judge."

The Chief stopped here to catch his breath, and fished a handkerchief out of his back pocket to wipe his face.

"You forget, Chief, that truth is a defense."

"You really think you can prove these allegations of money laundering and payoffs, Judge?"

"I do Chief. I truly do, thanks to Christi's efforts. This isn't a police state, Chief. There is freedom of speech. If I go too far, which I haven't, the injured always can avail themselves of a civil action, but of course, truth is a complete defense."

"Don't you give a shit about this community, Judge? You're going to tear it apart with these wild accusations."

"Whatever the truth is, I want it to come out in full. Whoever gets singed, gets singed. That's the way it works."

"God damn it, maybe I just better lock you up now as a material witness and throw away the key."

"You try any strong arm stuff and you're one who'll be staring down the barrel of civil ligation, you and the City. This isn't LA in the 30's. Why don't you start focusing on doing your job properly, instead of letting this investigation slide for your friends in high places?"

The Chief's mouth moved but he was so angry that at first no words came. Finally, he got control enough to utter in low and angry voice, "Get out. Get the fuck out of my office."

Chapter 40 - Wednesday

The Judge settled in at the breakfast table to read his paper. Outside the nook window, all of LA was covered in a thick fog, with only the skyscrapers of what locals referred to with distain as the 'downtown' poking up above the fog and into the sun.

Katy padded into the breakfast room about 7:30 with tousled hair, sleepy eyes, bare feet, and the Judge's bathrobe, that was miles too big for her. She'd rolled the sleeves up several times, the bottom of the robe was modestly below her knees, and the robe's belt almost touched the floor. She looked cute.

She felt with her hands for a cup and coffee pot, feigning she was still asleep as a show for the Judge. The Judge roundly applauded and then grabbed the pot and poured her a solid cup of joe.

She disappeared for a while after her coffee, and then showed up again, fully dressed in clothes she'd had packed in the trunk of the Cooper, full makeup, lipstick and eyeliner, looking crisp and professional.

"OK, Judge," she said. "I'm off now, but don't forget me. I'll be back. Tell any old girlfriends you have lying around that they need to look elsewhere." With that salvo out of the way, she swung her bag over her shoulder and marched for the door.

Around noon, after accomplishing some legal work that needed to get out the door, or in these days out the Net, the Judge was considering a cup of tea. The day had turned cold and blustery again. A strong breeze came in off the ocean, blowing the fog away, but bringing the hint of winter in its chill, along with the taste of salt. The sky was clear and blue, no clouds, and there were no whitecaps out on the Bay, but the chill was tangible. He could feel it in his bones.

His cell phone rang.

He picked up the cell and hit the accept button, walking toward his kitchen to make tea.

He never got that far. The voice on the phone was barely recognizable: low, gaspy, distressed, but the Judge knew it. It was Katy.

"Judge…Oh, God…help me. I...I'm bleeding...I...I think I'm going to pass out. I..."

The phone went dead.

The Judge scooped his car keys off the table as he made a run for the door, crossed the porch, and dived into the E.

He called 911, and then the police while gunning around curves, breaking every speed law in his sprint to Lunada Bay and Katy's townhome. He hoped she was there.

It took him all of eight minutes flat. He slammed into her driveway hard.

The door was ajar. He pushed it open all the way. He felt fear and sickness in his stomach as her living room swung into view. The townhome had been professionally tossed, just like Maddie's place: the sofa overturned, drawers pulled out of the bureau, all the books off the shelves.

There was a trail of very red blood on Katy's bright white carpet. It led from the middle of her living room into the hall, unraveling toward her bedroom like a crimson ribbon.

He threw the bedroom door wide.

The crimson trail continued across the bedroom carpet into the bathroom.

He could hear faint sickly gurgling sounds from the bathroom, punctuated by small soft sobs.

He rushed in.

She was there, her body half sprawled over the bathtub, collapsed into a frail bundle, her hands to her face, covered in blood.

Her nose was a mess, the cartilage smashed up, and bleeding profusely.

She was gurgling, and having trouble breathing from the blood pouring down her throat and cutting off her air passages.

He grabbed her head and pulled it gently up and back and held it there clearing her passages. She started to breathe again.

She looked at the Judge, her eyes wide with pain and fear, and then collapsed into his arms while he supported her body and kept her head up. Small little whimpers shook her narrow shoulders from time to time.

He held her steady for what seemed an eternity. Then the paramedics were there, surrounding them, efficient, unbuckling their yellow box, placing an oxygen mask over her smashed-up nose, careful hands replacing the Judge's hands at her head and back, taking her pulse, checking blood pressure, calling in to the Torrance ER.

A stretcher appeared onto which she was gently lifted, keeping her head elevated, and the stretcher was whisked back along the crimson ribbon, the Judge in close tow.

The Judge jumped into the ambulance with her, yelling to the police getting out of their squad car that he'd talk to them later. They seemed to know who he was and waved him on.

It was a long and noisy ride down The Hill, siren blaring as they slowed for each intersection.

Katy was wheeled into the ER. The Judge was told that he couldn't follow her any further, and was shooed off to an admitting nurse.

When the nurse found the Judge didn't know anything about Katy's insurance, wasn't her father (the Judge resented this question) and wasn't a close relative who was potentially a financially responsible party, the nurse quickly lost interest and suggested he wait in the lobby.

The lobby was packed with a collection of worried people, some in pain, some sick, some significant others or caregivers, some just kids or family in tow because there was nowhere else to leave them.

The Judge found several magazines, mostly out of date and filled with unflattering pictures of movie stars he had never heard of, and settled into a corner to wait it out like everybody else. It was an uncomfortable, miserable and unhappy crowd, evidence of how broken the American medical system had become.

After an hour, the Judge had had it. He detested lines and he detested waiting and he was worried, tired, bored and very angry. He marched to the window and inquired about Katy. The nurse pointed out that he wasn't a family member; the Judge countered that he had brought Katy in, and then finally used his judicial voice to order the nurse to let him back to see Katy. The nurse jumped when he used the voice, reacting as though he were an irritated doctor, and buzzed him back without further argument.

In the inner sanctum of the ER he found Katy sitting up in bed, a large clump of gauze and tape pasted over and under her nose. The gauze was white, but with a splotch of red growing slightly bigger a bit at a time across its lower expanse.

Her blue eyes were a bit glazed, partly from shock, partly from pain, and partly from the medication she'd no doubt received. She saw the Judge and reached out to him like a small and frightened girl, but immediately halted her forward progress, wincing, her battered nose protesting any movement or contact.

"They're going to take me into surgery in a few moments, Judge. Make me beautiful again." Hope flickered in her eyes.

"Absolutely," the Judge said softly, holding her hand in his and patting the top with his other hand, as though she were a child to be reassured.

She tried to give him her best brave smile, but between the trauma, the tape and the drugs, the best she could do was a lopsided painful-looking half-grimace.

"I'll be right here," said the Judge, "waiting to inspect the job when you come out. They do very fine work here. You may come out even prettier than when you went in."

She tried to give the Judge a small slug with her other hand, but it ended up only a soft paw.

"Judge, you have to be careful," she said earnestly, anxiety flooding her face.

"What happened, Katy?"

"I came home from school at the lunch break to pick up a file I'd forgotten. I used my key, stepped in, and stopped, aghast at the mess someone had made.

"I guess he hid behind the door as it swung open. Anyway, he tapped me on the shoulder from behind, startling me. As I turned around he punched me in the face." A small tear slid down from the corner of her eye and dampened her gauze.

"I fell on the floor and couldn't breathe. Blood flowing down my throat was choking me.

"He leaned down over me and said very clearly - I'll never forget those words -he said:

" 'Tell the Judge if he doesn't stop his snooping, next time you may be dead. He may be dead too'.

"Then he just left. Left me there, drowning in my own blood."

"What did he look like?"

"Didn't get a good look at him. After he hit me, I had tears and blood all over. Couldn't see very well.

"He was Mexican, or Latin American, and he had a Spanish accent. Big, over six foot, and built, like he worked out. And...he has a mean right hook."

She smiled weakly at him.

He thought she was wonderful and incredibly brave, and told her so.

They came for her then, transferring her carefully to a rolling bed, and carted her through the ER. The

Judge held her hand until they reached a set of solid steel double doors, beyond which he could not follow.

Then he turned and headed back through the lobby to the elevators, and up a floor, aiming for the cafeteria and the hot coffee he knew would be there. He wished they served scotch.

There was going to be trouble now. Serious trouble. The Judge was going to be making the trouble...lots of it. It was personal now.

He couldn't easily be pushed. It was his nature, like the elephant. At first he would ignore. Then he would stubbornly plant his feet. If you kept pushing, he'd finally start moving. But not in the direction you wanted. He'd be coming for you.

The Judge cooled his heels in the public lobby. Finally, someone came to tell him Katy was out of surgery, in recovery, and he could visit.

He bounded over to the elevator and waited impatiently for one to show up. He dashed aboard and pounded the keypad several times. He wound through the labyrinth of a nursing station and found Katy's room. She was just coming off the anesthetic, and looked about to throw up.

The Judge, having some experience in such matters, thought this highly unlikely since there was nothing in her stomach to give up. But it didn't matter either way. He wanted to be close to her for a while.

He sat on her bed and they held hands for a long time, much as lovers do anywhere when they first find each other. Finally, the nurse returned with pain pills, a sleeping pill, and determined instructions to the Judge.

He had to go now. The patient needed to settle in for the night and rest.

The Judge said his goodbyes, kissed Katy lightly on the forehead, and headed for the door, the lobby, the parking structure and then stopped. He didn't have a car. He'd ridden down in the damn ambulance.

He retraced his steps to the lobby, found the public phone, and called for a taxi.

Chapter 41 – Thursday

The Judge called Katy's room at 8:30 the next morning, unable to wait any longer. She was awake and sounding far better than the night before. The doctor had made his rounds and said she could go home around 3 p.m.

The Judge would have immediately played the AMA card (against medical advice) and left for home at once if he had been Katy. He detested hospitals. About the only real fun was to announce that you were leaving AMA. This always rattled the nurses, stirred up the doctor, panicked the medical records people usually behind in their paperwork, and frustrated the bean counter accountant somewhere in the bowels of the hospital who would lose expensive hours budgeted into his cash flow.

The Judge told Katy he'd be there with bells on and flowers in his hands at three, sharp. He could hear the relief in her voice.

The Judge arrived at Torrance Hospital at 2:30. He felt guilty…worse than guilty…he felt awful. It was his fault she was in the hospital.

His first stop was the gift shop where he purchased a dozen red roses arranged in a non-descript green vase. It was about three times the price it should have been. It didn't matter.

Katy was awake and alert when he stuck his head around the corner, his best smile on. He produced the roses with a flourish.

She smiled back at him, but it was a drawn smile, and there were circles under her eyes. Her nose was pink and swollen, but sitting straight on her face. It hadn't started to turn black and blue. It would.

"Hi, Judge," she said. "You come to take me home?"

"Damn right," he replied, "to my home. Where I can keep an eye on you. Hospitals are dangerous places for everybody concerned."

"Are you concerned, Judge?"

"I'm more than concerned."

This brought a better smile from her, and just a hint of the old light danced in her eyes.

She slowly sat full upright on the bed, swinging her legs over the edge, and then slid off, placing her feet on the floor. "If you'll pull that curtain around and hand me my clothes over there, I'll get dressed."

"I should step out."

"Won't see anything you haven't already seen, Judge. Just this sorry old ass, a little sorrier than usual…and my nose is a little bigger too. Thank God my mom brought some fresh clothes this morning."

She slid off the hospital issue gown, revealing her small firm breasts, flat tummy, and slim, hourglass figure. Very beautiful, thought the Judge, and very young. He could tell she liked him looking at her from the way she watched him, the full sparkle returning to her eyes. And he did indeed like looking.

She put on a light yellow bra and did the strap, pulled a pair of plain yellow panties over her legs and up to her waist, covering up a small runway of pubic fur etched on pale white skin. She wiggled into a pair of jeans that looked suspiciously too small for her. Then she donned a yellow T-shirt and reached for her roses, burying her swollen nose into the bouquet for a second.

She looks about 14, thought the Judge.

"All set Judge. I've already signed the paper work."

"Do you want a wheelchair or something?"

"No way. Let's get the hell out of here," she said, shifting the roses to her right hand, softly linking her left arm through the Judge's, and leaning close into him as they walked out.

They maneuvered through the lobby passing an older man in a blue coat, likely a volunteer by his age and uniform, who smiled at them, saying, "That's a lovely daughter you have."

The Judge was appalled.

But Katy started to laugh uproariously, then had to stop mid-stride because it hurt her nose. "Ohhh," she said.

"Serves you right," said the Judge, his pride still stung.

The Judge suggested that Katy bunk with him for a few days. He urged it was the safest course.

"Oh, Judge," Katy said, "that's the worse excuse for a proposition I've had ever. You know you just want to get laid."

The Judge turned to her, concerned she'd taken it all the wrong way.

But she quickly put her hand on his, saying, "I can't think of a better way to recover than to snuggle up to you. Besides," that sparkle came again, "I want to get laid too."

They got to the Judge's house and he suggested she take a nap.

She stripped to her underwear, then removed the bra and panties as well, and slid under the fresh sheets, settling in with a look of relief on her face.

Then she suddenly sat up.

"This morning I remembered something about the thug that hit me," she said. The Judge immediately returned to her side, perching on the bed.

"What was it?"

"The guy had a big tattoo on the back of his hand. It was scary.

"Sort of a grim reaper in a big robe and hood, lots of teeth in a grisly smile and a scythe over its shoulder. Holding a ball in one hand and scales in the other. With long skeleton hands."

"Can you draw me a picture?" asked the Judge, going to his side table for pen and paper.

"I can try."

It was the same image as the Judge had seen in San Pedro.

The Judge closed the blinds to darken the room and left Katy to get some rest, carefully leaving the door well ajar so he could hear her if she called, and so she would hear him working nearby if she awoke.

He took the tattoo drawing with him. It was the same as in the picture he found in Gloria's purse. The same as the one he saw on the hand of the driver in the hit and run car. It didn't take long to turn up the tattoo on the Internet.

It was a gang tattoo used by a powerful criminal syndicate. It was considered to be one of the most technologically advanced and dangerous Mexican cartels, with half of its revenues coming from drug traffic and half coming from a variety of other activities, both criminal and legitimate.

A gang like that, mused the Judge, would have a huge need to launder money.

Chapter 42 - Friday

The Judge hadn't slept well. Katy was loaded up with pain pills, and snored much of the night, breathing through her mouth because of her injured nose.

The Judge was stirred up, angry and fearful for Katy. He was determined to strike back.

As a result, his sleep was fretful. He woke up several times during the night to find himself in the middle of going over and over what he knew, and what he supposed might have happened to Christi.

He finally fell into a deeper sleep around 4 a.m. It was the fall sunlight, streaming into his bedroom window like honey that finally woke him up around 9:00. Katy was still asleep beside him. He tiptoed out of his bedroom, silently closing the door.

The Judge had several cups of coffee and plowed through his three newspapers, marking time. It was almost 10 a.m. It was time.

He called the Torrance Branch of the Superior Court and asked for Judge Potter's Clerk. After an extended interval, Marion came on the line. Marion had been Potter's clerk since Potter started judging some five years before.

The Judge identified himself, and said he'd like a quick conference with Judge Potter on a private matter, if it could be arranged. He said he was pretty much open up to 2:30, needed only about 15 minutes, and would work around Potter's schedule.

Marion seemed doubtful, but she was too cautious to dismiss him lightly. The Judge was known to be forceful and had friends in many places in the Court House. You didn't cross the Judge if you could avoid it, even though he might not be a sitting judge anymore. She took his number and said she would get back to him.

About 45 minutes later, the Judge's cell phone rang. It was Marion. Judge Potter could share the last part of the lunch break with the Judge, at 1:00, in the Court House private dining room.

The Judge took up Annie's leash, snagged her in the kitchen and hooked her up, and set off on his walk, down the street to the bluff road and then along the cliffs, musing about Christi.

He knew there was a conspiracy to stop his investigation. It was coming from a place of power, and strings were being pulled at City Hall, at Police HQ, and even at the School Board.

He suspected Harley & Johns were up to their necks in laundering Mexican cartel drug money.

He knew that whatever they were doing, Jake Benson was heavily involved. He knew that what Christi had discovered at the Harley & Johns firm that had gotten both her and Gloria fired.

He knew that Gloria had been killed under mysterious circumstances.

Harley & Johns weren't up to murder in his estimation. They didn't have the stomach.

But what of the people behind them, the Mexican drug cartel? Someone threatened the life of a

Katy and beat her. Someone ran down Gloria in San Pedro.

But would they kill a young girl from The Hill? The risk of notoriety, the investigation, the spotlight of publicity that they would wish to shun at all costs...They would have to be very desperate to take such a risk.

He knew the loss of the judgeship election had been engineered by Harley & Johns, and by Jake Benson. Not illegal per se, of course, but tricky.

He knew Judge Potter was receiving large sums of money from an affiliate of Harley & Johns while judging the case in which they were defendants: a very big conflict of interest.

He suspected worse.

Because of the size of the sums paid to Potter, because of the way they had been routed through supposedly unconnected entities using Jake Benson, because of the searches and theft of checks and ledger, and because of Potter's concurrent actions in quashing discovery at every turn, the Judge suspected Potter's decisions on discovery were being purchased. That the payments were out and out bribes in a desperate effort to hold back the discovery in the case so that embarrassing and perhaps damning information would not come out about how Harley & Johns had financed their business. And of course tilt the resulting trial heavily in favor of Harley & Johns.

And what of Christi?

No one considered her a suicide risk.

She seemed to be happy and well adjusted, with the normal stresses and strains of any teenager, but not suicidal.

But there were errant facts there too.

She was sexually active - the condoms in her car, and the racy panties.

That was what young people did these days. It was a far different from when the Judge was a teenager. Back in the horse and buggy days, he ruefully thought, you didn't get any unless you went steady for two years and were at least in your second year of college.

And there was another errant fact…Christi had a new boyfriend. He was reputed to be an older man. Christi and the new boyfriend had been lovers on the secret beach, and perhaps elsewhere.

From all reports, right up to the afternoon of her death, Christi was happy with her new love. If the Judge's suspicions were true, it could have been a dangerous liaison for the new lover. But it appeared to be a secret well kept, hardly a reason to kill someone.

But then again, hardly a reason for Christi to jump off a cliff.

And what about her ex-boyfriend, Jeff Harwood? He was angry and unhappy. Bitter at being dumped. Dumped for an older man. He was also controlling and abusive. Was he so angry he would push Christi off a cliff?

It was possible. He didn't have a good alibi for when she took her plunge.

He seemed unstable. Did he just lose it after coming face to face with the reality that Christi was gone?

He recalled the old law school saw: "I didn't break the pot…the pot's not broke…and…there is no pot…" All fair arguments a defense counsel could argue simultaneously in a trial, forcing the plaintiff's counsel to prove each fact separately.

How did that apply here? There was a death. There was a cliff. There was a neatly folded blue dress at the cliff's edge. You couldn't dispute those facts.

But perhaps there was no jump. Maybe Christi slipped. Or maybe Christi was pushed. Or perhaps there was no cliff. Maybe whatever happened, happened down on the beach. The neatly folded blue dress suggested a plunge from the top of the cliff. But it wasn't conclusive.

What really happened that late afternoon?

Chapter 43 - Friday

The Judge hadn't been to the Torrance County Court House in six months. Something had changed. What was it?

There were still the usual gang of pedestrians wandering cheerlessly out of the lot toward the building and returning to their cars, interspersed here and there with several portly looking attorneys and a few thin ones, all dressed and tied, briefcases dangling at their sides.

The clientele of the Courthouse fell into easily identifiable groups. There were the ones here to protest parking citations: housewives, businessmen, secretaries, each unlucky enough to get caught. Everybody drove over the speed limit in LA. The cops scooped people up like guppies out of a tank. But there were lots of speeding guppies and relatively few cops, each cop ticketing only one guppy at a time. The odds were in your favor…until they weren't. Much like life, mused the Judge.

There were also the people here for criminal proceedings. They looked less affluent than the traffic ticket lottery crowd, and more nervous. They slowly shuffled out of the parking lot either by themselves or with a significant other, wishing they were somewhere else. The more affluent among them had high-priced criminal lawyers at their sides, talking in low, guarded whispers.

Here and there were angry ex-spouses, keeping step with their divorce lawyers, typically with files under their arms. And occasionally there were businessmen, here to sort out civil litigation, heavily weighted with large briefcases containing their versions of the facts.

The building hadn't changed; the crowd hadn't changed - what was different? The Judge realized it was him: he'd changed.

He couldn't see himself again donning a black robe and ensconcing himself on top of a wood platform in a windowless chamber without daylight or fresh air for six to eight hours a day, five days a week.

Listening to the same litany day after day, having to deal with smart lawyers, dumb lawyers, tricky lawyers, unethical lawyers, lawyers who didn't know when to shut up, lawyers who said too little and had to have the facts and law coaxed out of them, lawyers who said too much and shot their client in the foot, cocky lawyers, timid lawyers, and perhaps the worst: unprepared lawyers, wasting the Judge's time.

No, he was having more fun on the outside. Lots more fun. It was like a release from jail. In hindsight, his career had extended too long, demanded too much, and left him with too few connections to the real world.

The Judge went through the security screening. The older marshals there recognized him immediately. They shouted, "Hi Judge!" and "How's life out there?" He supposed they felt the confinement of the place too.

They were chained to this dungeon for life, career police officers having few alternatives to hanging in for an early retirement.

The Judge made his way to the back of the first floor, to an inconsequential door at the end of a corridor. A bailiff was sitting in front of the door on a chair, reading a newspaper. He looked up, recognized the Judge immediately, gave him a big smile, and got up to open the door. This was access to the private dining room reserved for the judicial staff. Apparently, the Judge was still accommodated privileges, ex-judge though he was.

The dining room was as nondescript as the other common rooms in the Court House. Instead of the wood and gilt edges of the courtrooms, here were institutional grey walls and a linoleum floor in a 20-year-old pattern, though not quite as worn as the common hallways. Grey drapes allowed a small amount of light in through the covered windows. Utility lighting in the ceiling, inset in the standard foam white ceiling tiles, painted everything in fluorescent. Small metal tables with fake wood tops were scattered here and there, accompanied by modern metal chairs with pale yellow fiberglass seats and backs. It almost felt like an old hospital cafeteria, thought the Judge, looking at it anew after his absence.

At the back ran a counter with coffee and soft drink dispensers, and off to the left a small kitchen, where food was set out and sold; the same menu as the common cafeteria down the hall.

Judge Henry Potter sat sipping a cup of coffee in the right rear corner of the room, his back to the wall, scanning occupants as they arrived. He spotted the Judge and waved him over with a congenial arm. The

Judge nodded, then detoured toward the drink counter to grab a coffee.

Potter was older than the Judge, late 60's the Judge guessed. Grey hair framed his ears and cheeks, grown long and combed across the expanding bald pate on the top. The overall effect was of a frayed bird nest.

His face was pink, perhaps high blood pressure pink. This made his watery blue eyes stand out in his face. Intelligent eyes, but not friendly. Rather quick and bird-like, looking for advantage.

The Judge did not know him well, their contact being limited mostly to judicial meetings with all the County judges. The scuttlebutt said he was a competent judge, but inclined to let cases poke along in his courtroom. His periodic reversals at the Appellate Level suggested that his grounding in evidence and procedure might be less than stellar.

The Judge purchased a Styrofoam cup, filled it with coffee and a little non-fat milk, and headed over to Potter's corner.

"Hello Henry," said the Judge.

"Great to see you again," said Potter, extending his hand. He wore a broad smile that didn't quite reach his eyes.

The Judge presumed word of his investigation had already reached Potter. He suspected that had made it easy to get an interview. But it likely also accounted for the hidden hostility he sensed. This was not a social visit. Potter likely viewed it as a meeting of two adversaries.

"So I've only got about 10 minutes," said Potter. "What can I do for you?"

"I'm investigating a girl's death on the cliff in PV. That investigation has led me to take a closer look at a firm called Harley & Johns, a PV developer with connections everywhere, it seems."

Potter nodded his understanding, not saying a word. He wore his best poker face. He was not going to volunteer anything.

"There's a case before you right now where Harley & Johns are the defendants. I spoke to Plaintiff's counsel. They are quite frustrated by the progress in the discovery phase of the matter."

Potter raised his chin, put on his best appalled look, practiced over many years on the bench, and said in a thin steely voice, "You know I can't discuss any case before me on the bench".

He said it to close further discussion, and even started to slide his chair back to get up and leave, obviously intending a "flounce out". The Judge bet he had a very good flounce.

"Of course not," said the Judge quickly. "I just wanted to bring your attention to certain facts which leave you in a somewhat untenable position as the case judge."

The Judge suddenly had the full attention of Potter's now steely blue eyes. Potter shifted his weight back down into the chair.

"The problem is, Henry," said the Judge in his best kindly voice, "I ran across this company, GreenShoots, headed by Jake Benson, the father of the deceased. And the company it turns out is primarily funded, and well-funded at that, and thereby controlled, by Harley & Johns."

Potter was poker faced again and silent, but his lips had tightened into a thin line.

The Judge was quiet for several beats, deliberately letting the silence build. This didn't please Potter, who was standing pat, making no sound, just watching the Judge now with narrowed eyes…waiting.

The Judge obliged Potter's silent call of his hand, reaching into his pocket as he continued.

"It turns out that this same company has been making large monthly payments for I assume important legal advice, to a member of our bar who is also a sitting Judge, creating what would appear on the surface to be a very serious conflict of interest."

With this, the Judge took out of his pocket and slid softly across the table to Potter, a copy of the check for $10,000 made out to Potter, and a copy of the ledger showing continuing monthly payments out of the same account.

Potter took the papers and scanned them, never losing his poker face. But his complexion went a sickly white as the color noticeably drained from his face.

He looked back at the Judge, a hint of panic deep in the watery blue eyes, and said in a voice that had turned suddenly husky, "It looks like I should recuse myself from this case immediately".

The poker face was gone now; replaced by a hopeful look that this would placate the Judge. Put the matter to rest.

And it would for now, thought the Judge…but not forever.

"I think that's the best thing, Henry," said the Judge, reaching across the table and retrieving his documents.

The Judge had copies of the documents of course, but he wanted Potter to understand in a physical sense who was in control.

The Judge then stood up, and reached across the table to shake Potter's hand. Potter mirrored his gesture, diffidently.

"Always good to see you Henry," the Judge said, turning and walking out.

The next senior Judge who would take over the case was Judge Lawrence Martin, an ex-Marine, a stickler for procedure, detail oriented, and expansive in his discovery rulings ahead of trial. His integrity was unquestionable.

Judge Martin would be Harley & Johns' worst nightmare.

The Plaintiff's lawyers in the Harley Johns case were going to have some fun, mused the Judge, and rightly so. It couldn't happen to more deserving defendants.

Chapter 44 - Friday

The Judge returned home and spent an hour preparing a legal opinion for George Smith, a small project that came unexpectedly when George, a former client, had heard he was back on the street and more or less practicing. It was a nice gesture from an old friend. His clients had always been his friends. And his friends had been his clients…back before the black robes and the stringent, if often unwritten boundaries on fraternizing with practicing lawyers and their clients.

He decided to set the project aside at 2:30 p.m., about the time Christi had walked out of the Judge's house, and out of his life, exactly three weeks before. He collared Annie and the two headed down Paseo Del Mar, the bluff road just as they'd done that day, only earlier now.

The light was good, the sun was still bright, and a gentle breeze wafted up the cliff from the calm sea below. Very small waves lapped the sand. The tide was pretty much full out.

The Judge and the puppy headed directly to the trail, and carefully picked their way down to the beach.

No surfers out today. The surf was too small and flat along the beach, breaking on the rocks calmly with very little clap or clatter except for the soft rattle of small stones here and there.

He left Annie to run on the beach without her leash, technically against City law, but no one was around. Malum prohibitum, thought the Judge.

He leap-frogged in a clumsy way out to the farthest rock protruding into the sea he could reach. He was a big man, older and not agile. He thought he must look like a bloated toad jumping rock to rock. He slipped once and almost got his shoe into the sea, but recovered.

He turned around on the furthest dry rock he could reach, squatting down, barely above the seawater flowing around his perch. He imagined a surfer's view from there, looking back at the cliffs.

From what surfer Mark Daniels had said, Christie had enjoyed the company of a special friend somewhere on a beach here, hidden from the view of passersby.

Viewed from seaward, there was only one place that could serve such a purpose. Off to the right was a tall steep outcropping of rocky spur jutting out not quite perpendicular to the cliffs, running perhaps 50 feet into the sea. It looked possible to climb around the spur, although risky. If you slipped, there was a 15-foot sheer drop, and you'd fall amongst deep water, dangerously jutting rocks and swirling heavy surf, even now at low tide.

The rocky spur actually ran at perhaps a 60-degree angle to the cliffs to the south, shielding a small slice of what lay just beyond. But for the most part, the cliffs to the south were rugged and steep, running right into the sea with deep water and rollers crashing at their base.

Leaning way out from his perch, the Judge thought he could catch the occasional glimpse of exposed sand behind the rocky spur. Whatever was there was largely hidden from above by the overhanging cliffs, and further south by another formation jutting into the sea. It was only a narrow slice of the place that would be visible, and then only from seaward and very near a mass of unfriendly rocks. A place where a leash-less board might wash up.

The Judge leap-frogged back to the beach and retrieved the puppy, who was racing up and down, barking at each wave as it rolled in. As he surveyed the beach again, he noted an elderly gentleman sitting quietly in the shade under the overhang, placidly watching the sea slide in and up the beach with each wave, a large paper pad on his lap. He didn't move, seeming content for the moment to watch the waves marching like soldiers up the beach, tricked out in green sea and white foam. Perhaps that's why the Judge hadn't noticed him before.

The Judge leashed up the dog and walked up the beach to say hello.

"Good day," said the Judge.

The old man gave him a smile and a once over with clear blue eyes. Then reached down to pet the puppy straining at the leash to lick his hand. Annie's tail was moving like a windmill, threatening to knock the pad from the old man's lap. He didn't seem to mind.

He wore tan cargo shorts displaying scrawny legs punctuated by knobby knees and grounded in disreputable looking Jesus sandals. His tan safari shirt, the kind with multiple pockets, was of a larger size to fully cover his belly, which jutted out like a shelf above his skinny hips. His eyes were a startling light blue, clear, and overhung by white bushy eyebrows, and the sunburned and spotted face was shadowed under a floppy tan hat, also safari style. Several brushes poked out of one shirt pocket. A small palette with side pockets filled with water colors sat beside him on a rock, along with a jar of water, its lid resting beside it.

His pad was a large watercolor pad. Roughed out in light green and blue washes were the beginnings of the sand and surf in front of him.

The Judge guessed he was north of 80, perhaps considerably north. Every year would be significant at his age.

"They call me the Judge," said the Judge, somewhat ostentatiously, sending out his hand.

"Raleigh Graham," said the old man, shaking the Judge's hand lightly with a skinny and knurled old hand emblazoned with wrinkles and sunspots.

"Come down here often?" asked the Judge.

"Try to," said Raleigh. "I like it about this time of day, middle of the afternoon, when it's warmer. I get chilled easily."

"How's the trail down for you?"

"Oh, I'm more spry than I look." This was said with a smile, but the eyes still pinned the Judge's inquisitively. "My daughter gets quite aggravated though. Says if I fall it'll be all over. Guess she's right.

But who wants to live forever? Just want to be able to do the things I enjoy as long as I can. Especially enjoy this beach, sitting here, watching the waves come in, trying to capture the emotion of the place on a flat surface. Every wave's different you know. Each a separate and distinct treasure. You like waves?"

"Never gave them much thought," admitted the Judge. "Guess I've always been too busy to study them."

"That's a mistake young man. Sorry to be blunt. But whatever you find satisfaction in: waves, roses, art, vistas, whatever, you got to find time to step back from your living and just contemplate it. It's solace for your soul." The old man displayed a toothy smile now.

"I'm sure you're right," said the Judge, and meant it. "Are you down here every Friday?"

"Most every Friday afternoon."

"Were you down here the Friday the young girl jumped off the cliff, about three weeks ago?"

"I heard about that. What a shame. I was. About this time; might have been a little later. I remember it was starting to build to heavy surf. Strong wind was picking up. All from that tropical storm in Mexico I suppose. I couldn't stay long. Never would have gotten back up the trail. Would have been airborne trying," cackled Raleigh.

"See anybody else?" asked the Judge.

"You know, I did. Nice couple. Least she was. Really young. He looked a mite old for her I thought. But she was looking goo-goo eyed at him, the way lovers do at the start."

"Did you talk to them?"

"No, they were ahead of me on the trail down and I'm slow. They went frolicking across the beach, over there. She had on a blue dress. Took it off when they went wading into the surf. It was really too wild a surf to swim, but they just got their feet wet."

"Did they see you?"

"Oh yes. She waved at me. He kind of glowered. I think he would have preferred an empty beach."

"How long did they stay?"

"That I don't know. They climbed up over the cliff spur. Over there at the end of the beach. He pointed to the south incursion of the rock spur into the sea. Disappeared the other side."

"What's over there?"

"Not sure now. In the old days, when I could climb," Raleigh winked, "there used to be a small bit of private sand. At least up to near high tide, then the waves sweep in. I used to climb over and go skinny-dipping. Sometimes I'd talk a girl into coming." The blue eye twinkled with old memories."

"What did this girl look like?"

"Maybe 18, blond hair, blue eyes, nice figure I suppose, although I'm way too old to notice. If a woman can cook, and drive at night, that's what counts now." Raleigh cackled some more. "She had a nice smile."

"And the guy?"

"Older, early 30's, mid 30's. Not too tall. Tan, like he was in the sun a lot. I don't know. He kind of turned away after he saw me. Didn't look in my direction anymore. But his face was familiar. Seen him before somewhere."

"What was he wearing?"

"Blue swim trunks, red T shirt; think it said Billabong on the back."

"And this was what time?"

"About 4:00."

“Did she put her blue dress back on before they started to climb over the spur?”

“Ah…matter of fact she didn’t. Left it folded there high up on the beach on this side. Makes sense. She’d have gotten it wet wading over to the spur to climb up.”

“And you didn’t see them return?”

“No, I was getting chilled so I started my slow climb back up.”

"What time was it you saw them go over the rocky spur?

"About 4 o'clock, maybe a little before."

“Thank you very much, Raleigh.”

The Judge took out a pen and in his flipbook wrote down Raleigh’s contact information.

Chapter 45 - Friday

The Judge and the puppy set off for the south end of the Beach.

Reaching the rocky spur jutting out at an angle from the cliff, the Judge could see he would have to wade through some surf to climb up. He sat down on a dry rock and gingerly took his shoes and socks off, then rolled up his pant legs above his knees. He looked down at his knobby knees, just visible past the protrusion of his tummy, which he couldn't seem to get rid of no matter how hard he exercised and dieted, and thought how silly he must look. He certainly didn't look judicial. Just as well no one was around to see.

He tied the puppy's leash to a rock far up the beach that would stay dry even at high tide and set his shoes beside her. If he slipped and fell, she would be a beacon for where to look.

Steeling himself to what he knew was going to be icy cold water for an old guy, he timed his approach, and then scrambled through shallow water and up on to rocks beneath the side of the rocky spur. The spur ended in a sheer drop of about 20 feet, and at its base, deep water and foam swirled around jutting rocks and undertows.

From the base of the outcropping there appeared well-worn footholds and handholds, leading up perhaps

10 feet to a faint trail that traversed across the rocky spur, very near its sheer face.

The Judge carefully climbed up the outcropping to the faint trail, and then worked his way up the trail and around the face of the rock. The trail was suitable for a mountain goat with four legs, not an old goat with two. The path was narrow, ran steeply up another 10 feet to the crest, and then steeply down the other side. The rock was worn and slippery and few handholds were available.

All the while the tide surged in and out below the sheer face, exposing jagged rocks and coral, like some wet sea serpent breathing in and out, baring its fangs with each breath. The air was filled with sea mist, and occasionally, a particularly large crashing wave would fling full misting spray up toward the Judge.

The Judge found it a precarious scramble to the other side. There was no place to reverse course, and you had to keep moving forward to maintain your balance, if the word balance could be applied to the Judge's awkward crab crawl. Finally he rounded the spur and descended down the south face to the safety of a tiny beach. It was really just a sliver of dry sand, with large rocks and hollowed out places that weren't quite sea caves running its length at the back under the bluff.

It was mostly sheltered from prying eyes. The Judge had visions of "From Here To Eternity", and the famous beach scene from his youth. This would all be terribly romantic if you were young…and agile.

He dusted off his hands and looked around the tiny area. There was no evidence of occupancy, but the place would be washed clean with every tide.

The Judge thought back to his youth in the rugged hills of the Covina Highlands, and the pretty young girl with the blond hair and the blue eyes on whom he'd had such a terrible crush. They'd been juniors in high school together. And for a brief and bittersweet spring they had gone together.

That had meant a trip in his beat-up car to the A&W root beer stand where you stayed in your car and sucked down a float, an occasional sock hop dance aromatic with the scent of old socks, and occasionally a drive in movie when they could muster the price.

Half the time at the drive-in was spent watching the horror flick, and the other half was spent in mild sexual exploration. Kissing on the lips and sometimes the neck. The Judge had always been a neck man himself. There was no French kissing. There was also some close cuddling. You could feel soft breasts against your chest, perhaps the length of a thigh pressed against your own, all very exciting and yet safe. Nice girls didn't allow much fondling. And sadly, the Judge mostly dated nice girls. Times had really changed, he mused.

The Judge's crush had left him abruptly toward the end of the spring quarter when the high school's quarterback suddenly became available. It had been a sad and traumatic time. A time when everything seemed so important, and emotions ran rampant.

But when the Judge and his crush were together, they had played a little game. There was a rock wall they both had to pass on the way into school. Together, late one afternoon almost at dusk, they had spent considerable energy loosening one of the stones in the wall so it could be slid in and out.

This had been their secret place to leave notes to one another. The Judge never went past the wall without finding some excuse, a loose shoelace or something, to hunker down beside the wall and check behind the stone. There was often a note to recover or deposit.

And what about today's teenagers, all the pressures and stress over grades, college admissions, finances, and ultimately finding a job, and all the sexual liberation? The Judge wondered if there remained some universally romantic notions and customs that withstood the course of time, like his shared secret stone.

Christi and her mysterious lover had used this beach as their own. Had they played the game of hiding notes in their secret place? It was worth a look.

He stood up and began to systematically examine the face of the cliff at the back of the tiny strip of sand.

He visualized Christi's approximate height, estimated her reach on extending her arms upward, and drew an imaginary line along the face of the cliff. He then began a minute study of the cliff from that line down to the sand.

He came across a hollowed out indentation in the cliff, well protected from the elements. A three-foot shelf of strata protruded out, like a narrow shelf. And at one end was a purple rock, about a foot long, pock marked with holes. It didn't match the color or texture of the cliff.

The Judge pushed against it and it moved easily. He slipped it off to the right to reveal a hole underneath, lined with plastic, the plastic folded over as a flap on top.

The Judge opened the flap.

There was a beach blanket, carefully folded to fit into the space. Nesting on top was a small wallet and keys. Beneath that a blue corduroy book with faded gold lettering embroidered across its top:

It read, "My Diary".

Chapter 46 - Monday

Saturday and Sunday came and went. Katy had more or less moved in, bringing three carloads of clothes over in the back seat of her Mini Cooper and displacing the Judge from the larger walk-in closet in his bedroom. He didn't mind. In fact, he was elated.

Meanwhile, a motion to delay a trial scheduled for Monday had been denied, triggering an all-out effort to prepare the case over the weekend. Litigators tended to leave things to the last minute. The Judge didn't have to appear, but was helping on trial preparation, always a massive undertaking if it was to be done right.

The Judge came up for air early Monday morning. Leaning back in the black swivel chair in his library, he put his feet up on the desk, stretching them out to their fullest extent, and gazed out over the red tile roofs of his neighbors to the blue sea below. The sea fanned out in a 180 degree arc, sweeping from below him at RAT Beach, short for Redondo and Torrance State Beach, all the way around the Santa Monica Bay to Malibu, and beyond, to Point Dume.

He stared at the faded corduroy diary sitting beside his feet on his desk. It was the diary that Christi was never without, that she took everywhere. Yet it had been left in the shared hiding place, on the secret beach she shared with someone. Why?

Had she put it there on arrival, to keep it safe and dry? Likely. But she'd not retrieved it when she left. Nor the small wallet and keys that were underneath it. He suspected she hadn't taken the beach blanket out since everything was resting on top of the blanket. Why not? Wasn't the blanket for their tryst on the sand? Had the meeting been about something more than pure sexual fun? Perhaps more serious? Had she left in a hurry, forgetting her diary in the rush? Or had she intended to come back for it?

Was she hiding it there for safekeeping? Was she afraid someone knew about it and would try to take it away? Or was she upset, distraught, angry, leaving in a hurry without a thought for the diary? Did she ever leave the secret beach at all? Did her young life end right there?

What the hell really happened on that beach late Friday afternoon?

The Judge had no answers...yet.

But the diary had certainly been an interesting read. Much of it was lavishly written by a young, emotional and terribly vulnerable teenager exploring her life, her values, and her budding sexuality. Growing up under the Palos Verdes bubble.

Some of her story he'd already known. The diary filled in much of the rest, up to that afternoon when she collected her money from the Judge for house sitting, and confidently bounced out his front door.

She had ups and downs, small triumphs and defeats, many of which loomed larger to her then they really were. Also lucky breaks and unlucky disasters, but there had been steady progress toward maturity.

There had been lots of entries about her new, "more mature" lover, some obviously dashed out in the heat of passion. But there had been no name. Her new lover was still a mystery.

In the last entries, the Judge could see she was suddenly under extreme stress. Pressured to make some decision she was having difficulty facing. But again, there were no specifics.

It was never easy growing up, mused the Judge. And like life itself, no one got through the process entirely unscathed.

As to Harley & Johns, there was much more detail, as though she were documenting what she knew so as to protect herself.

Christi was a sharp girl. During her internship over the summer, she had observed much more about the Harley & Johns operation than they ever suspected.

It started with Harley's advances toward her, which were not reciprocated. She viewed him as a dirty old man. Referred to him as 'that octopus.'

He'd tried every tack to get into her pants. He started with romance…lots of compliments, flowers, small gifts and such. He'd moved on to experiences, offering expensive concert tickets, innuendos about the delights of an experienced lover, proposing a weekend getaway to Acapulco that might require him to bring his assistant, and perhaps, late in the summer, a joint 'business' trip to Paris.

When each of these advances had been politely but firmly rejected, he offered drugs, then significant cash, and then a highly paid ongoing staff position. Finally, he threatened her. If she didn't submit, he would fire her and leave a poor performance report in her work record and with her school.

Christi was both disgusted and fearful. She needed the job for college money. She didn't have a dad she trusted to turn to for advice. She didn't trust her mother's judgments on such matters after watching the parade of part time men who had populated Maddie's life after the divorce.

As part retaliation and part self-defense, she'd begun to document in her diary the things she saw at Harley's office that didn't square with her understanding of good business ethics.

Her observations included names, dates and transactions, overheard bribes of building inspectors and planning commission members, job kickbacks from vendors and unions, chiseling on the depth of foundations and footings in parking structures, and most interesting, the large deliveries of cash on designated late summer afternoons.

Cash delivered in two large leather satchels to Johns' office by a tough looking Latino with an ugly skull figure tattooed on his hand. There was always a small package of drugs for Harley tucked in with the money.

Christi had made a drawing of the tattoo in the diary. It looked all too familiar to the Judge: a large hooded skeleton, holding scales; a crystal ball and a scythe.

Harley's advances were ceaseless during the balance of August. He just wouldn't give up. Every day there was a new carrot and a new stick, some new threat of what could happen if she didn't give in. The Judge supposed it was this ruthless persistence that made

Harley such a successful real estate developer. At any rate, it didn't work here.

It finally all blew up just before Labor Day and her scheduled return to school. Christi just lost it. It was one push too many, particularly given what was going on elsewhere in her life.

They had a screaming match in his office one night when he'd kept her late on some trumped up matter. She'd told him he was a dirty old man, she found him disgusting, if he was the last person on earth she wouldn't screw him, and to fuck off.

The next day she was fired, purportedly for destroying the wrong records.

There was plenty to hang Harley & Johns in the diary. The chain of evidence had been compromised a bit by the Judge's independent investigation, but there were names, dates, jobs and bank account records. Once you knew what to look for and where, the whole story would be easy to document.

There were two questions the Judge pondered…

Were Harley & Johns and their silent partners involved in Christi's death? And what should the Judge do with the diary?

The second question was the easier one.

He was going to bring down the whole damn criminal enterprise.

He'd set his offense in motion with his visit to see Judge Potter. This was a clear shot across their bow, but it wasn't a hull shot that would sink.

He had formulated his next move.

When he was in private practice one of his clients had said, "You damn lawyers, you think in traps, in ever-extending pincer movements encompassing every damn advantage, smothering legitimate businessmen just trying to get ahead."

He had smiled at the time, but the client was right. That was how he had been trained at USC Law, to think and plan carefully, considering anticipated events and potential consequences.

His eyes narrowed as he gazed out at the water from his desk, choreographing the moves of the participants.

Judge Potter would recuse himself from the case, of that he had no doubt.

Judge Martin, the next senior Judge, and a real ball-breaker on fair and full discovery, would waste no time in discarding frivolous objections to extensive discovery in the case.

Harley & Johns and their silent partners would be grinding their teeth and cursing the Judge for his meddling, he was sure.

But in the end, Harley was a businessman. He would move to settle the case immediately, whatever the cost, in order to forestall any further discovery. The Judge was sure it would cost him dearly, but Harley would simply have no choice.

It likely would leave a large hole in whatever financial obligations were due their silent partner. That could be extremely dangerous for them both.

The Judge dialed Jeb Stewart, an old friend from his days before the bench.

"How the hell are you, Judge?" asked Jeb in a gravelly voice that implied years of smoking and bourbon, which as the Judge recalled were his two favorite things.

"It's been so long, I figured you must have died and gone to heaven."

"Doing great, Jeb," said the Judge. "How about you?"

"Same old, same old. Working for the government doesn't get you rich, but at my age it's secure work, and…it has certain satisfactions." The Judge could sense the smile in Jeb's voice. "Sorry to hear you lost the election, Judge. Must have been a bummer."

"It was a shock, Jeb. I was depressed for a while. But you know, now I look back, I'm beginning to think there should be more to life than being sealed into a windowless court chamber 9 to 5. My life feels like its expanding again, not stagnant. I'm beginning to think it's the best thing that could have happened."

"I'm glad to hear that, Judge. What can I do for you?"

"You guys still have that program where someone turns in information and you pay a bounty?"

"Sure, Judge, as long as it's not privileged info or something that we can't use."

"That's not an issue here. If I turned some information over and a bounty ultimately got paid, could I assign it to a charitable trust or foundation, maybe scholarships for kids here on The Hill, or the like?"

"Oh, I think so Judge. 'Course the bounty would have to be pretty big. If it's a small bounty, you'd just want to donate it to a 501(c)3 group with similar goals. You'd report the income of course, and then take a charitable deduction for the gift so likely it could all wash out."

"I suspect this bounty might be pretty big, Jeb. It involves laundering of drug money, payoffs to local officials, secret kickbacks from vendors and unions in the construction trades, over a course of many years.

"Let me write up what I know, and then I'll attach copies of pages from a hand-written diary of someone who is now unfortunately deceased. It will give you names, dates and bank accounts. Plenty of probable cause to follow up with a subpoena for bank records and books and records which should clearly tell the story."

"Great, Judge, let me give you my new address. Send it here:

Internal Revenue Service
Whistleblower Office
SE: WO
1111 Constitution Ave., NW
Washington, DC 20224

"If the amount not reported is at least $2 million, Judge, and the taxpayer makes at least $200,000, there's a 15% to 30% bounty that can be paid. That could be as much as $600,000 to start, and perhaps much more from the situation you describe.

"You just might have enough there to start your scholarship fund."

I just might, thought the Judge, and I'll name it the Christi Benson Scholarship. Maddie would like that.

"Thanks, Jeb. I'm going to Fed Ex this out to you in about an hour."

The Judge figured Harley & John would make whatever quick settlement they could on the civil litigation. They'd pay out an arm and a leg, several times the realistic settlement value of the case, just to avoid Judge Martin and his discovery orders. And a large part of what was paid would likely be their silent partner's capital. That wouldn't sit well with the Mexican gang.

They'd get it done fast too. They couldn't afford to wait until Judge Martin got rolling on case discovery. Their settlement money would be paid out well before they got wind of an IRS tax fraud investigation.

The whole criminal enterprise would come crashing down around their heads at that point. That's when their problems would turn serious.

How were they going to explain a very large loss of capital to their silent partner? The Judge suspected it wouldn't be pretty.

Harley & Johns were certainly culpable. They had treated Christi very poorly. They could be the indirect cause of Gloria's demise, complaining to their partners about her nosey record disposal, her inclusion of Christi in firm secrets, and her subsequent not so subtle hints about severance compensation. But it was the Mexican cartel that had threatened him on the phone, searched his house, cut the throat of his puppy and left her for dead, as well as brutally smashing up Katy's face, breaking her nose. And they had run down Gloria without the least qualm.

There needed to be some grief dealt out in their direction too.

He took his feet off his desk, swung around to the computer behind him, and found Barbara Johnson's phone number.

She answered at once.

"This is Barbara."

Her voice brought back memories of the old days before he had married. He and Barbara had been an item once. They now had a long friendship that extended over many years, although they rarely saw each other except for the occasional Christmas party.

She had married a doctor with a thriving practice in cosmetic surgery and a big house in San Marino. And she had built for herself an impressive record as a criminal lawyer for the Justice Department.

She was Supervising Manager for the Los Angeles Field office of the Federal Drug Enforcement Agency, or DEA. She was a NARC.

"Hello Barbara, how the hell are you?" he asked.

"Oh my God," she said, drawing each word out slowly. She was originally a Valley Girl, and although the dialect was long gone from her usual speech, she liked to lapse into Valley Speak with old friends. "Can this be the Judge?"

"It can be and it is," he said, smiling into his cell phone

They spent several minutes catching up. How was her husband?...Sorry about his election…How were her kids?…Was he back to working for a living, practicing law? …How was her career going?...Was he still living out in the boonies on The Hill?

Finally, after they had run through most of their catch-up questions, she said, "So what can I do for you Judge? I know you all too well. You wouldn't call without a reason. What do you need?"

"I'm hoping we can help each other," the Judge said. He gave her a rundown on Harley & Johns, and his suspicions about laundering drug money.

"That's pretty interesting, Judge, but not enough for a warrant." Barbara was a quick study and liked to get to the point.

"I was more interested in the people they may be laundering drug money for," said the Judge. "I suspect it's a Mexican drug cartel. They use a gang tattoo I think, sort of a skeleton dressed in a big robe, holding a ball and a set of scales, with a scythe over his shoulder."

"Tell me more," said Barbara, her voice shifting tone. He could mentally see her sitting up straight in her chair and reaching for a pad of paper, like a hunter who'd just caught a scent.

The Judge described the diary he'd found, and how it itemized deliveries of cash and a significant amount of drugs every other Tuesday. She suggested a tail. Perhaps they could follow the gang member back to the next level in the chain of command. The Judge knew this was what she'd suggest.

He gave her the address of Harley's office, and specifics from Christi's diary on the approximate time of delivery - 8 a.m., and the telltale sign: two large leather satchels being carried in by two Latinos, one tall and one short.

Barbara thanked him for the lead and told him she would let him know where it led.

They promised to have lunch together soon, a promise they both knew wouldn't be kept. They were both busy, and besides, they had history. They were old friends, but they couldn't ever again be too close as friends. They were too close once and had gotten…if not burned, then at least singed. Now they had different lives, and she had a permanent commitment to a husband.

The Judge set the phone down, stood up and stretched. For now he had done what he could.

It was much more than a shot across their bow. Would it be a "hull shot"? Time would tell.

Chapter 47 - Tuesday

It was close to sunset when the judge drove his XKE down to Paseo del Mar, to the cliff where the blue dress had lain.

A small impromptu shrine had sprung up, there on the cliff. Flowers in vases, some dried, some fresh, two small teddy bears, small battery operated candles, a coiled bridle with a picture of Christi on a horse tucked inside were all arranged in a half shell pattern facing the edge of the cliff. The Judge felt sad and more determined than ever to get to the bottom of what happened.

He clambered down the steep trail to the rocks below, watching the twilight surfers.

As the first of them waded out of the surf, the Judge approached with his best smile.

“Hi, I am looking for surfer with a cherry colored board, has the nickname "Lam", or maybe "Ham". Know anybody like that?

One young man paused, gave the Judge a careful look, and then said, "Yeah, think I've seen a guy like that."

"Do you know him, know his name?" asked the Judge.

"I don’t think anyone really knows him. Stays pretty aloof. Think his nickname is Ham. Has a nice board though."

"Seen him around today? Need to talk to him."

"Nope, haven't seen him around in 3 weeks or so. That's really unusual. He's almost always down here at twilight at least once during the week unless he's sick. He just suddenly disappeared.

One of the other surfers stepped forward. "I heard someone saw him down at Abalone Cove last week."

That'd be kind of strange too, said the first surfer. Abalone Cove's a crap beach, unfriendly crowd, smallish waves, way below his skill."

"Is his board a Billabong?" asked the Judge.

The two surfers looked at each other, then both shook their heads.

"Like I said, a real good surfer. Don't think we've ever seen the bottom of his board, that's where the logo would be if it's a Billabong. That would be an expensive board."

The Judge thanked the young men, toiled his way back up the steep trail, and glided away in the E, making a quick dash south toward Abalone Cove. When he got just past the Wayfarer's Chapel, a famous Church on the Palos Verdes Coast, he pulled into the Abalone Cove Parking lot.

The lot was mostly deserted, perhaps four cars there in all. But at the end of the lot a surfer was carefully loading an old blue board into the tail of his SUV. He had his back to the Judge, but he looked older than the other surfers, short brown hair, muscular.

The Judge pulled up, leaning out of the E, and asked "You Ham?"

"Who wants to know?" asked the man, turning around to face the Judge.

It was Hamilton Smith, Christi's history teacher.

His smile flashed to shocked recognition.

"You remember me, Mr. Smith, or I guess its Ham down here. I'm the Judge. I'm still looking into Christi's death."

The other man flashed a salesman's smile.

"Now that you mention it, I guess I did see her around on the beach with the other kids occasionally. Guess I didn't think to mention it since you were focused on her school work, her activities as a student.

"She went with one of the Bluff Cove Twilighters, Jeff Harwood, I think. So I'd see her on the beach occasionally. But I don't hang with the younger surfers. Just do my own thing. Surfing's really a pretty solitary sport. We didn't ever talk on the beach. Sorry I can't be more helpful."

The Judge decided to get to the point, the light was fading and he was getting cold.

"I heard you might have had a more intimate relationship with her," said the Judge bluntly, watching for a reaction.

"You heard wrong, Judge. She had a boyfriend; I'm happily married with two small kids. I'd never date one of my students even if I was single, and of course, she was under age.

"Surfers are not the most reliant source for information. They gossip a lot, and they are mostly focused on their waves."

"Didn't say it came from a surfer," said the Judge.

Ham wouldn't be rattled. "Well where ever you heard that, just was bad information, Judge."

"When did you see Christi last?" asked the Judge.

"I told you Judge, in my history class on Friday."

"And you still don't know of any reason she might want to take her own life?" asked the Judge.

"I don't," said Ham, "but then as I told you, I didn't know her that well. We may have had coffee once or twice in the school cafeteria to talk about history, I don't really recall. I try to be available for all my students."

"One more question: do you have a red Billabong surf board?"

"No, said Ham, just this blue one. It's a good board, steady. It's a Gold-Coast."

"You never had a red board?"

"Oh, sure. I had a red Pipedreams Board for a while. Sold it about 2 months ago. It had gotten pretty beat up over the years. But it wasn't a Billabong. Wish it had been. Billabongs are sweet."

"Thanks for the time, Ham." The Judge put the E in gear, made a U turn, and cruised out of the Abalone Cover parking lot.

Chapter 48 - Wednesday

Katy went out for dinner with her mom to explain about her new domestic relationship, and the Judge thought the better part of valor was to let her go alone. No, he corrected, he was just a plain coward.

It was about 10 p.m. when the Judge got a call from Barbara Johnson.

"Want to have some fun playing cops and druggies, Judge?"

"What's up?"

"We followed your drop guy on Tuesday morning. He went to a rickety old house in Wilmington, just off W.F. Street. We staked the place out. There are four of them sharing the digs, all with minor criminal records, all Latino. A little while ago three of them suddenly got very agitated, jumped in separate cars, and headed in caravan for the Palos Verdes Bluffs along PV Drive West. They are out there now, one of them camped out on a bluff overlooking the sea; the other two climbing discretely down a rugged trail to the beach."

"No kidding," said the Judge.

"We suspect there may be a drug delivery by boat this evening. We're going out there in force to see what happens. I have an extra seat on the copter if you want to come."

"I'm in," said the Judge. "Where do we meet?"

"You'll have to be quick. Can you get to Torrance Airport, the fixed based operator there, within 20 minutes?"

"Wouldn't miss it," said the Judge. "I'm trotting for the car now."

"See you there, Judge. Bring a coat."

The Judge fired up the E, pulling his old leather jacket from the trunk, and sped out of Malaga Cove, through the trees of Valmonte, down Hawthorne Blvd, over to Airport Drive, and pulled into the parking at the fixed base operator's office with four minutes to spare. As he pulled on his leather jacket, he heard the beating sound of 'copter blades. It was dark but the 'copter had only the minimum lights flashing.

As soon as the helicopter had settled firmly on the ground, the door opened and Barbara appeared, motioning the Judge to join her. He dashed across the tarmac, ducking under the whirling blades, and hauled himself aboard.

The Judge was excited, like a small boy on a fishing trip. He suspected his presence aboard was not exactly regulation, but Barbara's crew was a tight group and were used to keeping secrets.

As soon as his belt was buckled the chopper took off, leaving the ground like a giant dragonfly, only touching the surface for a moment.

"We're the surveillance part of the operation, Judge," Barbara yelled into the Judge's ears. "The Coast Guard is standing by with a go fast boat off shore, and we have two teams on the ground, bracketing the bluffs and the beach. We'll stay high and out of sight and see what happens."

The helicopter ascended to 1500 feet as it beat its way over the peninsula, turned on silent running gear, and then settled in a small circular hover above a cliff-enclosed sandy beach some three miles north of Point Vicente. Barbara handed the Judge his own set of night binoculars and the two of them began to scan the beach and the sea beyond.

The Judge picked it up first, a small sleek craft, perhaps 40 feet long, maybe four miles off shore, tearing through the water at perhaps 70 miles an hour on a dead run for the beach. The boat was painted grey and hard to spot, but its wake left a faint trail.

As it got closer to the shore, the Judge saw it had has three outboards mounted on the stern, blazing a trail across the reasonably calm ocean surface. There were perhaps 10 fuel cans stacked aft, and one occupant overseeing a continual transfer of fuel into the primary tanks to keep the engines going at a dead heat.
Two men were at the helm, one handling the wheel and one apparently working navigation equipment. It had no radar, no high projecting tower or rails above the water, and no lights. It must have been near impossible to see from down on the water and no doubt left a very small radar print. And it was very fast.

Down on the beach the Judge saw two people, one sitting smoking and the other holding a flashlight seaward.

As the boat neared the beach, the Judge picked up a flashlight blinking off and on in a coded pattern from the bluff above. The third man. The boat veered slightly, correcting its course for the beach.

About 100 yards out, the boat suddenly cut its engines, plopping down off plane, and its speed dropped to close to nothing, the boat coasting under minimal power toward the surf line.

The surf was very low and there was no moon. The two men waded out into the water up to their chests to meet the boat, and then loaded on their shoulders what looked like sacks of rice. Then they scrambled back to the beach with their loads.

They made several trips, stacking the sacks high up on the beach above tide level.

Once the last sacks had been offloaded, the crew immediately started to pull up the anchor, preparing to depart.

Suddenly a small grey boat with big outboards and an automatic gun mounted on the fore deck came tearing around the cliff and into the cove from the south, flying a Coast Guard flag.

The copter dropped low and spotlighted the two men on the beach, stunned, standing beside their stacked contraband.

Two NARC patrol cars turned on flashing lights on the road at either side above the cove, and teams from each side began a descent to the beach.

Because the smuggler's boat was not yet underway, it had no chance of escape. Its crew assessed this situation at the same time as the Judge. He saw the crew quickly throwing automatic weapons overboard. The Coast Guard boat came alongside and three of the crew clambered aboard, drawn guns in hand, while another manned the gun on its bow and its commander steadied their boat at the helm.

The two smugglers on the beach lay down flat on the sand with their arms and legs spread and didn't move.

The NARC teams quickly reached them and they were cuffed and frisked.

The Coast Guard boat took its prisoners aboard and steamed back south toward San Pedro, the go fast boat in tow.

In a matter of minutes, the cove was quiet and deserted again, as though nothing had occurred.

"There we have it," said Barbara with a victorious smile.

The Judge smiled too. The payback was overdue, but very satisfactory.

Chapter 49 - Thursday

At 2:24 the next afternoon, the Judge got a call from Barbara.

"I've got news, both interesting and disturbing, Judge."

"From the top," said the Judge.

"All right. One of the folks we nailed on the beach decided to cop a plea.

"He gave us the address of a rundown warehouse fronting on a rear alley in Vernon.

We put the place under surveillance for a couple of hours. From the comings and goings it looked like either a factory, or a warehouse for distribution of illegal drugs on a high volume basis.

"We got a search warrant and busted the doors down about an hour ago. It was a combined warehouse and processing lab. We think the inventory of drugs will have a street value well north of $40 million.

"It's going to put a big chink in someone's cash flow," Barbara said with satisfaction.

"And the disturbing news?" asked the Judge.

"Well, Judge, there were a lot of people milling around inside. We arrested them all. Among them was someone you know, one of your old law partners."

"Jake", said the Judge, stunned.

"You won the prize, Judge, it was Jake Benson. Even more interesting, he's in lockup right now pending a bail hearing, and who do you think he's asking for?"

"Don't know."

"He's asking for you, Judge."

There was a long pause while the Judge digested this information.

"What's he want with me?"

"I don't know, Judge. He's not talking to anybody, except a lawyer he hired who is preparing to argue bail. But he wants to see you privately at the jail as soon as possible."

"Well then, I guess I better put on my coat," said the Judge.

"Guess so, Judge. Let me know how it turns out…that is if you can…subject to privilege, and so on."

"Thanks Barbara." The Judge hung up.

The Judge changed into a white shirt and tie, one of his favorites - several white sheep, and in the middle, one all black with a pair of white eyes staring out…the proverbial black sheep.

An hour later, he walked into the new jail in downtown LA, and went through security, emptying his pockets and giving up his brief case and belt for scanning.

He was escorted down a long hall to a private room reserved for meetings between inmates and their legal counsel. Jake Benson looked haggard. There was no other word for it.

He shook the Judge's hand with a death grip, thanking him for coming. Then he sat down and got right to business.

"Judge - I really need your help. I need you to negotiate a plea deal."

"But I'm not a criminal lawyer," said the Judge.

" Look, Judge. I'll give them the head of the Mexican cartel and Johns.

"I can also name the addresses of the other six warehouses in Southern California, just like the one they raided. It will move their investigation along quickly and give them the tools for convictions.

"And," said Jake, lowering his voice to a whisper, "I'll set it up so the head of the cartel comes across onto US soil to meet me, so they can actually get him."

"In return?" asked the Judge.

"It's my first offense. Maybe 12 months, and a couple of years' probation."

"But what was your role in the enterprise, Jake? What are others going to say you did for the gang? That's going to be the first question the DA asks. How deep are you in?"

"Is this privileged, Judge? Are you giving me legal advice here so it's a privileged conversation?"

"Yes," said the Judge, "this is a privileged attorney-client conversation, even though you haven't hired me."

"I was mostly the go between for the money laundering. I didn't have anything to do with the actual drugs. I coordinated things between the Mexican Captain here in LA, and Johns. I arranged for the cash drops at Johns' office, kept track of the money advanced and the accruing interest, collected payments from Johns on the debt and forwarded it off to a British Virgin Islands company I set up for them.

"It was all bookkeeping and cash drops, payments made, deposits wired in, that sort of stuff. Money laundering, yes, drug distribution, no."

"What the hell were you doing in the warehouse with all the drugs, Jake?"

"Tortuga Loco's second wanted to go over the accounts with me."

"Tortuga Loco"?

"Yeah, that's what they call the boss man. Fat, short little toad, but mean like a snake.

"Anyway, they were all upset. Johns had stopped making payments. I explained about the lawsuit. About the lawsuit settlement. About how the settlement needed to be funded immediately to protect everybody.

"They didn't understand, or didn't give a shit. Just wanted their money, and at once.

"It was just fuckin' bad timing. If I hadn't happened to be there I'd likely be in the clear.

"They'd have had to turn one of the gang captains to reach me. But there I was sitting with my thumb up my ass when the cops busted down the damn door."

"Did they find drugs on you?"

"A recreational packet. Not enough to support a retailing charge, unless you add the 200 kilos of cocaine stacked around me in the damn warehouse. Shit, I was sitting on a stack of bricks four feet high when they blew the door."

"That's a problem," admitted the Judge. "But why me? I'm told you have a criminal attorney."

"You're the Judge, and my ex law partner. They all know you. They all respect you. Go talk to Justice.

See if they're open to a deal. I'll trade my information, testimony and cooperation for whatever they can do to lighten my load. You'll get a better deal than any defense attorney I'd trust in there. And honest to God, Judge, I wasn't selling drugs. It was all financial - cash to bail out the collapsing empire of Johns and his partner."

"And you'll give up Johns too?" said the Judge.

"Yes."

"What about his partner, Harley?"

"Harley must have known. Money doesn't grow on trees. Not the kind of money I was dumping into their company.

"But I didn't have direct contact with Harley. Saw him occasionally, but never discussed the cash with him. He was never there as far as I know when cash was delivered."

Too smart to be overtly involved. He's a smooth bastard."

The Judge sat back in his chair, considering.

He didn't owe Jake anything. In fact it was Jake's idea, or his implementation of someone else's plan, that had got the Judge defeated in his election.

Of course, as it turned out, the Judge now considered the election loss a favor.

Sitting in that airless, windowless court room for eight hours a day listening to people's complaints and troubles, watching all the greed, anger, and revenge play out. It was all a past life…No…more a lost life. A period of years wasted, never to be regained. But he wouldn't squander any more precious time that way.

"Where does Christi fit in to it all?" asked the Judge.

Jake's cautiously optimistic smile cracked and disappeared. He looked sad and old at the same time. A small quiver came into his voice.

"She doesn't, Judge. I am so, so sorry about her. She was a good kid. Straight arrow. Not like me.

"I tried to reach out to her after the divorce, but it was difficult. My assets were cut in half. I was scrambling just to regain some part of my former life. I stayed in the Valley and her and Maddie stayed on The Hill, an hour's lost drive from nowhere.

"I tried some…

"I'm the one that got her the job in Johns' office. I figured the internship job would be good experience."

"It didn't work out too well," said the Judge. "You know she found incriminating records, and saw the cash deliveries."

"Yes. She called me about that.

"I told her it was just a tax deal, tax planning, and maybe a little fudging on the side. I don't think she believed me. But I'm sure she had no idea drugs were involved."

"Why'd she get fired?"

"It wasn't about the records.

"It was Harley that fired her. Christi told me he badly wanted in her pants. Said he was like an octopus with 8 hands and bad breath.

"She said no. And no, and no, and no again.

"Finally she just told him he was way too old for her; that if he was the last man on earth, it still would never happen.

"So he found an excuse to fire her. That's what she told me."

"Do you think they had anything to do with her death?"

Jake blinked, caught off guard.

"No. She was confused, mixed up. She jumped off the damn cliff. How could they be involved?"

"Maybe she was pushed," said the Judge. The Judge had Jake's full attention now as he considered that possibility.

"Jesus, Judge, that'd mean I was responsible for her death. At least indirectly."

"I loved her, Judge. She was my only kid. I wouldn't put her in harm's way."

"I can't see Johns being involved in something like that. He's a financial crook. But he'd never have the balls to kill someone. Or even be involved."

"What about the Mexican gang?" asked the Judge.

It suddenly got very quiet in the little room.

Finally, Jake said, "I guess it's possible. Shit, if they thought she was a threat to their trade…in a heartbeat. They're totally ruthless. Behead people in Mexico all the time just for sport. But why would they think her a threat?"

"Perhaps because of the documents she had or what she'd seen and recorded in her diary," said the Judge.

Jake got very quiet again, and his face turned almost ashen.

"Shit, Judge, I don't know. I suppose it's possible."

The Judge switched gears again, turning to the plea deal issue.

"I'll make one call for you to the Feds", said the Judge, "float the idea of cooperation. Tell them I think you are serious, repentant and could considerably widen their net.

"Then your attorney's will have to take it from there."

"Thanks, Judge," said Jake, mostly still lost in thought.

The Judge offered his hand and Jake shook it distractedly. The Judge slid his chair back, stood up, and left the room, not looking back.

Chapter 50 - Friday

The Judge put the E's top up, and then squeezed in. Lately, it had become more and more of a squeeze with the top up.

He had agreed to talk to the Feds for Jake, and normally a personal visit to their offices would be the way to go about it, at their convenience, on their turf, where they could talk off the record.

But the Judge had a pretty good idea where this was going, and a quick intervention now might turn the tide, so he made the call from his car on the way back to The Hill. Sadly, that meant that the top had to go up. It would still be noisy, but manageable.

When Barbara came on, she said, "Well, Judge, two calls in one day, three calls in two days, and after no calls for a thousand days. I'd say my popularity is on the rise."

He could feel the smile in her voice.

"You know you're always popular with me, Barbara," he said.

"What can I do for you, Judge? Why do I think this is about Jake?"

"It is, it is," said the Judge. "He has asked me to approach your side with a plea deal, in exchange for information, cooperation, pinpointing of another six warehouses similar to the one you raided, testimony against the Mexican gang members you arrested, and testimony against the recipients of the drug money who used the money as their capital source, effectively laundering it.

"He says he had no hand in importing or selling drugs, only in the money laundering side. That your investigation will prove this out."

"He's still staring at 8 to 10," said Barbara. "And let's face it. He is a scum bag. A lawyer, an officer of the court, supposedly setting an example for the community. And without money laundering, there wouldn't be near as much traffic in drugs. The two crimes go hand in hand, supporting the criminal enterprise of the drug cartels.

"Hell, we caught him red assed, sitting on a stack of bricks. In a warehouse of cocaine having a street value north of four million dollars. Worst case, he is a direct part of the drug ring; best case from his perspective, he's an accomplice, an aider and abettor.

"I think he's pretty much earned a full ticket ride."

"It is a first offense," said the Judge. "No priors, I'm told."

"That and a dollar will get you a cup of coffee, Judge. Particularly when you're sitting in a warehouse atop your stash."

The Judge knew it wouldn't be easy, that this was pretty much how it would go. It was time to play one last card.

"I understand, Barbara. And I know your perspective will hold water with the court. But suppose Jake could contribute something more?"

"Like what?" Barbara responded, caution in her voice.

"Suppose Jake could lure the leader of the cartel, this Tortuga Loco, across the Border on to U.S. soil for a powwow, and you nabbed him?"

Across the ether the Judge could sense Barbara sitting up straighter in her chair, leaning into the phone.

"Tell me more, Judge," she said in her best non-committal poker voice.

"Jake has just been arrested. I assume there is no press on this yet; no one knows he's in the lockup. The gang is quite anxious to recover some money loaned out to a legitimate business. They will be even more anxious for their money now that the disaster at the warehouse has occurred and they've lost this inventory. Jake was the point man with answers about their money. They'll want to talk to him at the first opportunity.

"And since the warehouse is lost, Jake will be expected to appreciate how much more urgent the money question is. So urgent, that it could be a little dangerous for Jake if the money isn't delivered. He can be expected to be a little nervous about meeting.

"He's certainly not going to go to Mexico now. And he won't want to go to another warehouse in LA that might be vulnerable to a similar raid. And because of the raid, who can he trust on this side of the Border? Everyone will be looking at each other, wondering who tipped off the Feds."

"And so Jake will want to meet with the big cheese, Tortuga Loco, but on the US side, and soon," finished Barbara.

"That's the idea. You folks could flesh out the plan. Jake would have to be released but quietly kept in custody, and charges held pending but not filed while it all played out."

"And Jake would do this," asked Barbara?

"Yes," said the Judge, "I think so."

"Let me make a call. I'll get back to you."

Forty-five minutes later, as the Judge came back under the umbrella of cell phone service after traveling across Palos Verdes Drive North, his phone rang again. It was Barbara.

"Alright, Judge, if Jake can entice Mr. Big across the border, and if we can arrest him, and if Jake testifies against your "legitimate" businessmen who just happen to launder money, and if we get convictions there, the Justice Department will accept a plea to one count of money laundering and one count of tax fraud, no drug charge, and we'll support a reduced sentence of four years in the Los Angeles County Jail, and a $250,000 fine. Whatever he may owe in income tax and penalties, he'll have to settle that out separately.

"But this is strictly a 'No Ticki…No Laundry' deal."

"I think that will be acceptable, Barbara. I'll certainly recommend it. But I am out of my depth here, not my area of practice, so there should be an immediate discussion between your side and Jake's lawyer. I'll make the call now and have him contact you."

"OK, Judge, and don't be such a stranger."

"You've got it, Barbara."

The Judge hung up, then immediately called the number on the card Jake had given him - Jake's criminal defense attorney. He spoke briefly to the attorney, outlined his suggestion on how to proceed and the parameters of deal that might be crafted for Jake. The attorney seemed quick and competent. He said he would take it from there.

The Judge hung up.

That was all he could or would do. He was out of it now, and just as well. A sordid business on all sides. He settled back and enjoyed the last bit of drive into Malaga Cove, rounding that special corner to suddenly expose the vast view of the Santa Monica Bay, all dressed in bright blue today.

The Judge whipped up his driveway in the E, timing his press on the garage door opener, and sliding into his garage. He crawled out of the E with difficulty, vowing to lose weight as he did so, and then turned back and carefully folded the canvass top back down so he would fit next time.

Chapter 51 - Saturday

The Judge had put all the facts he learned about Christi and her death on 3x5 cards, and had been playing with them on his desk. He had sorted them in various ways, into stacks based on topic: sex, drugs, money, lawsuits, real estate development, political clout.

Then he shuffled them again and sorted them by relationships: Maddie Benson, Jake Benson, girlfriends Katherine, Paige and Hannah, Jeff Harwood, Gloria Tomlin, Mark Daniels, teachers Mary Roth and Hamilton Smith, Counselor Katy Thorne, Pat Harley and Mel Johns, beach painter Raleigh Graham, Police Chief Bill Wright, the new and mysterious 'more mature' lover, the weasel detective, John Broadman, and even the Judge himself.

Then he laid them out in a time sequence, adding separate cards with notes for various places he knew Christi had been the day of her death and why: his house, the beach, the cliff. He added in cards for places and facts he assembled for last spring, summer, early fall, two weeks before her death, the day she came to his house to house sit, and so on.

Then he threw them out on the desk in a random order to see if there was a trend he'd missed.

Finally, he laid them out one just overlapping the other into various piles, following some instinct he couldn't pinpoint.

The Judge's eyes fell on the Hamilton Smith Card, Christi's history teacher. His instinct whispered there was more there to learn.

Perhaps it was time he paid another visit to the history teacher.

He reached for the computer and did an address search in Palos Verdes. He wasn't surprised the address was behind the gates in Rolling Ranchos. A pretty expensive address for a high school teacher, but Katy had said the guy had married very well. His wife's dad was just about the wealthiest guy on The Hill.

He packed himself into the E and headed to the gate at the top of The Hill that accessed Rolling Ranchos.

He flipped his Judge Officer of the Court credentials to the guard and was cordially ushered in.

He traversed several winding country lane roads with white rail fences separating horse trails, then turned down a narrow road, and finally drove through an open gate which was marked as the residence of the Smith family, and up another long winding road, finally swinging around some trees and bringing a ranch style house into view.

He parked on the circular driveway, walking up to the hacienda style porch that ran the entire length of the front of the house, punctuated by several old wagon wheels, a well-worn buckboard, sans horse, and a variety of potted flowering plants. The double doors ajar in the middle turned out not to be the house doors, but an entry into a large interior patio, bricked, with fountain and koi pond, hanging pots and shrubs, and an atrium-like lattice ceiling, open to the sky.

A pair of heavily carved Spanish doors stood at the far end of the patio.

He pushed a small doorbell on the left and heard massive chimes ringing throughout the house behind the doors.

After a time, one of the two doors opened and a small, bird-like woman poked her blond head out. She may have been in her late thirties, but had a weathered and lined face, the result, the Judge surmised, of a very fair complexion and many years of trail riding and sun damage. She wore tight blue riding jeans and a red checked shirt, no makeup, and her blond hair was pulled back in a disheveled ponytail of sorts. Her faded blue eyes regarded him anxiously.

"Hi," said the Judge, putting on his best smile. "I am the Judge. I am investigating the death of a Palos Verdes High student, a former student of your husband's. Hamilton was kind enough to tell me a little about the victim. I was hoping he could provide a bit more information about her."

The mention of her husband seemed to stir something, perhaps anxiety, in her eyes. She held on to her side of the door and shook her head, saying in a small voice, "Ham isn't here."

"Oh, I'm sorry," said the Judge, "I should have called first. When will he be back?"

"I don't know. I never know where he is or when he'll come back. I'm sorry."

She stood away from the door now. The Judge noted the blue bruise marks on the arm that had been hidden behind the door, as though someone had grabbed a hold of her arm with two hands in a very powerful grip and mercilessly squeezed. She saw the Judge looking and said, "A horse bit me yesterday." quickly hiding the arm behind the door again.

"It looks like a painful bite," said the Judge, wondering how a horse could so closely imitate a man's bruising grasp. "Perhaps you knew Christi Benson?"

"No, no, not at all," said Mrs. Smith, perhaps just a tad too fast. "Just what I saw in the paper. Poor girl. Do they know who did it?"

"It appears to be suicide," said the Judge.

"Oh," she said in a small voice, nodding vigorously. "Well, I'll tell Ham you came by."

The Judge handed her his card, thanked her for her time, and turned, making his way back across the interior courtyard. He noted the surfboard leaning against the inside of the outer wall as he left.

It was a cherry red board; with a bright Billabong logo embedded in the fiberglass. Beside it was a cherry red wet suit, hung out to dry. A Rip Curl label was emblazoned on the breast.

Chapter 52 - Monday

The Judge spent the balance of Saturday and all of Sunday on case work, barely coming up for air. Katy looked a little bored since the Judge couldn't come and play, but she was beginning to appreciate that he was a workaholic. In many ways, his work defined him. It would always be so. If she were going to stay in a relationship with him, she'd have to make room for his work and accommodate it. At four in the afternoon, the Judge emerged from his office.

Katy was sitting on his couch opposite the door, curled up with her feet under her; blond hair all tousled, wrapped in his cream velour robe, which looked about 10 times too big for her.

The puppy was asleep at her feet, and a fire crackled in the fireplace.

The Judge gave her a big smile as her blue eyes pinned his with interest and affection.

The swelling around her nose had gone down considerably. It was almost petite again.

She uncurled her legs and stood up to greet him, his robe almost dragging on the floor.

He wrapped his arms around her, feeling like a huge bear, and felt her press her pelvis against his and snuggle her breasts into his chest. Then she tilted her head up for a kiss that lasted a while and involved interesting commerce between tongues. He was careful not to bump the taped area of her nose.

They finally unwound, and she settled back down on the sofa while Annie, who had gotten up and was waiting expectantly, insisted on being greeted and petted, her tail going like a small windmill.

"Judge," Katy said as the puppy settled back into her place by the fire. "Do you think the gang killed Christi?"

The Judge had filled her in on his discussions with Jake, and then Barbara. Pillow talk he supposed, although they weren't married and so conversations with Katy didn't technically fit the definition.

"I don't think she committed suicide," said the Judge. "She had absolutely no reason to jump off that cliff, and there is no indication of serious depression or other symptoms which suggest suicide."

"Wow", said Katy. "You think a murder was committed on The Hill. That never happens."

"Oh, it happens," said the Judge, "…infrequently, but it happens. The question is, did it happen to Christi, or was it an accident of some sort? I have a much better picture of Christi, but I still don't have all the facts."

"Perhaps we can get you some more facts, Judge. Your friend from the Coroner's office called about an hour ago and I heard the message. Said to call him back."

The Judge headed back to his office in quick strides, dialed Keith Kline, a senior assistant in the Coroner's office, and an old friend who had been an invaluable resource for early, and not yet released information out of the Coroner's office back when the Judge was in private practice.

After some brief banter, Keith said. "According to the Coroner's report, Christi had serious head trauma, probably from colliding with a rock in the water or something, and multiple cuts, bruises and contusions, likely from rolling for so long among the rocks and surf.

"But she died of drowning. Her lungs filled up with water and that was that. No alcohol in her system, no sign of drugs, a healthy and fit young female. No bullet holes, knife wounds or other signs of foul play. No broken bones either, a little surprising given the height of the cliff. Time of death was approximately 5 p.m.

"That's about it."

"Interesting," said the Judge. "Anything else of significance?"

Keith thought a moment. "Not really, that's pretty much it. Oh, one more thing though, probably not relevant, but kind of sad."

"What's that?" asked the Judge.

"She was about two months pregnant."

Chapter 53 - Monday

The Judge sat back in his chair, stunned. That would explain why Christi was upset. But would it explain a suicide?

There was something else in the coroner's report that didn't feel right. What was it? He just couldn't quite put his finger on it.

He turned to his computer on the console, brought up Google, and searched "Southern California Tide Tables". Then he specified Redondo Beach, which seemed to be the closest table to The Hill, and put in the date Christi died.

The tide had been quite a bit above average that day, with high tide about 1:20 pm, and low tide at 8:47 pm. Factor in the storm surge, and the crashing surf was explained.

He had seen Christi walk out of his house at 3 p.m., and seen her in the water at about 6:45 pm. Sometime during that 3 and 3/4 hour period, she had died.

The Coroner estimated she had been in the water approximately 1 and 3/4 hours, placing her time of drowning at approximately 5 p.m. That was consistent with what the Judge had seen.

That meant Christi would have hit the water about the time the tide was half way up the beach and falling. It would have been a good 3 and 3/4 hours before low tide, and before the water would start creeping up the beach again.

The Judge had seen Christi in the water at 6:45 pm. The tide was on the way out and receding, but it would have been further up the beach at her estimated time of death.

The Judge pulled up the tide information for the current date. The tide today was another high and low tide, just about the same as on the date Christi died. High tide was at 1:10, and low tide was at 8:35.

The Judge looked at his watch. Four-thirty p.m. On a comparison basis, Christi would have hit the water at a tidal point that would occur in about half an hour.

The Judge got up and walked across the living room, noting again the trim figure of Katy in his oversize robe, her head resting on one sofa arm, her legs together and bent at the knee, bare feet planted together at the other end of the sofa. She was reading a book, something about teenage emotions. The robe had parted in front at the top of her knees, exposing a nice swath of female charm to his angle of view. Sensing his attention, she looked up, catching him looking. She read the lust in his eyes, a smile rising from her lips up into her eyes.

He patted her on her head, whispering, "Later, I've got a date right now with the tide." It felt good to have her there, close by and safe.

He walked into the kitchen and got three white trash bags out from under the sink. He opened the patio door and walked out to a small lean-to shed filled with stored gardening tools. He opened the shed door, took out a shovel, and marched to the strip of garden that ran along the back fence. Finding a suitable location, he dug in with the shovel and filled each of the three trash bags with a large scoop of dirt.

He knotted each of the trash bags, put them carefully in the back of his old car, slid behind the wheel, and back coasted down the driveway and out into the street.

He stopped in front of the part of the bluff where it had all started, got out and retrieved his three bags. He walked over to cliff edge where he'd found the blue dress; it seemed like years before. So much had changed, both in the case, and in his life.

He checked his watch and waited five minutes, until 5 p.m. Stepping forward to the edge of the cliff, he dropped the first bag over the side, giving it a small forward push, as though someone might have stepped off or perhaps lunged off the cliff.

He swung the second bag back and forth for some time, getting the feel of it, and then hefted it out and over the cliff, lobbing it out into space to approximate someone backing up a few feet and then making a running leap.

Taking the third bag in hand, he backed up quite a way, and then ran toward the edge, lobbing the bag like an Olympic shot putter as far as he could, using the momentum of his body to further the throw. He hoped this would be the outside result of someone taking a long run at the cliff edge and jumping off on the fly as hard as they could, as though it were a broad jump.

He went to the edge of the cliff and peered over. The result was clear, but he picked his way down the steep path again to be sure.

Two of his bags were on the sand, dry sand for the first one, and wet sand for the second, with occasional tide surging around it, but only barely. The third bag was well into the surf and mostly submerged.

He noted also that at this stage of the tide, the water was low enough at the side of the rock formation jutting out on the right that one would be able to wade through the water up to it, climb up on the rocky outcropping to the faint foot path, and climb around to the small hidden beach behind it, which would be dry. But the water remained deep and churned dangerously around the rocks below the rocky spur at its sea end.

He got back into the E and drove off to the Redondo Beach Village for a Starbucks to wait for the tide, bringing his laptop with him as he entered. Being able to work anywhere was useful, but sometimes very debilitating, since it made it possible to work every waking moment. In this case, he felt he had no choice. He had let several other projects slip in his headlong pursuit of the facts surrounding Christi's death. He needed to catch up.

At 6:40 p.m., he drove back to see how far the tide had withdrawn, arriving at 6:45. This would have been approximately 1 and 3/4 hours after Christi's estimated time of death on the tide scale. It was about the time he had seen Christi's body, battered and bruised, bobbing and bouncing in the surf. The sea had gone down considerably. The water was just as deep and the surf just as tortured around the base of the rocky spur, and a riptide ran from the base toward the Judge's end of the beach.

He could see two of his white bags clearly enough. The surf had gone down, and in the process, apparently washed the third bag out to sea.

The surf was swirling up on the beach and lapping around several feet down the beach from the middle bag. The first bag was still high and dry.

At 105 minutes after her death, with a running jump off the cliff from the point of the blue dress, and assuming she was unconscious on landing, her body could have washed out into the rocks where the Judge spotted her. Perhaps even the second bag…in the post-storm surge of that afternoon, her body might have been washed out into the surf, but the Judge felt it was unlikely. If she had made merely a small step or lunge off the cliff with a desire to kill herself, her body would still be high and dry on the sand.

He looked over again at the rocky spur and the sea at its base. The water was deep there along the side of the spur, and swirling around in a violent froth. One could have swum through the tip of the spur he supposed, either to reach what was left of the hidden beach, or to return over the rock from the hidden beach to the main beach. But you'd have gotten pretty banged up. Any effort to swim out to the point of the rocky spur would have been very risky. It was deep water punctuated by rocks protruding from above the surface, all swirling sea and rip tide as the weight of swell after swell beached on its point.

He picked his way back down the cliff one more time to retrieve the first trash bag, giving up on the second one, which by now was also fully engulfed in the sea, and then climbed back, vowing it was the last time he would brave that beach unless an elevator were installed.

So if Christi had run has hard as she could off the edge of the cliff, not a typical way to proceed with a suicide in the Judge's view, she would likely have still landed on wet sand, if the coroner was right about her time of death.

If she were unconscious, then the tide could have rolled up the beach and taken her body out into the deeper water where the Judge had spotted it, rolling and crashing against the rocks.

But she had no broken bones. The Coroner thought that unusual given the height of the fall, and attributed it to her landing in the water. But the judge's experiment suggested she would have landed on the sand, perhaps wet sand, but not in the water.

To the Judge, it seemed unlikely that Christi folded up her blue dress and then jumped off the cliff.

He knew she played with someone periodically at the secret beach. He suspected it was Hamilton Smith. Mr. Billabong Surfboard. If she had been over on the face of the jutting cliff, coming or going, a fall there would have put her into deep water among the rocks about the right time. The rip tide could have drifted her body up to where the Judge spotted it.

That made more sense to the Judge. Besides, she was wearing a swimsuit. She'd taken her dress off. He assumed she had taken the dress off herself. There was no sign of a struggle, no torn dress. A swimsuit would have made sense if she had been going or coming from the secret beach. You'd have had to wade in and get wet in both directions.

And her diary, wallet and keys had been left in its secret place on the secret beach. Would she have left them there if she had gone for the day and didn't expect to return? The Judge doubted that. Gloria had said she mostly carried her diary with her and she'd certainly have needed her keys and her wallet.

But suppose she got so upset and angry that she forgot her stuff, following a boyfriend up and across the faint footpath over the rocky spur, perhaps arguing all the way. Upset, angry and distracted.

Suppose she fell from the jutting rock into the swirling water and rocks at the front of its face. Maybe it was an accident, and she slipped. Maybe she was deliberately pushed. But is that where it happened?

He looked again. It was nasty, deep water, swirling and pulling around in a tight area surrounded by slippery rocks. Waves continually rolled in to pound it.

If Christi had fallen in there, it would have been difficult enough to get out, assuming she had missed hitting her head in the fall. It was a good 20 feet from the faint trail cut on the jutting rock, on a vertical sheer down to the water, with rocks alternately exposed and covered by the boiling sea below. But with some luck, if you were a strong swimmer, you might navigate it, although you'd be bruised and battered along the way.

If she'd hit her head on impact and were unconscious, it would have been a different story. It could have been over very quickly. It wouldn't have taken long to drown. Her only hope would then have been that someone with her would pull her out.

That wouldn't be easy, but possible. One could slide down the sheer feet first, stopping one's progress on the small rocks at the base, then dive in, grab her and tow her past the clustered rocks and around to the beach.

The Judge supposed he would have tried. It looked do-able, despite the undertow.

The Judge turned and trudged back to the E. His little experiment, when combined with the Coroner's report, had answered several questions, but raised new ones. Was Christi alone on that rock? Did she fall or was she pushed? Did she hit her head? There had been a gash on her head the Judge recalled. The Coroner had said it was a serious one.

And if she were not alone, who was with her? Was it her new lover? Was that Hamilton? Had the new lover tried to rescue her? If not, why not?

Why hadn't he called 911? Why hadn't he gone for help? Why hadn't he come forward afterward?

If it was Hamilton, that was easy to answer: an affair with your underage student, and you married to a wealthy wife with two small kids.

The Judge was beginning to see how some of the pieces fit together.

Chapter 54 - Friday

The Judge awoke early, careful not to disturb his new bedmate, who was softly purring beside him. They both slept nude now, enjoying the brush of the other's skin from time to time. He could smell her, and perhaps a faint whiff of their sex the night before, a passionate coupling that had left them both gasping for breath and then laughing together like children in mutual delight.

It had been a long time since he'd had someone to sleep with. It was quite nice. He harbored a fear he would roll over and squish Katy, but so far this hadn't happened. He suspected she was considerably more durable then she appeared.

The Judge had been in San Francisco working with his client there for three days, having left early Tuesday morning and returning late Thursday night. It was amazing how much he'd missed the warmth and skin contact of sleeping with Katy. Their reunion last night had been passionate, as though they'd been apart for weeks. It was a heady experience having this young, super young, girlfriend in his life.

Unfortunately, his down time in San Francisco had been spent on long calls to Katy, followed by fantasizing she was with him. He'd given little thought to the Christi case.

But he was now determined to solve the mystery of her death. As he had drifted off to sleep after their wild love making the night before, he'd deliberately begun to turn over in his mind the facts he had learned in the case. When he had awoken, his subconscious was still sifting through the same facts, as it had been all night. He'd used this technique before, using the power of his subconscious to solve a vexing problem or suss a new solution to a tricky puzzle. It often produced valuable insights. The power of the unconscious mind always surprised him.

As he drifted out of sleep, he realized he had been dreaming of standing on that cliff after calling 911, the dusk before all the police lights and commotion. He had looked around at the people who had stopped to see what was going on. There was the professional looking neighbor lady in the violet raincoat, the small Asian women who looked like a lawyer, and the young couple passing by who had stopped and were all agog. Hadn't there been someone else?

A shadowy figure standing a little farther back. Away from everybody else. Yes, he remembered now, the straw hat, the green overalls…a gardener.

One of the many non-descript gardeners who tended the lawns and beds for the denizens of The Hill. Almost fungible in a way. Never really noticed unless they were your gardener, and only then on payday and when some specific specimen needed to be pruned.

The gardener had softly melted away as the police car arrived, likely illegal and not wanting to meet the police. But the Judge had a clear image of his face. There was fear in it even before the police car arrived.

Perhaps a little too much fear for an illegal, just passing by.

The Judge wanted to talk to that gardener, and right away.

It had been a Friday, and about 6:45 pm. This was also a Friday. The Judge decided he would take the puppy for a walk about the same time as before, or a little earlier, and see if he ran into this shy gardener.

Katy showed up at his office door about 10:30, wearing his robe and nothing else, looking like a teenager in the oversized garment. She was carrying a tray of freshly made coffee and buttered toast. The robe fell open to show the white curve of her small breasts as she set the tray down. She felt his hot glance wash over her and she looked up at him, a randy twinkle in her eyes inviting him to look further.

They shared the coffee and toast together over his desk, and she announced she was all better, and going back to work in the afternoon.

She did look much better, color in her cheeks, a spark in her blue eyes. The Judge smugly attributed that to periodic sex, mentally patting himself on the back. Much of the swelling had gone down around her injured nose. He told her she looked a lot less like Jimmy Durante. This earned him a slug on his shoulder.

After some idle chatter over coffee, she provocatively let the robe fall open again to expose her breasts, giving the Judge another suggestive look. He had been distracted, but he dropped all thought of work and got up, chasing her around the desk, through the living room and into the bedroom where he cornered her against the bed. She giggled all the way through the chase, then screeched as he finally caught her.

They whiled away a satisfying hour and a half, cuddling, petting, joining, and sleeping, locked in each other's arms.

She rolled out of bed and headed for the shower, swinging her hips a little extra on the way across the room for the Judge's benefit. The Judge was all eyes. She indeed had a cute fanny.

About 6 p.m., the Judge put on his coat, collected the puppy and her leash, and headed toward the bluff road. He began a crisscross pattern, briskly walking the side streets, all of which directly or indirectly fed back down to Paseo Del Mar. He listened for the telltale sound of a leaf blower or a lawn mower.

He found two groups of gardeners, but a close inspection of each crew did not turn up the face he carried in his head.

He was running out of territory when he heard a leaf blower start up near the old high school at the foot of Malaga Cove.

When he and Annie ambled over in that direction they came upon the leaf blower in full operation, and the man running it. He was just as the Judge remembered.

Perhaps 55 or so, deep brown skin, not only from his heritage, but also from his work outside in the sun and elements. Deep lines in his face, and large hands that had worked with yard tools in the sun for almost half a century. There was no tattoo.
He wore light beige pants and matching long sleeve shirt with lots of pockets. On top of his head sat a small straw

rancher's hat with the sides steeply rolled up. His dark boots were old and battered with worn rubber soles.

He worked the leaf blower methodically across the lawn, sweeping the gold and yellow leaves together toward one end in large swaths. Because he was concentrating, and because of the noise, he didn't hear the Judge approach.

The Judge gently tapped him from behind on the shoulder, and he jumped as though shot.

The Judge flattened his palm toward the ground and pushed it down a couple of times with emphasis, indicating the gardener should shut down the leaf blower, and he did so at once.

"Hi," said the Judge, "Nice day, huh?"

"No English," the gardener said, with a smile that showed jagged teeth that probably were in need of dental work. But his eyes weren't smiling. They looked fearful.

The Judge extended his hand to the man, announcing, "I'm the Judge."

The man accepted the hand and shook it carefully. "Carlos Pinto," he said, bowing his head slightly as he spoke.

"Six weeks ago you stood beside me," said the Judge, "down there on the cliff where the girl died."

Carlos immediately shook his head. "Not me," he exclaimed, and then he immediately added, "No English."

"Look," said the Judge softly, and slowly in the hope he would be fully understood.

"I think you understand just fine.

"You are a material witness to a crime. You can tell me what you saw and I'll see if we can keep you out of it, sort of behind the scenes. Or I can call the police and they will come over immediately and take a full report."

"No comprendo," said Carlos. "I know nothing." But now Carlos looked terrified.

"I want it all," said the Judge sternly, employing the judicial voice that used to rattle off his courtroom walls and make attorneys quake in their shoes. "I want to hear every last thing you saw, and every last thing you know about that girl and what happened, and I want it now…or the police can sweat it out of you. And you know they will."

The Judge put on a grim look. His clerk used to tease him in chambers, calling it the Hanging Judge look.

Carlos said nothing. He just stared at the ground, immobile and silent.

The Judge counted slowly counting in his head to 20, deliberately letting the tension build, then said, "Okay, let's have it."

More silence from Carlos.

"All right, if that's the way you want it," said the Judge, reaching into his coat, taking out his phone, and starting to dial.

Carlos looked up, the terror changing to anger at the Judge's threat. Then his face relaxed suddenly and took on a sort of *que sera sera* attitude that had probably served him well in times of difficulty. The Judge suspected there had been many such times.

The Judge slowly put away his phone and said, "Why don't we go over and sit in your truck for a few minutes and talk?"

Carlos put down the leaf blower and dejectedly headed to his truck. The Judge followed.

They crawled into the truck, some small protection from the cold and from prying eyes.

Carlos spoke in reasonably good English, just a hint of an accent. And once he started the words spilled out, like they had been bottled up too long.

"I finished this lawn early that day, so I walked to the bluff for a smoke."

"What time?" asked the Judge.

"About 4 p.m.," said Carlos.

"And what did you see?"

"Nothing, azure, the wind. It was muy bonito. But then there was yelling on the rocks below. An hombre and a young chiquita, muy bonita.

"She was very angry and so was he. Couldn't make out what they were saying, and then she started to yell, and he just turned away. She grabbed him with her arms from behind and tried to hold him, but he forced her arms away and turned and shoved her away really hard. She fell off the cliff. She hit her head on the rocks on the way down and then she landed in the water and floated face down in the surf, not moving."

"What did the man do?"

"He stared down at her, like me. I guess we were both hoping she would turn over and start to swim. It was deep water and jagged rocks, all churned up by the storm surf."

"And did she turn over and start to swim?"

"No, she just laid there, her body bouncing around in the water and banging against all the rocks."

"And then?"

"He just left. He just left her there. He could have slid down and swam over to her, got her back to the beach. It would have been muy peligroso, but he could have. He didn't. He climbed away, down the rock to the beach."

"What did you do?"

What could I do, Senior? I was on the cliff. If there was a way down, I didn't know. And he was still down there. I have no cell. I didn't know what to do.

"I was scared. I ran away, back here, to my next lawn. I thought he may have seen me. Thought he might come after me."

"You could have gone to the house across the street and called the police."

Carlos looked very sad now. "Yes, you're right, that's what I should have done. That's what a good man would have done.

"But I was afraid. I didn't want to be deported to Chile. If I go back to Chile, who would take care of my two small ones? My wife makes a little money, but not enough. Without this job they'd starve.

"And I was afraid I might be blamed.

"Those are all reasons, Senor Judge, but not good enough ones. I am a coward. I ran away.

"I went back after 15 minutes. I told myself maybe I could still help. Perhaps I could find a trail down there, I thought. Or perhaps she woke up and swam to shore. But I knew it would be too late.

"And then I saw you there, Senor Judge. You were already calling the police."

"What was she wearing?" asked the Judge.

"Not much," said Carlos. "Just a small swimsuit."

"How did she look when she was climbing around the rock?"

"She seemed all flushed. Very, very angry."

"And him? asked the Judge, "What did he look like?"

"It was a ways down. Medium tall, dark brown hair, maybe mid 30's, hard to tell.

Red swim trunks. Very strong looking, like he worked out. Tan, like a lot of sun.

"He was very angry too. Enraged, the way he was yelling at her. He was leading the way around the rock, and she was following right behind him, close. And then it all happened."

"Anything else?" asked the Judge.

"Only the clothes," said Carlos.

"What about the clothes?"

"Around the rock, on the beach on this side, they'd left some clothes. They didn't want to get their clothes wet wading to the rock I guess. When he came down around the rock and waded ashore, he took a yellow jacket and put it on. There was a blue dress too. Hers, I guess. He picked up the blue dress, shook it to get the sand off, folded it and put it under his arm. Then he jogged along the beach and disappeared. It was like he'd removed every sign she'd ever existed. It was very sad."

"Let's walk down to the bluff, Carlos," said the Judge. "I want you to point out exactly where you stood, and explain again what you saw."

They walked slowly back down the road to Paseo del Mar, and then along it to the bluff. At the edge, Carlos pointed out the rock jutting out into the ocean with its little patch of sand hidden to the south

It was around the face of that rock they had been coming, picking their way along down to the side where it was a short, shallow wade to the beach.

He pointed to the beach below the bluff, where their clothes had been left.

"Carlos, you said you saw him shove her away very hard, and she fell."

"Yes, Senor."

"Did he shove her hard and cause her to fall, or did he shove her away hard, and then she somehow lost her balance or slipped and fell? Did he shove her off that cliff?"

"I couldn't really tell, Senior. It happened all so fast. I can't say for sure he shoved her off the cliff. I was far away.

"Thank you, Carlos," said the Judge, walking back to his truck with him.

"Please don't call the police, Senior. They will send me back to Chile. My family will starve. Please don't."

"I am not sure I can keep you out of this, Carlos. It will depend on how it all plays out."

Carlos turned slowly back to his lawn, picking up the leaf blower with his weathered hands. He looked defeated. Fortune had thrust him into the middle of a death…an accident? Perhaps a murder? And now his fate was in the hands of a hombre judge. With his usual luck, this would not turn out well.

Chapter 55 - Friday

The Judge pulled into the high school parking lot, consulted a roster outside the principal's office, and then headed for the E Corridor, and Office E-18. It was after hours, but there were doors open and people working in several of the classrooms. As he got closer, he saw that the door to E-18 was open.

He knocked on the doorframe and then stepped in.

Hamilton Anderson Smith was there, poring over student papers at his desk. He looked up, and blinked a couple of times behind his glasses, and then his head snapped back as he recognized that the bulk of someone coming out of the late afternoon shadow of the door was too big to be a student.

He put his hand over his eyes to shield them from the bright desk light and looked again, this time recognizing the Judge.

They looked at each other for a minute, and the silent communication was clear. The Judge's face said he knew, and the panic behind Ham's eyes confirmed he knew the Judge knew.

Ham sat very still and didn't say a word, watching the Judge with apprehension.

The Judge stared back with level blue eyes pinning Ham to an instant in time.

Finally Ham lifted his chin and using his best Harvard accent to ask, "Can I help you?"

"I think you're partially responsible for Christi's death," said the Judge. "I think she fell, or maybe you pushed her. But then you just stood by and let her drown."

Ham went pale white. "Why would I do such a thing?" he said hoarsely, all trace of Harvard disappearing in an instant.

"You had a lot to lose if Christi started shooting her mouth off, Ham."

"Like about what?" Defensive now.

"Like the sexual affair you had with her all summer. You violated the ethical standards of the high school by having an affair with your student.

"Or like the two-month-old baby she carried in her womb. It was yours. She wanted to keep it. You wanted an immediate abortion.

"You had sex with her when she was under 18. You would go to jail and be branded a sex offender. Your life would be essentially ruined if the affair came out.

"And you have a wife and a child. A very rich wife as I understand. You could lose them both, and the lifestyle that went with all your father-in-law's money.

"The consequences of her talking and making a public stink would have been catastrophic."

"You have no proof of any of that," said Ham, rising from his desk, his voice raised in falsetto. "That's pure conjecture, and slanderous."

"DNA of the fetus will tie you to the baby, Ham. But there is much more."

"I have a witness. He saw you push Christi off the cliff face. He saw you just stand there. Just watch while she drowned."

"He even watched you pick up her blue dress, shake the sand out, fold it carefully, and carry it up the cliff, to be used as a decoy, as a prop to imply a suicide."

Ham gave something between a sob and a hard intake of breath. "I want a lawyer," he said.

"And of course you'll get one," said the Judge.

"I'm here as sort of a neutral party to suggest you get your lawyer now…immediately, and then go present yourself and your story to the police, before they interview the witness and come looking with a warrant."

"It was an accident," said Ham. "I didn't push her. I pulled away from her and she just lost her balance and fell."

"Why didn't you slide down the cliff face into the water and pull her back out?" asked the Judge. "You could have saved her."

"I don't swim. I was afraid of the water," he said.

"Bull shit," said the Judge. "You're a twilight surfer. If anyone is a natural in the water it's you. Why didn't you call for help?"

"My cell was in my car up on the cliff."

"So you just stood there and watched her drown? Very convenient."

"It wasn't like that. She was dead by the time she hit the water. She smashed her head on the rocks before going in."

"The only way to know that for sure was to jump in and drag her out. Something you couldn't, or wouldn't do."

"I…I…I didn't know what to do. I was stunned, shaken, not thinking clearly."

"But you thought clearly enough about her dress. You shook the sand out, carefully folded it up, and planted it at the top of the cliff so it looked like she had jumped from there."

Ham swung his head up, anger in his voice. "I didn't want it to happen; I loved her."

"You knew she was carrying your child," said the Judge

Ham dropped his head, staring at his desk with unseeing eyes.

"That was what the fight was about, was it not?"

"Yes," Ham said softy, sagging, suddenly looking older and battered. "She wanted me to leave my wife. She said she was going to have the child either way. I could leave my wife, or I could pay the medical and hefty child support. And to hell with the resulting scandal.

"So then I said it wasn't mine. That's what infuriated her. She just went nuts.
Called me all sorts of foul names, grabbed me from behind on that little path, said she wasn't finished with me yet".

"It's lucky we both weren't killed."

"Lucky for you," said the Judge.

Ham gave a big sigh, looked up at the Judge, and said, "What are my options?"

The Judge considered for a moment.

"You could do nothing. The witness will come in and testify to the police, they'll take it to the DA, who will check your DNA against that of the fetus. It will match up. Then a warrant will be issued for your arrest, and in about 48 hours the police will show up to arrest you."

"You could run. Mexico, the Caribbean, perhaps South America. It's a miserable life on the run, particularly if you don't have money to fund a lifestyle. And it's very likely you'd ultimately get caught somewhere. The world becomes a smaller and smaller place every day."

"You could hire a lawyer and go in of your own accord tomorrow afternoon, probably the earliest you could get set up with a lawyer, and tell your story."

"It won't be pretty. But I don't think there was any premeditated murder here, or any lying in wait. I would guess the best the DA could plead would be manslaughter, or perhaps negligent infliction of grave bodily harm."

"And such a case has problems. There's no corroboration that the fall down the cliff was anything but an unintended accident. My witness certainly can't be sure it was otherwise. The troublesome part is you standing there watching her drown. That won't sit well with a jury."

"But my guess is the DA will play it safe and just go for statutory rape, illegal sex with a minor. That's a slam dunk to prove, what with the DNA of the unborn child, and likely remnants of sperm in Christi as a result of your tryst earlier that afternoon."

"And a jury won't like that you were also her teacher, a position of trust. You had a responsibility not to parley your professional relationship with one so young and inexperienced into a sexual liaison."

"You may want to try copping a plea on that charge alone and see if they'll let the rest go. They may give you a little credit for 'fessing up at sentencing."

"But that's a question for a criminal lawyer. I'm not a criminal lawyer. If I were in your shoes, I'd get a criminal lawyer now, a good one, and see what might be negotiated."

"You're better off taking the initiative."

The Judge walked to the door, turning around as he reached it. "I'll give you until tomorrow at 5 p.m. to choose whatever course you consider best. If you haven't turned yourself in by then, I'll bring my witness in to give his testimony."

The Judge left the classroom, leaving Ham still staring blankly at this desk, his face pale and drawn as he contemplated his options.

Chapter 56 - Sunday

The next morning, the Judge rose early, leaving Katy in the middle of his bed, curled like a large cat, softly purring in her sleep. They seemed to have a need to touch while they slept, so they had been meeting like this in the middle of the bed, lying pelt to pelt as they slept.

She was an absolutely adorable creature, thought the Judge. But way too young.

He moved into his bathroom and started to shave, noting the small adjustments there.

Nothing pushy. He still had total occupancy of all his drawers, cupboards and closets, except for his walk in closet in the master, the best closet, which was now filled to the gills with her stuff. And except for the larger bottom drawer, invaded by bras and panties. On his bathroom counter were neatly arranged, four bottles containing God knew what. One looked to be some sort of astringent for makeup removal, another was some sort of cream, the third was also a cream, and the fourth was marked 'scrub'.

To the right on the counter sat two plastic travel bags. The smaller one, partially opened, appeared to have sufficient lipsticks, eye liners, rouge, nail polish and other cosmetics to repaint the Sistine Chapel, along with a ghastly assortment of torture tools and implements that belonged to the Inquisition. The larger bag was always kept carefully zipped. The Judge could only imagine what grizzly things it might contain.

There was a new brand of soap in the soap dish, one that didn't smell like soap. And the Judge had noticed the addition of several new plastic bottles on the floor of his shower next to his combo shampoo and conditioner.

There was also a new box of tissue on the counter and a fluffy bag of cotton balls that were used at all hours of the day and night.

The lid on the toilet seat seemed to be continually down these days as well. The Judge suspected this was a silent protest.

It was a source of amusement to him that while a man could be perfectly happy visiting a friend's house with only his toothbrush and a razor, and could often even borrow a razor, a woman traveled only in full cosmetic mode.

At any rate, the risk of harm that had propelled her into his bedroom and his arms was now fully abated.

And it wasn't healthy for a beautiful young woman like Katy to be wasting her time on an old geezer like the Judge. He loved her dearly, it was true, but he wanted the best for her, and the best was someone her own age with whom she could build a life. She needed to meet some up and coming young man who was looking to settle down.

He resolved to have "The Conversation" with Katy tomorrow morning, perhaps over breakfast at the Yellow Kettle - the conversation you had when it was better for one or both if they went their separate ways.

He didn't want to be the one responsible for wasting Katy's time. He cared too much. He would let Katy go. It was the way it had to be.

He finished dressing and sped out the door, off to his meetings and a busy day. He needed to gin up some new legal business.

For the first time in a long time he relished returning to the fray of practicing law. Perhaps an old dog couldn't learn new tricks, but the things he already knew would make him a formable advocate and a tough adversary. He just needed to snag a couple of clients and he had a pretty fair idea where to go for that.

Chapter 57 – Saturday, Three Weeks Later

The Judge stood on the cliff where he had found the blue dress so many weeks before, and stared out at the vast Santa Monica Bay. Finding the dress had been a life changer.

When he had walked out of Ham's office late that afternoon three weeks before, he knew he was done with Christi's case. He had gotten to the bottom of how she died. That had been his assignment.

In pursuing his investigation, the Judge had put things in motion. The Judge had watched the concentric circles ripple out in all directions.

Judge Potter had decided to retire permanently from the bench, and indeed from the practice of law. That was a wise decision in the Judge's opinion. Particularly since the tax fraud investigation in progress in the offices of Harley & Johns was bound to spill over into Potter's lap. The Judge doubted very much that Potter had "reported" his monthly consulting fee.

Jake had made his plea deal and fully delivered, enticing the Mexican gang's drug lord over the border for a meeting. But the bust hadn't gone well. A gun battle had ensued and three of the gang members had died. Jake came out unscathed and none of the police were hurt. The risks Jake undertook to setup the sting would stand him in good stead with the court when it came to the penalty phase of his case.

Jake would likely be out in a year or two with good behavior. He would never practice law again, of course. But perhaps the striped-suit vacation would free him once and for all from his drug habit and he'd be able to turn his life around. The Judge hoped so.

The DA had asked the Judge to come down and view the three casualties of Jake's sting operation to see if the Judge could identify the man who broken into the Judge's house, and attacked his puppy.

The Judge explained that he never saw the man, and suggested he bring Mrs. Holland, the Judge's neighbor. She was the one who saw the unknown gardener cutting his front lawn.

Betty Holland was all too pleased to view the bodies. She came back with a lurid story of it all, which she recounted with gusto to friends on The Hill. She'd pause for effect when she came to the part about the body with the tattoo of a hooded skeleton on the back of his hand, and her friends would all gasp.

"This was the man pretending to be the Judge's gardener", she said. She was certain. No doubt the same man who had broken Katy's nose and likely run down Gloria .

The Judge had connected the dots for the police in the ongoing investigation of Gloria's hit and run death in San Pedro, and Harley & Johns' business of laundering drug money. They had searched Gloria' apartment and found on her computer, in a coded file, blackmail letters directed to Johns, threatening to expose vendor kickbacks, inspector payoffs, and drug money laundering, unless the company paid a six figure termination benefit. The Judge suspected Johns had complained to one of the gang members about the email. The Judge doubted Johns understood how quickly and violently the gang would react. Poor Gloria.

The development firm of Harley & Johns was pretty much in ruins. With the loss of the drug money, they couldn't make the mortgage payments. Every day, another of their properties went into foreclosure.

Harley and Johns, the two principals of the firm, had been indicted for operating a criminal enterprise, money laundering, bribing public officials and tax fraud. A receiver had been placed in charge of what was left of their dwindling assets.

But it had gotten worse. When the staff came back to the fancy Harley & Johns offices to pick up personal items, they found Johns hanging from the rafters in his office, a silk curtain tie from the fancy drapes wrapped around his neck, a chair he'd stood on kicked over beneath him.

Some thought the Mexican cartel had murdered Johns. The Judge was of the view that Johns had done it himself. But there was no note.

Johns had made the making of money his life's work. The money had become his security blanket, his reason for living, his identity, the measure of his self-worth; his religion. It had all been whisked away in one turn of the cards. Life was like that some times.

Johns had seemed unstable when the Judge had met him. The Judge believed he'd just cracked, a combination of the demands and then the threats from the cartel, the stress of his untenable position, and then the sudden loss of the fortune he had been so desperate to accumulate and protect. But no one could be sure.

Harley on the other hand, smooth to the end, was mounting a spirited defense against the criminal charges lodged against him. Given the surviving gang members' willingness to turn state's evidence, the detailed records of payoffs to inspectors and others Christi had found, and other records subsequently uncovered, the Judge expected Harley would be going away for a long time. But you never knew. Juries were often fickle, and so far no evidence of direct contact between him and the cartel members had been turned up.

The Judge had sat down with Maddie on her sofa and walked her through everything he had learned. It had been a tearful conversation. She had taken it as well as could be expected, nodding quietly and clutching a picture of her child.

The Judge hoped it helped in some small way that Christi hadn't committed suicide. But Maddie still blamed herself, he could see. And he supposed there was some justification there, although he'd never put words to that thought.

The binge drinking nights when there'd been no real supervision, Maddie's conflict and adversary approach when Christi had needed her parent to be tough, the relaxed attitude about rules of the house, the failure to monitor Christi's circle of friends or to sense the budding affair with an older, married man…

Had Maddie been more proactive, perhaps Christie wouldn't have been out on that secret beach, emotionally distraught, pregnant, angry, distracted, and with someone who hadn't the guts to go in after her when she fell.

It would take a long time for Maddie to recover from her loss. In many ways, she never would. Some things in life can't ever be fixed. You just go on.

Ham had shown up at the Police Chief's office at noon the next day after his conversation with the Judge, in tow behind a high-priced lawyer.

He told his story, admitting an affair with an underage student at his high school. He claimed Christi had slipped on the face of the rock, smashed her head on the way down the rock face, and lain motionless face down in the water. He said that the water was too rough and there was no way to get down the rock face to her aid.

He claimed he panicked after that.

He admitted he should have called 911 but had no cell phone, it being up the cliff in his fancy car. He could have called 911 from the top of the cliff though, upon reaching his car. He could have gone for help at a nearby house. But he hadn't.

His explanation was he just panicked. He wasn't thinking straight. Sort of a Chappaquiddick moment…or so he said.

Of course, he had a lot to lose if his affair was discovered. Sex with someone under 18, divorce, loss of his wife's family money and life style, loss of his teaching job, and perhaps lifetime branding as a sex offender.

And this pregnant teen posed an even greater problem. Christi had been outspoken, accusatory, very angry, and seemed determined to keep the baby, a combination that was his worst nightmare.

But his alleged panic hadn't kept him from snatching her dress from the sand, folding it, and leaving it on the top of the bluff. This was to make it look like suicide and to draw attention away from the cliff and the hidden beach where he knew Christi and he had been seen.

The police questioned him sharply about her fall, but he stuck to his story that Christi had slipped on her own. He hadn't pushed her or caused her to fall in anyway, or at least in any physical way.

The matter had been turned over to the DA, who initially elected to file charges for illicit sex with someone under 18. The Judge had quietly talked to the young lawyer in charge of the case at the DA's office, and made arrangements for him to talk unofficially to the gardener, without any involvement by immigration.

The DA eventually decided to stick with only the illicit sex charge. Other charges could have been brought, but proving them up at trial would have been difficult. The only witness was the gardener, and he didn't want to be involved, didn't want to testify, and in the end wouldn't be a very credible witness after defense counsel got through with him. More importantly, the gardener didn't see Ham push Christi off the rock. What he saw was Ham roughly shove Christi away from him, and then Christi fall, banging her head against the rocks as she tumbled down the cliff and into the swirling tide.

The DA wouldn't go for much of a plea bargain, given the way Ham failed to go to her help or go for the help of others. The Judge suspected Ham would be going away for at least two, and perhaps three years.

Meanwhile, Ham's wife had filed for divorce, her lawyer shoving the prenuptial agreement her daddy insisted Ham sign prior to the marriage under a judge's nose and waving it about the courtroom. Since she had custody of the kids, it left Ham pretty much penniless.

The high school had immediately fired him, and he'd find it difficult to continue a teaching career once he got out. The consequences of what in the best light was poor judgment would follow him for the rest of his life.

Should Ham have slid down the cliff and done his best to reach Christi and pull her out around the rocks and into shore? People had different opinions about that, even in the ranks of the police department, the fire department, and the DA's office.

The Judge, old guy that he was, wasn't sure whether he would have tried had it been him…except of course if it'd been Katy. He'd have been in the water in a heartbeat if it had been Katy.

The Judge had had his "Conversation" with Katy the day following Ham's arrest. That hadn't played out the way the Judge anticipated.

He'd chosen a public place, the Yellow Kettle, of course, on the oft quoted advice among males that it was better to have "The Breakup Conversation" in a public place, making it less likely the female would yell, scream, cry, or slap, all well-known and feared female tactics.

The Judge had been quite logical and persuasive, even elegant, he thought, presenting his reasons in specific and quite graphic examples of how the age difference was just too great for them to plan a future.

When she was 40, he'd be 61; when she was 57, he'd be 78, having run out of life expectancy. Woman lived typically 5 years longer than men, so she'd have a lonely old age of some 26 years without him, having wasted her youth on an older man.

He'd launched into the generational differences that made for different interests and attitudes. And the physical differences that led to different levels of physical activity, different sports pursuits, and ultimately, the prospect of a relatively young woman dealing with an old fart on his walker.

Thus, he summed up, it was better to break things off now before they got any further involved. It had been fun, of course, truly wonderful, actually. He would miss her forever, but it wasn't fair to her. He'd ended with a large sigh for effect, thankful he'd gotten it all off his chest.

He'd then leaned forward to see how she was taking it. She had been attentive, nodding at each point and showing no sign of tears. In fact, there was not even a hint of disappointment in her face, which miffed the Judge just a tad. He'd expected her to feel at least a little crushed, just as he did.

The Judge now shook his head with perplexity, recalling that conversation. He would never understand women.

Then the Judge turned back to look at the street that ran along the edge of his bluff. A racing green XKE Convertible, top down, sat there beside the road.

Squeezed into the passenger seat, happily waiting for his return, all smiles and expectant, sat a regal looking golden retriever.

The dog was perched in the lap of an equally all smiles and expectant young lady with clear blue eyes, gazing fondly at the Judge.

Their conversation of two weeks ago that he had so carefully planned had run entirely off the track.

Once he'd finish his summation, he finally got a reaction. But it wasn't what he expected.

Katy's face had become completely distorted…with laughter. She laughed and she laughed, and then she laughed some more.

The Judge didn't know what to think.

Then she put her hand across the table on top of his and said, "Dear, you're not getting rid of me that easily. You belong to me now. I attracted you and I've caught you fair and square. You're mine. I'm never letting you go…ever.

"We belong together. We're soul mates. We both know that. Either one of us could die tomorrow. That's the way of life. It's what makes each day so precious. You and I…we're spending our precious days together from here on out, for so long as they last."

He'd looked at her then and smiled. He knew deep down inside she was right. He wanted her more than anything. Just to be beside her made him so happy.

That's when he made his second mistake.

He brought his coffee cup to his lips, perhaps in part to hide the unmanly tears that lay just beneath the surface of his eyes.

Katy said, "Besides, Judge, I'm looking forward to having a LITTLE JUDGE in the not too distant future."

The Judge had been so stunned that the coffee cup slid out of his hand, its contents puddling into his lap. This had made Katy laugh even harder. And then he had started to laugh too, standing and leaning over the table in his soggy pants to give her a kiss.

The Judge stood on the cliff overlooking the cove and breathed in the smell of the sea. It was a fresh, slightly ionized scent, a mixture of breeze sweeping across a thousand miles of empty Pacific, mingled with the faint smell of drying seaweed on the beach below, washed up from the recent storm. The sea was blue green this afternoon, the waves small and frothy as they broke on the rocks and sand below.

The Judge turned on the bluff and looked again at the pair in the car, waiting expectantly for him. Katy smiled, relaxing in the last rays of the setting sun. Annie was squeezed in on her lap, muzzle sampling the breeze and intent on what her lord and master might do next. Perhaps there might be a walk in the offing, or better yet a treat.

The Judge retraced his steps toward the E, and marveled at how special it felt to be so loved.

Chapter 58 - Saturday, Three Weeks Later… Epilogue

The Judge dropped Katy and Annie off at the house, and continued down to Malaga Cover to pick up groceries for dinner. Katy had given him a list and promised a fantastic meal after she caught a brief nap. It had been the eight week anniversary of their first meeting at the Yellow Kettle. It seemed more like years ago they met, it felt so comfortable.

As the Judge pulled into the driveway, he heard Annie making a racket in the back yard. She was barking the deepest bark she could manage for her puppy size. That damn raccoon is back, he thought to himself. The neighbors would be on his tail if this continued. He'd have to call animal control in the morning and see what could be done.

He parked the E, walked down the driveway and retrieved the mail, including a new issue of Yachting Magazine that he was pleased to see. One of these days he would set up his law office on a yacht. He was sure of it.

He opened the front door and walked toward the table to put the mail down. The Master bedroom door was closed, which meant Katy was enjoying a nap.

He sensed another presence in the room.

Too late he turned to find himself looking down the barrel of a snub nose revolver. Behind it was a large man, who had been standing behind the door as the Judge opened it. He was Latino and rough looking, one hand holding the gun, the other resting on a long hunting knife strapped to his leg. There was a tattoo on the back of his hand - a hooded skeleton holding a reaper and a scale.

"So here he is, the big fancy Judge," said the man in an angry voice with a slight Spanish accent, the muzzle of the gun pointed at the Judge's belly and never wavering.

"The big mover and shaker who pulled all the handles on the machinery that killed my brother and destroyed our business. So now it's your turn, amigo…Time for pay back.

"You think you're so smart. Figured it all out, what happened to that bitch girl."

"Just so you know, you were all wrong amigo…all wrong. Stupid gringo."

"See, Gloria told Johns about the girl's snooping and her diary. So the girl had to die. I followed her. I was looking for an opportunity to grab her, encourage her to tell me where the diary was, have a little fun maybe, then put her down. A nosey bitch with a big mouth."

"I laid out on the edge of the cliff above their little beach love nest. I watched it all. The love shit on the sand. The big argument. "

"When she slipped, I thought that chicken shit surfer dude was taking care of it for me. He just stood there and watched her scrawny ass float in the water and rocks. Then he ran off. Grabbed her dress and hightailed it up the trail."

"But she was tougher than any of us thought. By the time he disappeared up the top of the cliff, she'd managed to fight her way almost around the rocks."

"So I hustled down to the beach as soon as he left. She'd dragged herself up on the sand, all beat up and dazed, just lying there. It was just too good a setup. I figured no one would bother with a diary if she was gone."

"So I grabbed a rock and hit her hard on the side of the head. Then I rolled her back into the surf, waded her out a bit and held her face down in the water, just to be sure. Didn't take long."

"I even carried the rock I used back up the cliff with me. I figure no muss, no fuss."

"It would have worked out fine it you hadn't stuck your nose in."

"But you had to play big time judge didn't you? Swan around with your fancy questions and stir it all up. You screwed it up good for everybody. Got my brother killed in the bargain in that fancy sting you set up. Did you think you would go unpunished, amigo?"
The man's nostrils flared."

"Tell you what's going to happen. I am going to shoot your balls off. Then I'm going to drag you in your bedroom and let you watch while I fuck your little girl in there. She's too young for you anyway. Then I'm going to slit her throat. We'll watch her bleed out together."

"Then I'm going to slit your throat and it's going to be your turn to bleed out. And that's it, that's the end of you, my fancy judge."

The man had a grim smile of satisfaction on his

face, anticipating how it was going to be.

The Judge stood motionless, his hands clasped behind his back, dropping all the mail but the yachting magazine to the floor.

His head was clear. But the odds weren't good. His hands behind his back had quietly rolled the Yachting magazine up into a tight tube, the only thing he could think of as a possible weapon. He now held the roll up magazine behind his back in his right hand. But the gun was held steady and he just wasn't close enough.

He saw movement behind the man in the hallway. It was Katy, fire poker in hand from his fireplace in the master bedroom. She crept up quietly and then made a lunge, swinging the poker at the back of the man's head. It seemed almost in slow motion. The Judge admired her courage.

But the man sensed her presence at the last second, dodging. The poker came crashing down relatively harmlessly, deflected by his left hand as he turned. The gun was still in his right hand.

But it was all the distraction the Judge needed.

The Judge stepped in close to the man, desperately brushing the gun hand aside with his left hand as he slammed the end of the rolled magazine, end first, with all of the force his 200 plus pounds he could muster, into the man's throat.

There was a satisfying feel of collapsing cartilage telegraphed through to the Judge's hand.

The man's windpipe collapsed from the blow. His eyes flew wide in surprise, then in panic as he realized he couldn't breathe. Both hands went to his throat, the gun forgotten and dropped to the floor. He toppled

backwards into the wall, and then slid down it.
He made small gurgling sounds, his eyes filled with equal amounts of hate and terror as his oxygen starved body began to die.

The Judge kicked the gun out of range, and then grabbed the phone, dialing 911. But he knew no one would reach them in time. It would be only a matter of seconds now.

He supposed he could have gotten a kitchen knife and improvised some surgery to create a hole in man's throat for air. But all things considered, he decided he didn't owe this man anything.

He scooped the gun up off the floor, held Katy tight, and they cautiously walked around the man and out the front door, leaving him to die alone.

A NOTE FROM THE AUTHOR:

Thank you for reading my book. If you enjoyed it, won't you please take a moment to leave me a review at your favorite retailer?

Thanks so much!

Davis MacDonald

Acknowledgements

The people, places and events depicted in this book are all fictional, and any similarity to any real people or events is unintended. Names have been chosen at random, and are not intended to suggest any particular person. The place bears a striking resemblance to a certain community on the coast near Los Angeles. Let me acknowledge that the actual community has the finest police department, motivated teachers who practice in schools that routinely win state honors as the best in the country, and dedicated citizens who selflessly donate the their time and talents to their city government, their schools, and their community for the benefit of all its residents. The facts, circumstances, and plot of this book were created out of whole cloth for dramatic effect, and bear no relationship to the actual community's inhabitants.

I'd like to thank my principal editor, Jason Myers, a noted writer in his own right, for his tireless work on this book. And special thanks to Dane Low (www.ebooklaunch.com) for the smashing cover design.

I hope you have enjoyed reading this book as much as I've enjoyed writing it,.. and perhaps here and there it made you smile a little...:)

Davis MacDonald

About DAVIS MacDONALD

Davis MacDonald grew up in Southern California and writes of places about which he has intimate knowledge. He is a member of the National Association of Independent Writers and Editors (NAIWE), and hold a Juris Doctorate from the University of Southern California. Many of the colorful characters in his novels are drawn from his personal and business experience. "THE HILL" is his first work introducing "The Judge". The second book in the Judge Series, "THE ISLAND", is scheduled to be
published in late 2014.

HOW TO CONNECT WITH DAVIS MacDONALD

Connect with Me: Davis.MacDonald1@gmail.com.
Website: www.DavisMacDonald-Author.com

Follow me Twitter: http://twitter.com/DavisMacdonald1

Friend me on Facebook: http://facebook.com/DavisMacDonald

Blog: http://davismacdonald.naiwe.com/professional-profile/

LOOK FOR THE FOLLOW-ON NOVELS IN THE JUDGE SERIES FROM DAVIS MacDONALD

The Island (set in Avalon, Catalina Island), Book 2 in the Judge Series

Silicon Beach (set in Santa Monica and the LA West Side), Book 3 in the Judge Series

The Bay (set in Newport Beach), Book 4 in the Judge Series

Cabo (set in Cabo San Lucas), Book 5 in the Judge Series

The Strand (set in Manhattan Beach, Hermosa Beach and Redondo Beach), Book 6 in the Judge Series

The Lake (set in Lake Arrowhead)– Due out in the Fall, 2018

Recipes and Philosophy from A Los Angeles Semi-Serious Epicurean and Bon Vivant.
(Recipes from Certain Memorable Dinners Prepared by Amazing California Chefs and Cooks).

Following are excerpts from Chapters 1 and Chapter 4 of Book two in the Judge Series, "THE ISLAND".

Excerpt from Chapter 1
The Island

Some omens are subtle. Others hit you over the head. Like a tablecloth angrily pulled out from under a loaded dinner table. There's a huge crash. Drinks, food and plates fly. The person sitting across gets wet. Waiters get nervous. Dining room calm is shattered. All heads turn to gawk.

The Judge should have known then the weekend was going to take a turn for the worse. A superstitious person would have known. But then the Judge had never been particularly superstitious.

The Casino Dining Room was well lit…20 soft chandeliers hanging from the high ceiling cast light and created shadows over the gold gilt, moldings and 1920's fixtures of the great circular room. The dining room sparkled with silver, china and stemware laid out on sixty linen covered dining tables. The tables were spread around the ballroom in a three quarter circle. The final quarter boasted a small stage where a five-man orchestra was pumping out elegant music from the 20's and 30's.

Young waiters, kids really, bustled about in long white tails, serving the diners.

It wasn't really a casino in the Vegas sense, of course. There'd never been any gambling. Not even in its heyday in the 1920's. But it was a circular structure of old world design and Italian definition.

The tables were filled with stiff looking tuxedoed men and flowingly dressed women, mostly a little older, all with the scent of money. It could have been a 'Great Gatsby' Party, moved forward 90 years and transported to this rugged island off the Los Angeles Coast, except that the assembled throng was a bit too weathered.

The Judge and Katy, his intimate other…Was that the term these days?…Sat together amongst a collection of tables more or less reserved for the Yacht Club contingent of which he was a member. Many of his fellow members were well into their cups, and having an uproariously good time.

Conversations were flowing easily. Discussions of sail boats and motor yachts, new nautical equipment, naval electronics, repairs, and close scrapes anchoring or crossing the channel, competed with discussions of business among the tuxedoed men. The women talked of kids, grandkids, weddings, births, deaths, divorces, and juicy stories of domestic life.

The level of noise was intense. It had been an extra-long cocktail hour. Just the way they liked it. People had only now settled into their assigned spots in the great ballroom. The band had struck up soft mood music suitable for ingesting food over light conversation.

The tables were broken up into twos, fours, and sixes. But this didn't preclude cross table discourse, carried on loud and lusty amongst the Yacht Club contingent. They were used to making themselves heard across wind and tide. They weren't bashful about carrying on conversation at the top of their lungs.

Suddenly a two-person table by a window erupted in a spat of angry words loud enough to carry over the din. The couple, husband and wife, had arrived late and had to settle for the smaller table.

She had on a flowing green dress, see-through chiffon on the outside, and an underskirt barely long enough to be decent. Not long enough to hide long slim legs that seemed to go on forever. She'd thrown an ivory silk scarf around her shoulders for effect, offsetting bright blue eyes, blond curls, and a slightly sunburned face with white circles around her eyes and across the nose where sunglasses went. She looked to be in her mid-thirties.

Hubby had on a Giorgio Armani tux, tailored to fit to a T. It made him look taller, thinner, and more buff then he was. Iron grey hair at the sides, mostly missing now on top, set off a bald pate, balanced by a large hawk like nose a little too big for his face. He had blue grey eyes, small and squinty, funneled with lines from age and too much squinting into the sun. He looked to be mid-fifties, a little older then the Judge, and well moneyed by the confident way he held himself and gave direction to the waiter flitting back and forth to his table.

Suddenly, there were more angry words between the pair, the volume rising. Then the husband leaned over in his seat, grabbed the table cloth some third of the way across the little table, and with one quick and vicious yank, pulled it out from under the assembled silverware, china and stemware, sending a portion of it tumbling into his wife's lap. The balance crashed on to the floor.

Noise in the room stopped as though by a switch. All heads turned. The wife, flushed with anger and embarrassment, stood up, dashed the remaining wine in her glass across the table in the direction of her husband's face, muttered in an audible voice, "You son of a bitch" and turned and stalked out.

Hubby sat very still for a time, whether in shock or in anger was unclear. He seemed oblivious to the crowded room, silently staring at the exit door through which his wife had stormed. Then he carefully wiped his wine-splashed face with a napkin, still ignoring the rest of the room. He threw the napkin down, slowly got up, and stalked out in the direction his wife had taken, out the side door a few steps away, his face twisted in anger.

"Who was that?" whispered Katy to the Judge.

"That was Marty Clark and his wife, Daisy," replied the Judge. "They seem to be fighting a lot these days".

"Wow, I'll say."

"Marty has the biggest yacht in the Club, the Santana, a 95-foot motor yacht. He's from Munich originally, immigrated here in the late 80's. He got a green card and later citizenship because of his aeronautical engineering skills, but went straight into real estate, buying, fixing, managing and sometimes selling apartment buildings across four counties.

"Smarter than the rest of us…He has a collection of several 50 unit buildings he owns outright now. Mostly just counts his cash flow. I understand he was a pretty tough customer back in the day. Used to carry a gun and collect his own rents door to door in some of the toughest parts of San Bernardino, Riverside, and Southeast LA."

"And his wife?"

"Daisy, his third wife, married about a year. A trophy wife I suppose. They don't seem to be having much fun."

"Not like us, Judge?" She moved her hand to rest it on top of his arm.

"Well, we're not married, he said."

She wrinkled her nose at him. "I could be your trophy wife, honey. And are you going to make a honest woman of me some day? " Her crystal blue eyes pinned his.

"Err, well, we'll have to see how it goes I suppose."

She flounced back in her chair, her hand leaving his arm as though scalded.

She gave him a cool look, and then spotted the twinkle in his eyes. She slugged him as hard as she could on his shoulder.

The both said " ouch" at the same time. The Judge had a solid shoulder.

The Judge diplomatically changed the subject, suggesting they dance. At her nod of assent, he rose immediately and slid her chair back as she got up, taking her hand and leading the way to the dance floor.

It was a cha-cha-cha. Katy was a very good dancer. Unfortunately, the Judge was not. He had a certain rhythm. But he danced to his own timing, rarely in sync with the music. Their compromise was to choose dances where they could each do their own thing, as with the cha cha cha.

She'd go left and he'd go right. But just like the old song, "Papa Loves Mambo", he'd invariably get ahead of or behind her a few steps at each turn. Because she tolerated his clumsy effort with great affection, he'd become emboldened to actually go out on the floor and dance, or attempt to. He grudgingly admitted he found it somewhat pleasurable, particularly if he'd first had sufficient libation so as to forget the awful figure he must cut on the floor for all to see. Sort of like a lunging bear, he supposed.

The Judge was a tall man, almost 6'3. Broad shouldered and big boned with just the beginnings of a paunch around the middle, hinting at an appetite for fine wines and good food. He had the ruddy, chiseled features of his Welsh ancestors, a rather too big nose, large ears, and bushy eyebrows on the way to premature grey. He was rugged looking, but not particularly handsome. The first thing people noticed and the last thing they remembered were the large piercing blue eyes, intelligent and restless. They ranged the space around him continually and missed little. Now in his early 50's, he cut a large figure in his tux and floppy bow tie Katy had insisted on getting for him, and took charge tying.

They danced two dances while the noise level picked up again and the waiters silently carried off the debris from the crashed tabletop. The crowd, particularly the Yacht Club crowd, was in a party mood. They were not to be deterred by a domestic flap, however dramatic.

Katy was tall, perhaps 5' 8," slender, all arms and legs. She wore a flowing gown in a yellow Easter egg pastel color setting off her pale face, not tanned like much of the Yacht Club crowd. Long brown hair, twisted together in a ponytail, bobbed around as she performed her cha cha cha with the smooth rhythm of a natural dancer. She had small, delicate features and lots of smile lines. She had the most extraordinary eyes, all vivid blue like the Caribbean, large and intelligent, with long lashes. In her late twenties, she had been focused on the Judge all evening, almost to the exclusion of the crowd around them. The obvious affection in the way she looked at the Judge was the envy of several younger males in the ballroom, but she appeared not to notice.

The evening wore on, dishes were cleared, and a Baked Alaska Parade was performed, all flame and marching around by a cotillion of waiters. Katy had untied the Judge's floppy bow tie and allowed it to hang down on both sides around his neck, unbuttoning the top of his tux shirt for effect. The Judge felt a little silly about it, like he'd been partly undressed. But she assured him it looked right, was practically 'de rigueur' in European circles.

The Judge wondered why it was that females once attached in some way to a male, immediately assumed as if by natural right the power to outfit, dress and adjust their male's ensemble, as though he were a small boy. Hormones, he supposed. But it gave him pleasure in some secret place to be fussed over. And he knew she knew he secretly enjoyed the attention, in the intuitive way females know certain things that never rise to words.

They danced some more after the Alaska. As the music receded with a strong flourish (after the band played an old Beatle song of vintage well before Katy's memory) they separated, the Judge heading back to their table while Katy went off to powder her nose.

As the Judge reached the table, a tall brunette separated herself from a young man she had been dancing with at the edge of the dance floor. She was in her late thirties, shapely, with deep cleavage well packaged and displayed in an ivory gown with plunging neckline accented with an expensive gold necklace, matched by jeweled pin in her soft brown hair, cascading long and free over her shoulders and down her bare back. She had lively brown eyes and touched the Judge's arm with an easy intimacy that suggested more than casual knowledge.

The Judge jumped guiltily at her touch, involuntarily leaning away.

"Great to see you Judge", she said with an honest smile, her brown eyes softening and focusing deep into his.

The Judge smiled back. He couldn't help himself. "You too, Barbara."

He'd of course spotted her in the crowd when he and Katy had arrived. It's different after you've shared another's body. The special intimacy created with the coupling continues long after you're no longer partners. He'd felt Barbara's eyes at various times during the evening. But it had seemed the better part of velour to avoid her, given Katy's close drill watch at his side.

"I see you have a new friend," said Barbara.

"Understand you two are quite an item. She looks a little young though."

The Judge winced, despite himself. It was a sore subject with him.

He should have been angry. It was an impolite thing to say, even catty. But he and Barbara had history and he knew her well. In some ways it was a compliment - a signal of her continuing interest. He could sense she was still wistful about what had once been. The underlying message was "availability" if he wanted to change horses, so to speak.

"We are very...compatible," he murmured to her, mentally kicking himself for sounding so lame.

Barbara leaned closer, like a snake preparing a strike, thought the Judge.

"I miss our old times together," she whispered, "particularly now I'm divorced."

Barbara leaned back and pinned the Judge with the soft brown eyes, now letting sexual heat flash in them for an instance.

Images of a wild night on a fur rug beside a fire, and another of a beautiful woman bent over on a hillside trail overlooking city and sea, arms locked on knees, bare buttocks grinding against his groin, flashed though the Judge's mind.

The Judge shook his head to clear the images, tried to put on his best non-committal face, and said. "That was a while ago Barbara; how are things going now?"

Barbara leaned forward again to answer, just a tad too far into the Judge's personal space to be polite, and then froze.

The Judge felt a disturbance in the ether surrounding him, much as a fish senses movement in the water. Before he could turn to look, a cool feminine voice shot from behind his shoulder with a smooth: "Who is this, Judge?" while a quick small hand shot forward to land territorially on the Judge's other shoulder.

Katy had returned.

The two women eyed each other with all the affection of dueling pit bulls while the Judge fumbled with introductions.

Barbara gave Katy an up and down appraisal, raised one eyebrow slightly, murmured without conviction, "Nice to meet you…" and turned away to retrieve her parked date across the dance floor.

Katy silently watched Barbara's departing back with a certain underlying venom. The Judge watched too, admiring the trim hips and fanny despite himself. After all, he was male.

This was the second bad omen. The Judge should have recognized this one more easily.

Perhaps if he'd been more alert, he'd have ended the evening right then. Taken Katy to bed early to smooth her feathers and for a quick romp. Left at first light for "Over Town", as the sprawling Los Angles plain was called by Islanders. Left before the weekend could deteriorate further.

Deteriorate into something very different.

"Who the hell was that, Judge?" Asked Katy, hawk like, her chin up, her nose in the air.

The Judge had a premonition he might be the worm.

“Just an old acquaintance,” tried the Judge, looking around the room for any possible reprieve or distraction; avoiding Katy's eyes.

"She looked more than that, Judge. An old lover perhaps?"

"Perhaps," the Judge grunted under his breath, his words almost unintelligible. How in hell were women so damn intuitive about such things?

"An old lover who's still interested in you perhaps?" Katy's voice rose an octave.

Another low, affirmative grunt.

"Used to be married, did she?" Another octave up.

"Err, yes, how'd you know that?"

"Feminine instinct"

"You responsible for the breakup with hubby?"

"Katy? Why'd you think that?"

"You slept with her while she was married?"

"Well, uh, a gentleman never tells." The Judge tried his boyish charm, putting on his best hopeful smile, hopeful this would all go away.

"So you've slept with married women…" Katy's tone was flat now.

"Well, perhaps just once."

"You slept with her just "once" while she was married? Or she's the "only" "married" woman you've slept with and carried on an affair with?"

"The former...I mean, the latter...I mean...Give me the question again."

The Judge could feel himself getting rattled. And Katy wasn't even trained as a lawyer.

"Humph!" was all that came out of Katy.

The Judge could feel the temperature dropping over the balance of the evening. Conversation was stilted from there, with Katy having little to say. But the Judge suspected the flush of color in her cheeks didn't bode well for later.

Excerpt from Chapter 4
The Island

They were skimming the water about 30 yards off shore, Charlie shining their light alternately along the rock beach and then seaward, both wondering if they'd come too far and this was a wild goose chase. Stony Beach, the boat yard, and the Washington Dime restaurant were coming up to starboard, the last outpost of civilization before the undeveloped wilds of the Island took over and ran to the Southern tip of the Island and Seal Rock.

It was then the Judge spotted a dark shape above the tide line on Stony Beach. The Judge tapped Charlie, who sent the rays of the hand held over to the beach, as the Judge swung the nose around and headed closer to shore. There was something there, all right: the dark lump of a sea lion perhaps, asleep on the beach. Or something else?

As they got closer the Judge could see the color of fabric, dull green in Charlie's light, but very like the color of Daisy's dress at the casino. The Judge goosed the engine hard and then at the last minute, popped the outboard prop up and out of the water as the dingy slid up toward the beach, grounding its nose in the sand a few feet from the water's edge. There was only minimal surf and the judge threw a small anchor over the side and then hauled on it to set the flukes.

They both scrambled out, getting their shoes and pants wet up to the knees, the Judge carrying the dingy painter and Charlie carrying the light toward the green shape on the rocks.

It was Daisy. She was on her back lying on the rocks, not moving. Her legs were spread wide, her green chiffon dress pulled up to her waist, her panties down.

She'd been a beautiful young lady in life. She wasn't beautiful in death. There was a nasty bruise in the middle of her forehead. But worse, her ivory silk scarf had been wrapped tightly around her neck several times and tightened to cut off air. Her blue eyes were blank of life. Her mouth was gaping in what had been a silent scream.

The Judge felt sick. He reached into his shirt pocket and dialed 911."

THE ISLAND
by Davis MacDonald

Made in the USA
Lexington, KY
13 December 2019